"I don't know what to make of you, Jeri."

"Make of me?" she asked.

Dan sat down beside her, stretching out his long legs and crossing his feet at the ankles. "I hadn't counted on this."

She sat up straighter, the first spark of fight easing the sexual tension she felt between them. "Counted on what?" She turned and stared at him. "The fact that I'm a woman?"

He looked at her with amusement. "No. *That* was obvious from the first night I saw you."

"What, then?"

"A fire chief isn't supposed to be attracted to one of his volunteers."

Her voice croaked. "Attracted? To me?"

"Yeah, you," he murmured, then abruptly stood. "Aw, what the hell." He pulled her to her feet, lowered his head and kissed her.

Dear Reader,

This story is close to my heart, not only because it takes place where I live, but, more important, because it was inspired by true-life heroes and heroines—neighbors serving on our local volunteer fire department.

When we moved to rural northwest Arkansas, the availability of emergency services concerned us. In the spring of 1994 we were baby-sitting two of our granddaughters, Katie (two) and Callie (five). During their last evening under our care, Callie accidentally pulled a heavy brass lamp off an end table, cutting her head open. Blood spattered everywhere, little sister Katie became hysterical, and Nana and Grandpa were understandably flustered. Living a considerable distance from the hospital, we had little choice but to call 911. Within four minutes our volunteer first responders and EMT arrived, tending to Callie and soothing the concerned grandparents. (Thankfully, damage to our emotional state was worse than Callie's wound, which proved superficial.) When I walked out to the ambulance, which made the trip from town within fifteen minutes, I was overwhelmed to see seven more members of our volunteer fire department standing by to offer assistance! That evening we learned firsthand about the dedication, caring and skill of the men and women who serve their communities in this important work.

Wherever you live, may you be blessed with heroines and heroes like these, who go the extra mile to assure your safety and well-being!

Sincerely,

Laura Abbot

P.S. Your letters are sources of genuine pleasure. Please write me at Box 2105, Eureka Springs, AR 72632-2105.

WHERE THERE'S SMOKE...
Laura Abbot

Harlequin Books

TORONTO • NEW YORK • LONDON
AMSTERDAM • PARIS • SYDNEY • HAMBURG
STOCKHOLM • ATHENS • TOKYO • MILAN
MADRID • WARSAW • BUDAPEST • AUCKLAND

ISBN 0-373-70747-9

WHERE THERE'S SMOKE...

In grateful appreciation for the selfless efforts of those men and women serving in volunteer fire departments and with special thanksgiving for my friends and neighbors in the Grassy Knob community.

To Jim and Linda Lemon
for their counsel, encouragement and friendship

CHAPTER ONE

THE MEN CLUSTERED outside the fire station watched warily as Jeri Monahan followed Smitty Dingle into the attached building—the Eagle Point Community Center. One tough-looking veteran ran a beefy hand through his grizzled hair and harrumphed disapprovingly.

Jeri glanced back at the men, who shuffled their feet and averted their eyes. She shrugged. Yes, fighting fires could be dangerous, but if they could do it, so could she.

Her father had always urged her not to be afraid to attempt anything the boys did. To please him and to prove to herself she was no sissy, she had, and generally been successful. Somehow, though, he invariably made her feel she fell short of his expectations. Nobody, however, had ever called her a quitter!

The rural Arkansas lake community depended on volunteer firefighters, and she was as able-bodied as the next person. Besides, she had training they needed—first-aid certification and two summers' experience driving a truck. A delivery truck, but still a truck.

Not that she was overlooking the element of fear, but she'd been afraid before—leaning in at the batter's box when her older brothers hurled their inside fastballs. When she'd completed her one and only scuba dive. And, worst of all, coming home that first time after her mother's death, walking through the doorway of the house her mother would never again enter. She winced at that last. Too painful. No time to look at it now.

"You comin'?" Smitty, the Monahans' longtime neighbor, gestured toward the corridor behind the meeting room. "The chief's office is back here. I'll soften him up. Wait outside till I call you."

Jeri paced restlessly as Smitty, audible through the half-open door, droned on about her recent return home and her qualifications. Soften him up? What did *that* mean? Then she heard a gruff second voice.

"I'd hoped the Eagle Point Volunteer Fire Department would never be put in this position, Smitty. You didn't tell me you'd recruited a female."

Jeri's lips pressed into a pencil-thin line. Clearly the chief was not pleased.

"Give her a chance, Dan. She's one spunky gal." Smitty maintained his reasonable tone. "You said yourself the department is shorthanded."

"What I said was under*manned*. We have enough worries without having to coddle a woman!"

Adrenaline propelled Jeri through the door. "Just a darn minute!" She placed both palms on the desk and leaned forward, staring down into squall-blue eyes. "Coddling won't be necessary, believe me."

Smitty chuckled. "What'd I tell you, Dan? Hellcat, ain't she?" He took hold of Jeri's shoulders. "Kiddo, now that you've got the chief's attention, it might be good to introduce you. Jeri Monahan, Dan Contini."

The muscular man with the bristling mustache and cleft chin glared at her. She glared back, determined not to look away first. He finally spoke. "Ms. Monahan, I appreciate your willingness to help, but the fact of the matter is, I'm not enthusiastic about women in the department."

She planted her hands on her hips. "Not enthusiastic about someone with first-aid training who could be an emergency first responder? Or about a licensed truck driver with experience?" She sat down on a wooden office chair, crossing one denim-clad leg over the other. "I'm curious. Why aren't I welcome in a *volunteer* fire unit, especially one that's understaffed?"

Dan Contini slumped back in his chair, his deeply tanned face creasing in displeasure. "It's not a matter of welcome. I've got my reasons, good ones."

Smitty chortled. "You two have gotten off on the wrong foot. Relax." He shot Jeri a warning look and faced the skeptical fire chief. "I'm telling you, Dan, we could use her. In a resort-retirement community like this, the average age of us volunteers is probably sixty, and we sure as hell ain't gettin' any younger. We're short one first responder and we need another driver. Who else have you got?"

Jeri watched the chief run his fingers through his short curly black hair, the fluorescent lights highlighting the occasional silver glint. He swiveled in his chair and studied the opposite wall as if seeing the ideal solution written there. No way would she beg for the job, but he was fooling himself if he thought she couldn't hold her own. Did he think she was some hothouse flower?

Then he turned back and shrugged. "I'm not crazy about the idea. But since you're here, you may as well stay, Ms. Monahan, until I—"

She interrupted. "Call me Jeri. I just want to be one of the boys." She couldn't restrain the sarcasm.

"Very well, *Jeri*." He rose to his feet, pinning her with his angry gaze. "I'll try you, but only because we do need help. You'd better be sure this is what you want." He leaned so close she caught a whiff of his balsam aftershave. "And you'd better be damned good!"

She looked up from under thick lashes and met his gaze, her mouth set in a deliberately disarming smile. "Count on it, Chief!" She stood, all five feet four inches poised for challenge. "Trust me, you won't have to coddle this female!"

She exited, firmly shutting the door behind her, and strode down the hallway. She'd not only show him, she'd relish every minute of it!

She entered the meeting room, took a metal folding chair near the back and looked around. Many of the firefighters, including several old-timers she recognized, were already in their seats. Smitty sat down next to her, a smug look on his face. "Give him time, Jeri. Contini's a cautious man, but he's fair. He'll come around."

"In my lifetime?" Jeri bent her head close to his. "What about the others?"

"Most'll welcome an extra hand. Do your job and leave any doubters to me."

So the fire chief was her major obstacle. Growing up with three brothers, she'd survived only because she'd learned both to take it and dish it out. This wouldn't be the first time a male had underestimated her.

AFTER THE MEETING Smitty adjusted the thermostat, then paused in the doorway of the community center. "Good meeting, Dan. Thanks for giving Jeri a chance."

"I'm reserving my judgment. You're right, though, we need help. I just wish your Jeri had been a man. Good night, Smitty."

"Night." Smitty, the last of the volunteers to leave, waved and sauntered toward the parking lot.

Dan stepped outside and locked the door. Pausing in

the fading June twilight before climbing into his Jeep, he gazed across the road at the distant Ozark hills silhouetted against the faint orange-tinged sky. He never tired of the beauty and tranquillity of this place. Before him an arm of Eagle Lake glimmered, the surface mirror smooth. Overhead the first evening stars pierced the darkening sky. He sighed contentedly as he climbed behind the wheel and started the engine.

Driving the familiar winding road back to the marina, he reflected on the enormity of the change he'd made since spring a year ago when he'd resigned his commission and left the U.S. Navy. Fourteen years of reacting to the whims of military bureaucracy, of taking orders and enduring the close confinement of sea duty—characterized by monotony and occasional cottonmouthed fear—had finally worn him down. All he'd wanted was to find a place near water, far from the noise and frantic activity of port cities, and be answerable only to himself.

For a man who, except for a brief time in San Diego, had never been west of the Appalachians, being the owner of a marina on a lake in northwest Arkansas, of all places, was quite a change. His service buddies had thought he was certifiable. But what did they know?

He grinned, braking to avoid a doe dashing across the road in front of him. He'd learned the marina business working for a couple of months alongside the former owner, Raymond Bell. Then, last July he'd bought the property outright. He'd owned it almost a year. A year of hard work. The marina had needed some renovation and required constant maintenance. Soon, though, he could begin to consider expansion.

The effort was worth it. The slower pace, the natural

beauty of the Ozarks and the friendly people daily confirmed the wisdom of his decision.

He rounded the last curve, his headlights briefly illuminating the sign "Eagle Point Marina, 1/4 mile." The floodlight mounted on the gas dock created a V of light across the surface of the lake and allowed him to see the sterns of the speedboats and pontoons in the first row of slips beyond the office. Out in the middle of the cove several sailboats, moored to buoys, bobbed gently. He backed into his parking space to facilitate a quick departure in case of emergency, then walked to the dock and double-checked the lock on the gate to the boat slips before turning toward the small brown A-frame house that had come with the property. Aside from the occasional drunken boater, fishermen who repeated the same stories over and over and the demanding few who held him personally responsible for their crafts' mechanical failures, he had no complaints.

Inside the house, he greeted Bull, the boxer he'd bought as soon as he'd sealed the marina deal. For him, a major drawback of sea duty had been the inability to keep a pet. Trailed by the eager dog, he moved from room to room opening windows to let in the cooler air and night sounds. He enjoyed falling asleep to the accompaniment of mournful hoot owls and awaking to the dawn chorus of birds. A nearly perfect existence.

He stretched and yawned. Nearly perfect except for Smitty's harebrained idea of having a female member in the volunteer fire department. Neither his traditional upbringing nor his military training and experience had disposed him to favor women serving on ships and in combat. He shuddered and tried not to picture Ensign Adams, Virginia L., whose naval career had abruptly ended when burns from a flight-deck accident had scarred her porcelain skin forever.

Hell. When a man joined the service, he expected danger. Some even sought it. The underlying knowledge you could be wounded or killed any time, that sour sense of impending doom, contributed to the brotherhood, the esprit de corps. That and the shared sense you were protecting values worth fighting for—family, home, country. And in the Contini family, you protected women; you didn't hand them a helmet, arm them and order them to the front. Other duties, okay, maybe—but not combat. He could recite by heart the official navy line why women qualified, but he'd never bought it. He guessed he was old-fashioned. He'd seen plenty of wounded men in his career, but disturbing as that was, it wasn't unexpected. However, the jolting impact of Adams lying mummylike in sick bay had torn him up. Reasons? Well, he had them, all right, so he could hardly be expected to welcome a female firefighter with open arms.

He opened the refrigerator and pulled out a beer and a half-consumed tin of sardines. Where the Sam Hill were the crackers? Finally locating them, he carried his snack into the living room and set it down on the hatch-door coffee table. He crammed a sardine between two crackers and stuffed the sandwich in his mouth.

Jeri Monahan. She probably wouldn't last long. Wait till, dressed in full gear, she tried to get her cute little behind up a ladder. Or tried to control the writhing anacondalike end of a fire hose.

He smiled. Those hazel eyes had burned pure indignation; and when she'd wheeled out of his office, the air had practically crackled. Smitty'd said she had spunk. He'd give her that. How old could she be? Not much more than twenty-seven or eight. She made him feel every bit of his thirty-six years. Despite his reservations, it'd been hard to ignore her compact body, firm in all the right places with enough tantalizing curves to get the attention of any red-blooded male. Her short curly hair was the color of butterscotch, and her skin...

He took a swig of beer. *Dangerous thinking, sailor.* Physical beauty was no qualification for fighting fires. Dammit, he didn't want to be responsible for her—or for any woman—for *any* reason. The past was a powerful teacher.

He propped his feet on the table. If he had anything to say about it, he wouldn't be responsible for long. Jeri Monahan would have to be made of sturdy stuff to withstand the training he had in mind.

JERI PARKED the Explorer in the carport and quietly opened the screen door on the main floor of her family's split-level home. Like most houses in the area, it was built into the slope of a hill. In the great room, open to the kitchen and dining area, only one dim lamp lit the pine-paneled interior. Her father must've turned in early. Beneath her, from the walkout ground level, she could hear the pulsating bass of her seventeen-year-old brother's stereo system. She'd been back in Arkansas only a short time, but she'd noticed definite changes in Scotty. Liberated from his braces, now shaving at least every other day, he was no longer an awkward adolescent. Her baby brother had metamorphosed into a teenage heartthrob. Scary.

As she set her purse on the sofa table and reached to turn off the lamp, she heard the flick of a cigarette lighter from the screened-in porch. She opened the sliding screen door. "Dad?" Hank Monahan was rocking back and forth in the glider chair and gazing absently at the lake. She raised her voice. "Dad?"

He started, then turned. "Hi, honey."

She walked over and settled into a chaise longue. "You must've been a million miles away."

He drew on his cigarette and exhaled slowly. "I guess I was. Lots of things on my mind...but nothing you need to worry about." He straightened. "So tell me about the meeting."

She'd much rather talk about the "lots of things" on his mind, but he was a man who kept his thoughts to himself. Especially these past few months. Congenial and outgoing, with the trustworthy appearance of a news commentator, he always had a quip, a new joke, something to deflect attempts at intimacy. His glibness, coupled with business acumen, made him a topnotch real-estate developer, but something of a personal enigma. His emotional detachment had always served as a challenge to her. No matter how hard she tried—in school, athletics or her career—Jeri never felt she quite measured up. Even now she craved his approval. Yet she'd always suspected him of having immense vulnerability. Had her mother pierced that shell?

"The meeting?" She considered her response. "The good news is I'm the newest member of the Eagle Point Volunteer Fire Department. The bad news is that Chief Contini's reaction to my being female was less than enthusiastic."

"Well, I can't say I'm overjoyed to have you take those kinds of risks, either, but I guess it's a little late for me to turn cautious with you. Kind of like locking the barn door after the horse is gone."

She smiled. "Yes, wasn't it you who had me up on water skis practically before I got my permanent teeth and who encouraged me to try out for the *boys'* Little League team?"

"Hmm. You've got a point." His face lit up. "And you made it!"

"Not only made it, Dad. I was the leading hitter. Sixteen years ago, for a girl, that was quite a feat."

"That's right. I'd forgotten."

"If it hadn't been for you, Chuck and Doug egging me on, I might've been a l'il ol' Southern belle—" she drawled for effect "—and y'all would've had to chase away those handsome beaux clustered around your delicate rosebud of a daughter."

She was gratified to hear him chuckle. These days it was hard to coax even a smile from him.

"Other than Chief Contini's gender bias, what did you think of him?" Her father rolled his cigarette between his thumb and forefinger.

"Think of him?" She could hardly tell her father that, Dan Contini's sexist views aside, she found him disturbingly attractive. He was intensely masculine, carried himself with authority and expressed himself in a straightforward manner. The truth was that, despite her commitment to paying attention at the meeting, his blue eyes and graceful movements were major distractions. "He seems to know his business."

"That's all?"

"All—except I imagine I'll have some interesting challenges ahead of me."

"And so you should. I want you well trained."

"Then, Dad, I think you can relax. I'll be in good hands with Chief Contini." She was thankful for the darkness. She found herself responding warmly to the image of being in Contini's hands.

"Raymond Bell was tickled when Dan bought the marina."

"Did you handle the sale?"

"Sure did. I was surprised it sold to someone from the East, instead of a local."

"What brought him here?"

"Liked it, I guess. When he got out of the navy, he was looking for a business to buy near water. Saw our ad in *Field and Stream*." Her father stubbed out his cigarette and yawned. "Think I'll turn in."

Lights from the lower level spilled out over the sloping lawn leading down to the private dock. "I take it Scotty's still up."

Her father stood. "Looks like it." Jeri detected weariness and tension in his voice.

Her stomach muscles tightened. "Something happen while I was gone?"

Her father sighed. "I don't know how to talk to the boy. He's been out of school since Memorial Day. He's had a week's vacation. I told him it was past time to find a summer job."

"And?"

"He told me in no uncertain terms he wasn't going to mow lawns again or flip burgers in some fast-food joint. He told me to leave him alone, that he'd handle things."

Jeri mentally counted to ten. "Maybe that's exactly what needs to happen. Maybe he wants to prove to you he *can* handle things." She sat up straighter and looked at her father. "Before you lower the boom, give him a chance to line something up himself."

Her father shrugged. "Maybe. I never had these problems with Chuck or Doug."

"Scotty's not Chuck or Doug." She drew a tight breath. "And...things have changed."

He seemed to shrink in the doorway. "Your mother would've known how to handle him."

"She's not here," Jeri said quietly. "You are."

"And you." He cleared his throat. "I'm grateful for that." He paused and squared his shoulders. "You coming in?"

She brought up her knees and hugged them to her chest. "Not yet, Dad."

"Good night, then."

She listened as his footsteps grew fainter. Across the expanse of water she spotted the winking lights of a boat anchored near the far shore. As a kid, when she'd made a big enough pest of herself, her older brothers had occasionally taken her along on their night-fishing excursions. The lazy rocking of the boat, the gentle slapping of water against the hull, moonlight glinting off the limestone cliffs—the stuff of treasured memories.

From the time she was small, Chuck, four years older, and Doug, two years older, had been patient with her, teaching her to cast, gut fish, water-ski, sail—you name it. They'd taken genuine pleasure in her accomplishments, as if their sole mission in life was to create the consummate tomboy. She'd been eleven when Scotty— "the afterthought baby"—was born. Immediately she'd found herself torn by competing tugs of affection— playing mother to her infant sibling and competing in the rough-and-tumble world of her big brothers and their friends. No wonder Chuck and Doug were her heroes or that Scotty, with his mischievous fun-loving personality, occupied a special place in her heart.

She clasped her knees more tightly, distantly aware

of the throb of the rock music, and stared at the loblolly pines profiled against the moonlit sky. Scotty. Where had the fun gone? His moods were more than teenage sullenness. She sighed. How long would it take any of them to move beyond the emptiness created by her mother's death eight months ago? Her father, so pensive, so alone with his thoughts. And now, as if she needed more problems, he and Scotty were at loggerheads.

She felt suddenly overwhelmed by responsibilities. It had been her choice to leave the Dallas high school where she taught phys ed and coached girls' basketball to fill a similar vacancy this fall at the local high school, her alma mater. But she also faced a summer of trying to bridge the gap between two hurting stubborn males and attempting to fulfill, however inadequately, her mother's role as companion, confidante and—face it— family pivot point.

Jeri stretched out her legs, forcing her body to relax. What ridiculous hubris had possessed her to think moving home could make things better?

Her self-sufficient father, who'd never asked her for anything before, had put it to her bluntly. "Jeri, I could use your help. I'm up to my ears in the start-up phase of Cedarcrest. This is the first resort development I've been solely responsible for, and it's a helluva challenge. It's bad timing personally, but it's critical professionally. I can't begin to give Scott the attention and supervision he needs this summer or in his senior year. Is there any chance you'd consider accepting the vacancy at River Falls High?"

Recent budget cuts threatening the girls' sports program at the Dallas high school, coupled with four years of big-city living, had made her decision easier. But she'd never imagined that home would be so empty, so charged with tension.

She steeled herself not to remember the way it used to be. Yet all around her was evidence of the mother who wasn't there mulching the azaleas, swimming off the dock with her powerful backstroke. Jeri pictured her tanned athletic mom grinning with exultation, her short no-nonsense Norse-blond hair gleaming in the sun, her well-toned arms braced, hands gripping the sailboard-mast bar, leaning dangerously near the water as she executed a rapid turn. A fitness nut, she'd positively glowed with health, competence, well-being.

Jeri sat up and crossed her legs, her hands clenched into fists on her knees. One moment her mother was alive, the next she was gone. In the mere blink of an eye. None of the platitudes had made a dent—"She didn't suffer," or worse, "It was God's will."

Jeri smacked her knees, stood up and gazed out at the lake, its surface calm and serene. No God of hers deliberately set out to cut down a woman like Pat Monahan in the prime of life. An accident of nature. A cerebral aneurysm, probably the result of a congenital defect, the doctor had said. Jeri shook her head. This remembering was too immediate, too painful. How many times, as a coach, had she told her team not to dwell on the past, on the losses, but to look forward to the next opportunity for victory? In this case, though, it was difficult.

Indulging in tears and imprecations against God wouldn't bring her mother back, though, wouldn't alter her obligations to Scotty or her father. Her mother's voice echoed in memory: *Go get 'em, Jeri. Don't let those boys win. You can do it!* She smiled faintly. Mom had always been her staunchest ally, her most vocal cheerleader. And she *would* do it! She'd hang in there, day by day, and get them all through this. Somehow.

"Jeri, where'd you hide the chips?" Scotty stood at the screen door, bare-chested, wearing frayed cutoffs. She turned, suddenly aware of the quiet—no Nirvana sending waves of sound through the house.

Taking in his blue eyes and tousled blond hair, so like their mother's, she moved past him, toward the kitchen. "I *hid* them in the cupboard where they belong. I found them sitting on top of the TV."

He trailed after her. "You trying to civilize me?"

"Is it possible?" She handed him the bag and perched on a bar stool at the kitchen counter watching him eat. "Want some milk?"

"I'll get it." He opened the refrigerator, took out the carton and drank straight from it.

She started to object, then caught herself. "Have any plans for tomorrow?"

He wiped his milk mustache with the back of his hand and rolled his eyes. "Yeah. Job hunting." His tone conveyed the enthusiasm of someone being led before a firing squad.

She bit back the lecture on pulling one's weight, being responsible. "Any ideas?"

"Thought I'd see if the Lakeview Inn needs a waiter."

Jeri groaned inwardly. "Don't they serve liquor?"

"Yeah. So?"

"You may be too young." When Scotty grimaced, Jeri quickly added, "But it won't hurt to apply. Maybe you could bus tables."

"Jeez, I'd rather flip burgers."

Oops! This was one of those no-win conversations. "You've got to start somewhere."

"Yeah, that's what Dad'd say." He balled up the

empty chip bag and tossed it across the room into the wastebasket.

"You have to admit Dad has a point. It's tough to pay car insurance without income."

"But I just got out of school. Why can't he let me have a break for a while?"

"Maybe because by then the good jobs will've been taken?"

"Okay, okay. I read you loud and clear." He saluted. "Tomorrow."

Not used to playing the heavy, she didn't want to end on this note. "If you're not busy Sunday, wanna crew for me in the regatta?"

"When was the last time you raced?" He eyed her skeptically.

She clambered down from the stool, placed her hands on his shoulders and looked him straight in the eye. "Oh, ye of little faith! The Monahans are not only going to race, we're going to win." She socked his chest playfully. "Now, let's turn in." She scooped up the empty milk carton and threw it away. Then she grinned at him. "Gotta be at your best for those job interviews."

He held up his hands in surrender. "Yeah, yeah, yeah." He paused and his voice dropped. "Jeri, I'm glad you're home." Then he walked out of the kitchen, stretching to touch the door header, and disappeared downstairs.

Wiping the potato-chip crumbs off the countertop, she considered this brother of hers. She'd never backed away from a challenge, and her family situation was no exception. She smiled as she draped the dishcloth over the sink divider. Just like she was going to show the Great Contini—he with the air of command and the body that made hers go into overdrive.

CHAPTER TWO

THE NEXT MORNING Jeri was puttering about the kitchen, thumbing through her mother's recipes for a simple dinner dish, when Scotty appeared, dressed in clean chinos, a blue button-down shirt and a flowered tie.

"Do I pass inspection?" he said.

She eyed him up and down, then nodded. "You look nice. I might hire you if…"

"If?"

"If I thought you'd work hard, be prompt and display a cheerful attitude."

"Uh-oh, the A-word."

He sat on a stool at the counter as she pulled a plate of soggy pancakes from the microwave and set it in front of him, along with butter and syrup.

Then she moved back to the counter and tamped down the recipe cards, arranging them in a neat stack.

"There's a lot to be said for a positive attitude," she told him.

"Whose side are you on, anyway? You sound like Dad. I thought we were pals."

"I didn't know it was a matter of taking sides."

He ate hungrily, sopping up the excess syrup with his last forkful, then shoved his dish across the island counter. "All I know is, I can't seem to do anything right."

Careful to mask her mounting frustration, she picked up the plate and rinsed it off. "I don't mean to sound preachy. It's just that this is a difficult time for all of us. I'm caught, too. I'm not Mother—" she saw pain flash in his eyes "—but I'm more than the sister who puts in an occasional holiday appearance. Dad's expecting things of me, as well. Let's pull together and lighten up a little, whaddaya say?"

He slid off the stool and stuffed his hands in his pockets. "Maybe. But I don't like being bossed around. After all, I'm nearly eighteen."

It didn't take a genius to see she'd offended his fragile masculine pride. "I'm not trying to be bossy. I want what's best for you, and after all, I *do* have eleven years' additional wisdom to offer." She extended her hand and lowered her voice. "Scotty, it's okay. I hear you. Truce?"

He pulled his right hand from his pocket, a grin flitting across his face. "Okay. Truce." They shook. "Well, here goes nothing."

"Hey, the A-word? Paste on that happy face."

"Right." The screen door slammed behind him.

"Good luck..." Her words trailed impotently into the sudden silence. *Mom, how did you ever manage four of us?*

She slipped the recipes back into the file box and double-checked her grocery list. Her cooking skills were definitely limited, so feeding two big eaters put the pressure on. She'd run some errands, do the shopping, try to prepare a meat loaf and then take a good long swim. She needed the exercise. Being domestic affected *her* attitude, too. She picked up her car keys and was just starting for the door when the phone rang.

"Jeri? Dan Contini." He paused as if expecting a particular response.

"Yes, hello." Silence.

"How're you coming with that manual I gave you last night?"

Like she'd rushed home and plunged right into it. "I'm planning to look it over this afternoon."

"You'd better do more than look it over, especially the first section. Memorize it, internalize it, make it second nature."

He sounded every inch the military officer she understood he'd been. She resisted the urge to respond, "Sir, yes, sir!" Instead, she said, "Not a problem. I'm a fast learner." Her diaphragm seemed to be having difficulty pushing air through her voice box.

"Good." The word was clipped. "Then you'll be ready for tomorrow."

"Tomorrow? Saturday?"

"Yes. The full-dress training session and controlled burn."

Her heart skipped a beat. She'd assumed they'd *ease* her into the ranks. To Contini, training apparently meant trial by fire. She cringed at her unintentional pun.

"Jeri?"

"Yes, of course, I'll be there." She paused. "With the manual committed to heart." Darned if she'd let him guess she hadn't had the foggiest notion her attendance was expected at an immediate training session.

"I hope so. Meet at the fire station in the morning at nine."

"I'll be there."

"And, Jeri, since we have to drive to the site of the burn, you'll get to show off those truck-driving skills of yours." Clearly the gauntlet had been thrown down.

"Thank you, Chief, for calling to remind me. I'll be prepared."

"That's the *Boy* Scouts. Goodbye."

As the phone clicked in her ear, she realized she was holding the receiver in a death grip. So *that* was the way it was. She banged down the phone and scooped up her purse and keys. *Okay, Contini, let the games begin!*

JERI TAPPED her brakes and gave a resigned sigh. The out-of-state car in front of her was literally creeping up the hill. Gritting her teeth, she reminded herself that a simple trip to the grocery store in tourist season took on the proportions of a half-day excursion. The annual invasion was in full swing—senior citizens arriving by the busload for a day's diversion from the country-music shows in the nearby town of Branson, families camping at the lakeside parks, well-heeled couples haunting the galleries and antique shops of River Falls, a quaint Victorian spa town spilling down the mountainside at the confluence of two rivers.

Yet it was this same relaxing pace that caused her to love the little town, where, in the late 1800s, visitors had flocked to take the natural spring waters, credited with medicinal value. Many stayed permanently, erecting elaborate three-story gabled homes with wide front porches and gingerbread trim. Others built summer cottages, wedged tightly against the porous limestone cliffs and perched precariously over steep serpentine dirt roads. A tourist mecca, River Falls was noted for its historic downtown district, charming bed-and-breakfast establishments and fine restaurants.

It was Contini who had put her in a hurry mode. Contini and his darn manual. By the time she ran her errands and fixed the meat loaf, it would be midafternoon. Fast learner, indeed! She'd need osmosis.

Seizing a break in the oncoming traffic, she turned down a narrow winding shortcut and wheeled into the bank parking lot. She needed to transfer her account.

While she sat waiting for the customer-service person to prepare the paperwork, she felt warm hands on her shoulders and heard a familiar deep voice. "Tag? Is that you? I heard you were back."

She craned her neck, then jumped up excitedly. "Mike!" She threw her arms around the short curly-headed man in pin-striped pants, crisp white dress shirt and paisley suspenders. "Let me look at you." She stepped back and held him at arm's length. "I can't believe it. Wall Street right here in River Falls. How's the brokerage business?"

"Best Monopoly game I ever played." He grinned an elfin grin, then sobered. "But it's more than a game when you're dealing with other people's money. I like it, Tag. Every day is different."

Mike Parsons was her brother Doug's best friend and one of hers, as well. He'd teased her unmercifully as long as she could remember and had dreamed up the name Tag, short for Tag-along, but she loved him like a brother. They'd dated briefly when she was a freshman in college, but had quickly agreed romance would ruin a great friendship. "I guess you know I've come back to take the job at the high school," she said. "And to be with Dad and Scotty."

"Yeah, your father told me." He lowered his voice sympathetically. "He's had quite a time, Tag. He was relieved you agreed to make the change."

"I hope I can help." She brightened. "Friends like

you make coming home fun. I don't intend to turn into little Susie Homemaker.''

He hooted. ''You? No way! Hey—do you want to join us tomorrow afternoon? We're going out to the island for a picnic.''

She quirked an eyebrow. ''Us?''

''Sorry to disappoint you. It's nothing romantic. Just a big group. Whaddaya say?''

''I hate to turn down my first invitation, but I have a previous engagement.''

''Can't you get out of it?''

She laughed ruefully. ''Not likely. I've joined the Eagle Point Volunteer Fire Department, and tomorrow is my first drill.''

Mike grabbed her by the shoulders. ''You're kidding! You've joined the fire department?''

She nodded. ''Something wrong?''

''I didn't mean it like that. In fact, it's just what I'd expect you to do.'' He rocked back on his heels. ''How'd Dan Contini react?''

''He didn't exactly roll out the red carpet.''

''It figures.''

''Oh?''

''I've visited with him at the marina. He strikes me as a pretty traditional kind of guy. Probably thinks a woman's place is in the home.''

''From my limited exposure, I'd say that's a fair statement. But...''

''You're just the woman to change his mind.''

She snapped his suspenders. ''Bet on it!''

He hooked his hands in the back pockets of his pants and eyed her with relish. ''Nobody should sell you short in the battle of the sexes. Give him hell, Tag.''

"I don't want to defeat him, just hold my own. After all, I like being a woman."

He winked. "I doubt Contini will be immune to your female charms." He leaned over and kissed her on the cheek. "It's great to see you, Tag. I'll call you."

"Bye." She sat back down. Suddenly the idea of giving Dan Contini hell wasn't nearly as satisfying as being a woman to whom he might not be immune. Even his brusque voice on the phone this morning had put her in touch with decidedly unfirefighterlike feelings about him.

"Miss Monahan?"

How long had the new-accounts representative been sitting there staring at her? "Sorry, I was daydreaming. Where do I sign?"

SATURDAY MORNING Dan stood clutching a clipboard, checking names off as the volunteers assembled at the community center. He glanced at his watch. Eight-fifty-eight. Several men lingered around the coffeepot, but most had settled into their seats in anticipation of the briefing. Only Simmons and Rojas were missing. Oh, and Monahan. No point adding her name to the roster until she showed up. She'd probably taken one look at the manual and changed her mind.

He flipped back the roll sheet, scanning his agenda as he strolled to the front of the room. The door swung open, and Simmons and young Rojas entered, followed by a red-faced frazzled-looking Jeri Monahan. She glanced at the wall clock and smiled broadly at him— she'd made it with all of ten seconds to spare. He watched her slither into an empty chair next to Earl Gunderman. The chatter died away, and he faced twenty sets of probing eyes and one pair of triumphant ones. *Go ahead,* he told himself. *Get it over with.*

"Men, some of you met Jeri Monahan, our newest volunteer, the other night." He paused. "Smitty Dingle recommended her. She understands this is tough dangerous work and has assured me she can pull her weight. This will be her first training drill. Give her all the help you'd give any rookie—" his eyes narrowed on Jeri "—but no more. Every man, er, person in this unit is important. We need to be able to count on one another. So, no special favors. Understood?" He noted Jeri's emphatic nod, as well as the undercurrent of mumbling from the back of the room. "Any questions?"

A thin ropy-looking man raised his hand. "Chief, you sayin' *she's* gonna do everything we do?"

"Within the limits of her size and strength." The questioner frowned, muttering something that sounded like "So much for stag night."

Dan arched his eyebrows, anticipating further questions. Jeri raised her hand and stood up. "I imagine some of you aren't real happy about my being here, and I guess I can understand that. But I do have some background and training to offer. I'm not asking for anything except a chance to help. Please judge me by my actions." She sank back into her chair.

Dan let out a relieved sigh. At least she'd had smarts enough to defuse the situation. She'd displayed none of the cockiness she'd shown in his office Thursday night, and only the two spots of color on her cheeks gave away the effort her diplomacy had taken.

"This afternoon's burn will simulate the conditions of a structure fire. So listen up and we'll review the procedures."

After he finished the briefing, the men scattered to their tasks—inventory and equipment checks. He assigned Smitty to outfit Jeri and explain the uses and limitations of each item. Out of the corner of his eye it appeared that even the smallest coat hung below her wrists and that they'd have to special-order a pair of boots. Smitty had no trouble, however, finding a helmet to fit. A grin tugged at the corner of his mouth. She did look kind of cute, like a kid playing dress up—dwarfed by the equipment, her short honey-colored curls tucked into the hat, her shoulders hunched under the weight of the coat, only her fingertips poking from the sleeves. Yet she didn't appear helpless. With her lips pressed firmly together and her brows drawn in concentration, her expression was one of single-minded determination. She listened attentively to Smitty, nodding occasionally. Well, anybody could wear the gear, Dan thought. Wait till she had to walk the talk.

He sidled over to her. "Equipment okay?"

Her forehead was beaded with perspiration. "Fine. Except for the boots."

"For now, you'll have to wear extra socks. What's your shoe size?"

"Eight." She demonstrated the slippage of the oversize boot and then turned her hazel eyes on him expectantly.

"If you complete the training satisfactorily, we may order you some."

She jutted out her chin. "Not if, *when.*"

"To begin with, what are the causes of Class B fires?"

She didn't blink. "Flammable liquids, greases and gases."

"Procedure for notifying the air-evacuation service?"

Again she reeled off the correct information.

"Book learning saves people's lives only when it's applied quickly and accurately. I'll be watching you this afternoon."

He turned and sauntered toward his office, aware of having sounded high-handed. Something about those big amber eyes peering from beneath the brim of the helmet unhinged him. He'd be watching her, all right. Looking for a way he could wash her out—a safety breach, a technicality, anything to rid himself of her disturbing presence. Disturbing in more ways than one. Why did his body respond so automatically every time she walked into the room? Was it just those tight jeans and that form-fitting T-shirt?

One more compelling reason women had no business in a man's world. He was responsible for a number of people, and he sure as hell didn't need hormones doing his thinking. If he was stuck with her, though, why couldn't she look more like a prison matron?

As THE SLOOP eased from its mooring around noon the following day, Sunday, the mainsail filling with air, Jeri and Scotty waved to their father, standing on the weathered dock. From her place in the stern Jeri steered the boat out of the cove, reflecting on Scotty's resemblance to their dad. Lanky and broad-shouldered, her brother had the same mischievous grin, though she hadn't seen much smiling from either of them since she'd been home.

She squinted at the telltale atop the mast to determine wind direction, adjusted the tiller and trimmed the mainsheet for the run to the starting line of the Eagle Lake

Yacht Club's June regatta, where, like so many white gulls, billowing sails dotted the expanse of blue water.

Scotty looked relaxed as he hoisted the jib. Since coming home after a fruitless job hunt both Friday and Saturday, he probably needed this carefree afternoon.

A sudden gust sent the boat skimming. "Ready, mate?" she yelled.

Leaning over the leeward side, Scotty scooped up a handful of the cold water and flung it at her. "Not until the skipper's wet!" He laughed, ducking to avoid the boom when she called, "Coming about!"

By the time they were into the second leg of the race, their boat was trailing the leader and being hotly pursued by a sleek teal-colored challenger. They were on a broad reach in a freshening wind when the teal boat nosed up on the leeward side, catching a draft. Gritting her teeth, Jeri glanced at the telltale and braced her foot against the centerboard trunk, arching her body farther over the water.

"Here he comes!" Scotty shouted. Despite their efforts to head it off, the teal sloop split the water cleanly. As the two boats neared the marker, the competitor eased past Jeri and Scotty, tacking to round the buoy slightly ahead of them. Completing her own tacking maneuver, Jeri looked up just in time to catch a glimpse of the skipper, a dark mustached man, eyes shielded by sunglasses—a man who looked very like Dan Contini. Startled, she realized it *was* Dan Contini.

Yesterday's indignities roared in her ears. *"Monahan, dammit, the nozzle!...Faster, faster—the whole house could burn down waiting on you....The truck is twenty years old, lady. You can't gun it like that!* Did she ever once see an approving nod or hear a *Nice job,*

Monahan? Never mind that Smitty told her she'd out-performed most rookies.

Something ignited in her head. She clenched her fingers around the mainsheet. He might've been a navy man, but she'd show him he'd met his match as a sailor.

During the final leg, Jeri frantically implemented every trick she knew to outmaneuver Contini. "Scotty, we've got to come about quicker!" Her brother responded with a thumbs-up, and the next tack was cleaner. The distance was closing. Jeri's heart hammered from the exertion of the battle for second place. She had to beat him! Although he'd tolerated her at the training session, his pointed criticism and indifference to her accomplishments had rubbed her raw.

She found more wind and, nearing the final buoy, eased the mainsail until the boat, lifted by a timely gust, swept past the bow of the Contini boat by a scant two feet. *Yes!* She raised her fist over her head in a victory gesture. "Scotty, we did it!"

Unable to resist the temptation, she turned, hand lightly on the tiller, to look back at the third-place finisher. One muscular tanned leg braced on the deck, Dan Contini helped his crew to the stern. Some crew! A lithe sun-baked goddess with a long shimmering blond ponytail fell toward him, her bouncing breasts barely contained within the strip of fluorescent orange passing for a bikini bra. Jeri felt a gut-wrenching stab. Putting his arm around the blonde, he curled her to him and planted a playful kiss on her carmine lips.

Wasn't that just like him! Flaunting his perfect trophy girl. Jeri ran her tongue over her own wind-chapped lips and combed her fingers through her damp unruly mop of curls, unable to account for her irrational anger. Anger? She'd won, hadn't she?

Suddenly her hand stopped on her head. A sick thought surfaced. Could she be...jealous? Of what? Of that Barbie doll? She didn't even *like* Contini! But she did feel a pleasant shudder when she imagined his hands enclosing hers as he helped *her* to the stern of a boat, warming *her* against that hard bare chest, pressing soothing lips to *her* wind-burned skin.

She watched the couple rocking contentedly in the teal sloop to the slap of the waves. Sailing off into the sunset, for Pete's sake. *Forget it. The important thing is we beat him.*

"Jeri," Scotty said, "are we gonna sit in the middle of the lake all day?"

She blushed, then gestured at the tiller. "Want to skipper her home?" Carefully they exchanged places. Jeri held the jib sheet lightly and leaned back, letting the breeze play over her body like soothing fingers.

THAT EVENING Dan stood by the barbecue, the hickory smell mingling with that of the pungent sauce he ladled over the chicken pieces grilling on the rack. He carefully shut the lid and sprawled in a green Adirondack chair, one of two on the deck. Raymond Bell's willingness to help out at the marina gave him an occasional break—like today. He'd enjoyed getting out in the boat; hadn't really cared about the race itself, more the relaxation of a day off. Until... He frowned. What was it about that Monahan woman? No sooner had he recognized her than he'd gone from "at ease" to "man the battle stations." Too little, too late, though. With some skillful boat handling, she'd outmaneuvered him. Damn, he needed a drink.

As if reading his mind, Sissy Hayward emerged from the house, slipped a gin and tonic into his hand, sat down and raised her glass to his. "Cheers." She was wearing some gauzy flowered saronglike thing over her revealing bikini. Hell, he should've cried "foul" in the race—he'd been distracted by his own crew. She eyed him over the rim of her glass. "Your drink okay?"

"Fine."

"Salad's made and the potatoes will be ready in fifteen minutes." She dangled a hand across the armrest of his chair. "I like the view you get from here."

He liked it, too. The last few pleasure boats had headed for shore, and the Sunday-evening hush had fallen over the lake. A few fishermen still trolled along the opposite bank, but the surface, so recently roiled by water skiers, powerboats and the small one-person Wave Runners, was rippled now only by the slight breeze. A tall oak shaded Dan's deck from the setting sun, and he felt contented sitting here quietly listening to the water kiss the rocky shore.

"Can I get you anything?" He'd almost forgotten Sissy. A beautiful woman, but a nervous one. She always seemed to be fussing—combing the hair off his forehead, straightening the magazines on his coffee table, refilling his coffee cup. She'd come to the marina several times inquiring about boats for sale. He'd taken her out to demonstrate a ski boat, and one thing had led to another. She still hadn't decided on the purchase. He'd permitted their relationship to drift from business to personal. Why, he really didn't know. Something to do, he supposed.

"No thanks." She sat there sipping her drink, apparently sensing he didn't want to make small talk. She was undeniably attractive—sleek, long-legged, inviting. That was part of the trouble. From the way she moved her body when he pulled her against him, he knew she was expecting something more. Something intimate. He wasn't opposed to the idea, but sex hadn't been natural, spontaneous, not since Vicki. It was more like an obstacle course.

He stood up and checked the chicken. The prospect of Sissy in his bed should be appealing. She was everything a man would want in a woman—feminine, sexy, capable of making him feel important. Yet she was all surface, frothy and insubstantial. Maybe he wasn't being fair. After all, she wasn't Vicki, his exwife, and he shouldn't tar her with the same brush just because they had similar carefully cultivated good looks. Besides, Vicki had been more than insubstantial.

He grimaced. *Try blatantly unfaithful.* It was hard to remember now why he'd married her in the first place. He supposed there had been some good times, but they didn't last long. About all he had to show for the disastrous marriage were a badly damaged ego and a teenage daughter he hardly ever saw. Vicki used every trick in the book to keep Tiffany and him apart.

He felt Sissy come up behind him and wrap her slender arms around his waist, her exotic perfume mingling with the hickory smoke. Catlike, she rubbed her cheek against his back. He could feel her breasts pressing against him. He stood stock-still. Frothy, insubstantial…and suffocating!

Disengaging her arms as he turned toward her, he looked into her eyes, swimming with invitation. Damn. Why couldn't he want what was available? She wasn't looking for commitment, but he'd never been comfortable with the idea of a casual fling. He cleared his throat. "Chicken's ready. Would you bring me the platter?"

She paused, searched his eyes uncertainly and then

said, "Sure." She walked gracefully across the deck and disappeared into the house.

What was the matter with him? There weren't that many attractive unattached females in this neck of the woods. And if Jeri Monahan was any indication, few of the sort he preferred—gentle, feminine, placid. She was all mouth and fire. He'd been hard put not to laugh yesterday at the grim look on her face as she'd doggedly kept at a task until she'd mastered it. But he sure as hell wasn't going to give her any satisfaction. She'd wanted the job and, as far as he was concerned, still had a lot to prove. Grit, *that* he'd have to give her. Just like today. He'd been able to see the strain of every muscle as she'd willed her boat forward in that last run toward the finish. When she'd stood up to give her crew a high five, he couldn't help admiring her deliciously curved body. Quite a contrast to the comical picture she'd made buried in the heavy fire coat.

Hell! Why had he thought of that? Now he'd probably be mentally undressing her every time there was a fire call. He felt an unwelcome quickening in his groin area.

"Will this do?" Sissy stood in the doorway holding up a wooden cutting board.

He wilted. "Platter's in the cupboard over the refrigerator." Just then the undeniable odor of burning chicken assailed his nostrils. "Damn!" He opened the grill and flopped the charred thighs off to one side.

THE NEXT MORNING Jeri, who'd agreed to help out with the bookkeeping for her father's business, watched Hank spread bills out on the kitchen table. He pointed to one stack. "These should always be paid in full just before they're due. These others—" he gestured to the rest "—well, depends on our cash flow." He handed her the checkbook. "Any questions?"

"I'll be fine, Dad. And I'm not bashful about asking."

"Okay. I've gotta run." He swigged the last of his coffee and carried his cup to the sink. "Where's Scott?"

"At the marina doing some sail repair."

"Still no job?" Displeasure was evident in his voice.

"He's trying, but no luck yet."

Hank scoffed. "He's not apt to find a job in the cockpit of that boat."

"He's going to spend the afternoon looking." Jeri sighed, aware she sounded defensive.

Hank picked up his briefcase and headed for the door. "See you tonight. Call me if you run into any problems."

"I will." She bent over the invoices. Cedarcrest was an ambitious project. Her mother had encouraged her dad to undertake his dream of a planned resort-retirement community. The first phase included a condominium complex, a subdivision of retirement homes, a nine-hole golf course and a clubhouse. He'd invested deeply in it and, with the help of several substantial backers, had broken ground just a month before her mother's death. Much of his enthusiasm for the project seemed to have died with her. Generating buyers was more a matter of survival than fulfillment.

Scotty, too, seemed merely to be going through the motions, his fun-loving self, with a few brief exceptions, hidden somewhere in his fast-maturing body. When she'd first come home, she'd tried to talk with him about their mother, even about grief counseling, but he'd stiffened and angrily spit out, "I don't want to talk about it!" Further efforts had met with similar rebuffs.

She laid down her pen and rubbed her temples. It was hard to know what to do. Both Scotty and her dad sidestepped any direct mention of her mother, averting their eyes if she tried to head into the subject, as if avoidance were a kind of anesthesia. Maybe it was, even for her. There was little, really, Chuck and Doug could do living so far away with families of their own to consider. Sometimes she felt all alone.

Jeri looked vacantly past her mother's large loom sitting silently in one corner of the great room and watched the finches and chickadees vying for position at the birdfeeder outside the window, one of the many her mother had filled faithfully throughout the year. Dammit, she didn't *want* to forget. But it was easier not to think, not to remember.

Jeri stretched her arms over her head before bending back to the check writing. At noon she finished; and as she gathered up the neatly addressed envelopes, she heard a car pull into the drive. Scotty was back.

"Jeri, guess what?" She braced for the inevitable slamming of the screen door as her brother burst into the kitchen, his face alive with pleasure.

"I can't, so tell me."

"He gave me a job! Six dollars an hour for the rest of the summer. Isn't that great?" Scotty headed automatically for the cookie jar, extracting three brownies.

Anticipating his next move, Jeri opened the refrigerator and poured him a tall glass of milk. He looked so happy she didn't care if his job was apprentice cat burglar. "Start at the beginning. *Who* gave you a job?"

With his mouth full of chocolate, Scotty sputtered,

"Mr. Contini, at the marina. I start tomorrow. Great, huh?"

"Mr. Contini?" Jeri sank onto a kitchen stool beside him.

"Yeah. He saw me working on the boat this morning. He said he was impressed with my crewing in the regatta and wondered if I wanted a job. I'll be doing stuff like cleaning the rental boats, running the gas pump, maybe helping with the little kids' sailing program." He crammed another brownie into his mouth, crumbs littering the table. "The only bad part is I have to be there at seven in the morning. Jeez, I'll get fired before I begin."

She smiled. "You can do it, Scotty, I know it."

"Yeah, guess so." He picked up the third brownie and headed for the lower level. Contini to the rescue. Her father would be pleased. She knew she should be, too, for Scotty's sake. But the mere mention of the man's name caused conflict in her—annoyance and attraction. Judging by the hero worship in Scotty's eyes— and her own quickening heartbeat—she was in for a steady diet of Dan Contini.

CHAPTER THREE

THREE WEEKS LATER Jeri stood, gasping for breath and surveying the charred hillside. The stench of burned grass filled her nostrils. A thin coating of soot had settled on her body and she'd have killed for a drink of water. Her first fire.

Dread and excitement had coursed through her when the radio call came. She'd been the first driver to reach the firehouse. Luckily she was familiar with the remote location. The eight responding volunteers had managed to contain the blaze in fairly short order. Three of the crew were sticking around to be sure they'd doused all the hot spots.

Earl Gunderman offered her a canteen. As she swigged the lukewarm water, she didn't know when anything had tasted so refreshing. When she handed it back, he grinned and nodded his head approvingly. ''You know, I think maybe we'll keep you.''

She suddenly felt light as a feather. ''Thanks, Earl.'' The older man winked at her, then set out for his pickup, parked high on the ridge.

Smitty Dingle walked up, tilting his helmet back on his head. ''Looks like we got her contained. Let's turn this old fire wagon toward the barn, Jeri.'' He paused. ''Wait'll I tell Dan what a good job you did. He'll be proud.''

Jeri rolled her eyes. "I doubt it. After all, he wasn't here to see for himself."

Smitty loosened his coat nonchalantly. "Ain't you bein' a little hard on him?"

"Smitty, the man is never satisfied! In training I've manned the hoses, I've crawled on top of a roof, I've hacked in a locked door with my ax, I've demonstrated I can drive this old brush buggy. What more does he want?" With the back of her wrist, she swiped the perspiration from her forehead.

Smitty picked up the fire hose Jeri had coiled and hoisted it onto its hanger alongside the water tank. "Don't mind him. The important thing is we got the job done."

Jeri climbed in the driver's seat and coaxed the jerry-rigged fire truck to life. When Smitty joined her in the cab, she asked, "Do the others still resent me, too?"

"Nah. They just worry about you. And we're all grateful for another hand."

"Then what's Dan's problem? He's one of the younger guys. You'd think his attitude would be more...liberal."

"Kiddo, you're a victim of his navy experience. He was a safety officer on an aircraft carrier. Him and his fire crew were on the flight deck right in the thick of it. Dangerous as hell. He nearly got turned into a fireball himself when a pilot misjudged a landing and the plane crashed and burst into flames a few feet from him. He's got some mighty strong feelings about women in combat. He's just flat-out against putting women in harm's way. But you shouldn't take it personal."

Jeri downshifted over some deep ruts in the old logging road. "That helps explain his attitude, but it

doesn't excuse it. I'll just have to change his mind."
She accelerated over some dead limbs.

"Well, nobody's complainin' about you today. You
did a great job of gettin' us to the fire before it got out
of hand."

"Without all the rain we've had, that would've been
a tinder patch."

As Jeri backed the vehicle into the fire-department
garage, Dan strolled out of his office to watch her position the truck. "Just a little farther," he yelled, indi-
cating the distance with parallel palms. "Stop!"

Jeri bit her lip as she clambered down from the truck,
unbuttoning the heavy fire-repellent coat and shrugging
gratefully out of it. After securing it on the hook marked
Monahan, she turned to find Chief Contini frankly ap-
praising her. She squirmed, feeling the sweat pooling at
the small of her back, aware of how bedraggled she
must appear. She met his stare. "Area secured, Chief."
It took all her willpower to refrain from saluting.

She felt Smitty's callused hand on her shoulder.
"Dan, she did great—especially for her first call."

"Good. Sorry I didn't make it out there to help."
Dan turned abruptly toward his office, hesitated, then
faced her again, his expression more mellow. "You
okay? The first one can be scary." He moved toward
her. She stood, rooted, her heart pounding.

She looked up, defiance draining and tears smarting
at the back of her eyelids as she crumpled from the
release of stress. She was safe, the danger past. "I'm
fine, thank you." Her voice echoed reedily in her ears.

The hint of a smile played around his mouth, though
concern still lingered in his eyes. He reached a forefinger to her cheek and gently wiped off a smudge of soot.
"Good. When you get something to drink and wash up,

we'll fill out the report." He turned and entered the office, closing the door behind him.

Jeri shook her head to clear it. Why was she so close to tears just because he'd uttered a kindness? Why had her legs almost buckled when that gentle finger strayed across her cheek? Damn the man! There she stood, quaking, not from the relief of danger averted but from out-and-out physical attraction.

She sat down on the running board of the truck, took a few calming breaths and eased her sore feet out of the heavy ill-fitting boots. What caused her to react so powerfully to Dan Contini? She supposed she could chalk it up to a dry spell in the romance department this past year in Dallas. She didn't meet many eligible men teaching school, and the ones she *had* met included a healthy share of jerks. Brent Faxon had seemed like a viable possibility—witty, caring and great fun; but as they became more intimate, she found his competitive nature distinctly at odds with hers. So although the sex was satisfying, they'd finally decided to go their separate ways.

Why couldn't she let a man get close to her? Why did she always have to challenge? Sometimes she wished she could just wilt, permit herself to be taken care of like the very hothouse flowers she'd scorned. But here she was again—pitting herself this time against Contini. She shivered, then reached up and touched her cheek. The motion of his finger had been soothing, approving—and had activated a trembling nerve deep inside.

LATE THE NEXT SATURDAY afternoon, Jeri, grease-spattered and frustrated, turned up the heat under the chicken she was attempting to fry for the monthly community potluck supper. The recipe had certainly *looked* easy. She had just rearranged the pieces when her father appeared in the doorway, combing his fingers exasperatedly through his thick graying hair. "Where *is* that kid? The inside of his Toyota looks like a garbage dump!"

"He's—"

Hank held up his hands, warding off her answer. "Don't tell me. He's listening to that weird music. If he's not at work, he's holed up like a monk. Doesn't he have any friends?"

Jeri put a lid on the skillet, retrieved a beer from the refrigerator and handed it to her father. "Sit down, Dad."

Hank slumped onto one of the stools, contemplating the beer can for a moment before popping the top and taking a long swig. "Maybe I better start again." He drew a deep breath. "Where's Scott?"

"Showering and changing for the potluck supper and dance."

"Damn, is that tonight?"

Jeri waved the fork in the direction of the stove. "Yep. You forget?"

"Sure did." His features crumpled in defeat. "Anyway, it's hard—" he took another swallow of the beer "—to go to those things...alone."

Jeri started to object and then reconsidered. Softly she said, "You mean...without Mom?"

He looked up, blinking rapidly. "Yeah. Business is one thing, but these social occasions really throw me. People tell me I'll get used to it, but I don't know..."

Jeri felt suddenly old. "I miss her, too, Dad. So does Scotty."

"Hell, I know you do. Sometimes I don't think I'm dealing with all this very well."

"Nobody expects you to be Superman."

He gave a sardonic laugh. "No danger of that." He contemplated the beer can again. "Am I too hard on him?"

"Scotty?"

"Yeah. He's changed. We used to be buddies, but now...I haven't a clue how to talk to him. He resents everything I say."

"What do *you* resent?"

He shrugged. "His carelessness, his self-absorption. He's downright inconsiderate. And moody as hell."

"He's hurting."

"I know, but—"

"Cut him some slack, Dad. He's a teenager. A year ago he was a skinny kid, all elbows, knees and braces. Just the changes in his body account for some of his behavior. All of that would've happened, anyway. Mom's death on top of it...well, it's been especially traumatic for him."

Hank smiled sadly. "How'd my daughter get so wise all of a sudden?"

"High-school teachers who survive are quick learners." She shook the fork in his face. "Now go shower and get ready. I expect to be escorted by the two handsomest fellas in the place."

As THE LADIES of the Eagle Point Volunteer Fire Department Auxiliary bustled about the community-center kitchen clearing away the potluck-supper dishes, the musicians gathered on the small platform. Minnie Werther adjusted her ample bottom on the piano stool,

Gerhard Mann wheezed a few chords out of his accordion, and Chester Vinson rosined his fiddle bow.

Her cheeks flushed from the kitchen heat, Jeri removed her apron and adjusted the hammered-silver belt that molded the bright orange broomstick skirt to her waist. She pushed up the sleeves of her peasant blouse and dimpled with pleasure when Margie Atwater said, "You sure do look pretty tonight, Jeri. You won't lack for dancing partners."

Jeri grinned. Dancing partners? Balding old men with music in their hearts and arthritis in their knees, or adolescent boys, dancing on a dare. Still, it would be fun. Much to her disgust she found herself scanning the crowd for Dan Contini. What could she be thinking? But the fire chief was nowhere in sight. He was no doubt working late at the marina.

The musicians launched into a rousing rendition of "There'll Be a Hot Time in the Old Town Tonight," and several couples began two-stepping around the floor. Leaning against the serving counter, Jeri saw her father persuade Murray Forster's ancient widow to dance. She smiled. At least he was trying.

When the trio segued into "Peg o' My Heart," Smitty Dingle tapped her arm. "Hey, kiddo, how about a turn?" She barely had time to place her hand on his bony shoulder before they began swooping and dipping like a two-person whirligig. When the music stopped, he released her and wheezed into the nearest chair. He nudged the occupant of the next seat, who lounged in bored repose. "Scott, get out there and dance with your sister."

"Jeez, Smitty. That's old people's music. It sucks."

"Just try it, son. See if you can keep up with us old geezers."

Scotty reluctantly rose to his feet and took Jeri by the hand. "Here goes nothing." The band struck up "My Blue Heaven." Scotty awkwardly embraced his sister and swayed in place to the music. "Gimme a break," he muttered.

Jeri giggled. "You're doing fine."

An hour later, after Jeri's partners had squeezed, pumped and galloped her around the dance floor until she was breathless, the familiar strains of "In the Mood" filled the community center. Smitty grabbed Jeri and twirled her under his arm in a creditable jitterbug. Midway through the song, dizzy from the spinning, she felt Smitty's hand leave hers as he gently shoved her at someone standing on the edge of the dance floor.

Dan Contini. She flushed, overcome by an unwelcome headiness. He placed a warm palm on her back and clasped her right hand with his left. "I think I have this dance." Expertly he turned her into the crowd, holding her so that her left cheek was embedded in his broad shoulder. Only when they reached the center of the floor did he release her hand, fanning her beside him as they executed a side-by-side turn and then gathering her up again into a series of traveling spins. She had no time to react, to permit nerves to tangle her feet. She certainly wouldn't have figured him for a fabulous dancer.

With the final refrain still echoing through the community center, the crowd began to applaud. Minnie rose from her piano stool to take a bow, then plopped down to begin a dreamy version of "As Time Goes By." Looking up into Dan's eyes, Jeri felt herself melting into his body, now moving languorously to the classic Second World War love song. She breathed in his woodsy scent and let herself relax into his lead, enjoying the giddy sensations the smell and feel of him excited.

When the music ended, he gently moved her away, holding her by the upper arms and studying her with indecision. Then his eyes deepened with resolve. "It's warm in here. Could you use some fresh air?" She let herself be steered through the chattering crowd, out the door, past the huddled smokers, beyond the parking lot to the gazebo overlooking the lake, shimmering in the moonlight.

She sat on the worn wooden bench and hugged herself in a spasm of awkwardness, unnerved by the storm of feeling he'd aroused. For a long time he stood, hands in his pockets, his back to her, gazing out at the panorama of lake, trees, hills and sky. Finally he turned. "I don't know what to make of you, Jeri."

"Make of me?"

He sat down beside her, stretching out his long legs and crossing his feet at his ankles. He rubbed one hand through his thick black hair and then locked his fingers behind his head. "I hadn't counted on this."

She sat up straighter, the first spark of fight easing the sexual tension she felt between them. "Counted on what?" She turned and stared at his handsome profile. "The fact that I'm a woman?"

He looked at her with amusement. "No. That's been obvious from the first night I saw you."

"What, then?"

A half smile played across his face. "A fire chief isn't supposed to be attracted to one of his volunteers."

Her voice croaked. "Attracted? To me?"

"Yeah, you," he murmured, standing abruptly. He hesitated for the briefest of moments, then said, "Aw, what the hell.'' He pulled her to her feet, lowered his head and kissed her.

The kiss, tentative at first, grew more urgent. One hand strained against her back. Caught by surprise, she tried to resist, but the tide of her own response swept her on. When at last he disengaged his lips, he cradled her head in the hollow under his chin. She dared to open her eyes and breathe, noting gratefully that the earth had stopped spinning and reason was returning.

His hand moved tenderly over her head, the fingers capturing and releasing tendrils of sun-bleached hair. ''I was afraid of that,'' she heard him whisper.

''Of what?''

''That kissing you would be as good as I thought.''

She pulled away to stare at him. ''As you thought?'' He'd been thinking about her? Hard to believe.

His eyes twinkled. ''I think about you quite a bit. You're a challenge.''

His words nipped any trace of desire in the bud. ''That's what I am? A *challenge?*'' She backed away.

''Whoa, there. Don't knock *me* for rising to a challenge! Aren't you the female who wants to be a firefighter?''

Jeri poked him in the chest. ''There's a big difference between fighting fires and carelessly lighting the sort you just did!''

He grasped her hands and gazed at her solemnly. ''I never light a fire I can't handle.''

Oblivious to his sincerity, she rushed on, ''Well, Chief, this may be one fire you can't handle. So do us both a favor. Go soak your head in a bucket of cold water!'' She shook off his hands and fled toward the lights and noise of the community center.

His teasing voice followed her, hanging on the night

air. "No matter what, Jeri, you'll never be just one of the boys!"

Damn him! Her chest felt tight with a mix of anger and frustrated desire.

"Jeri, that you? Can we go home now, *pul-leeze?*" Scotty hopped off the hood of the Toyota, which was parked near the entrance of the center. "Dad left with Smitty."

"Nothing I'd like more." She opened the passenger door and threw herself into the seat. "Go!"

As Scotty backed out of the parking space and put the car into first, he cast her a sly glance. "Pretty neat you and Mr. Contini dancing, huh? He's a cool guy."

"Yeah, real cool," she muttered as her brother revved the engine and spun the Toyota out of the lot, scattering gravel in his wake.

IMMEDIATELY UPON returning home, Dan collapsed onto the worn vinyl sofa. "Bull, I've made a huge tactical error." He absently scratched the boxer between the ears. "I wasn't even planning on going to the damned dance." The dog looked up, sad eyes commiserating with his master. "What got into me?"

But he knew what. Jeri Monahan. He'd spent far too much time thinking about her ever since she'd stormed into his office that first night. "I should've had more control, boy." He'd always been a sucker for moonlight. And the kiss...well, he'd enjoyed the hell out of it, even if she *had* misinterpreted his words.

He heaved himself to his feet and set off for the shower. "I need this aggravation like a hole in the head." Bull padded along behind him and set up camp on the bath mat as Dan stripped, then stepped into the tub and turned on the faucet. He rotated his aching shoulders under the needles of hot water. Today at the marina had been frantically busy, and a fishing party was going out at five in the morning. He quickly soaped his body, rinsed and stepped out, wrapping a towel around his waist. He ran his fingers through his wet hair and scowled when he heard the phone ring.

"Eagle Point Marina, Dan speaking," he answered.

"Hello, Dan." His mood plummeted when he recognized Vicki's flat nasal voice. She hadn't called him in months.

"Hello, Vicki. Is Tiffany…?" The unspoken question hung in the air, knotting his stomach.

"She's fine," Vicki said dismissively. "Out with her friends celebrating somebody's birthday."

Dan clutched the towel, tucked the phone under his chin and picked up his watch from the dresser. "It's nearly midnight where you are."

"Don't turn overprotective on me, Dan. Not after all this time."

Her grating condescension made it hard to keep his voice steady. "She's only fifteen."

"Welcome to the nineties. I'm not running a nunnery."

He gritted his teeth. *That's for sure.* "So did you get my letter?" He'd written Vicki to ask her formally to send Tiffany, at his expense, to Eagle Lake to spend part of the summer with him. His custody agreement, allowing him four weeks, had been hard to manage when he was still in the navy, but there was no reason it wouldn't work now.

"I'm considering it."

Gee, thanks a lot. He hadn't spent any extended time with Tiffany in years. She was his daughter, and he was entitled! "What does that mean?"

"Well, to be perfectly frank, Dan, she doesn't want to come."

"Too damned bad. In case both of you have forgotten, I'm her father."

The line crackled. "Her *occasional* father."

Dan gripped the phone and tried to calm his rising ire. "Let's not rehash your resentment of my navy career. Now that I can manage it, I'd like for Tiffany and me to spend some time together getting to know each other."

"I'll talk it over with her and let you know."

"Since when is a fifteen-year-old in charge?"

"You don't have much choice, Dan. What do you expect me to do? Hogtie her and send her kicking and screaming?"

"If that's what's necessary." His voice hardened. "I don't really want to take this thing back to court."

He heard her resigned exhalation of air. That remark must have cooled her jets. "Okay, Dan, I'll get back to you."

"You do that. Soon!" He slammed down the phone and sat, exhausted, on the edge of the bed. Bull whined sympathetically and plopped down at his feet. Vicki and her game playing. How he always managed to come out the villain was a mystery. She was the one who'd sulked and blamed the navy for all their problems, who'd acted as if he had personally cut his own orders for sea duty, and who couldn't keep her pants on the minute his ship cleared port. The divorce had been the easy part, a relief, in fact. Tiffany was the hard part. He couldn't raise a kid from the flight deck of an aircraft carrier.

But he hadn't counted on the insidious job Vicki had done of alienating Tiffany. Age three: "Mommy says you don't love us or you'd stay home wif us." Age seven: "I know you're too busy for me. It's all right. Lotsa my friends don't have daddies, either." More recently, in answer to his queries about school, friends, interests: "What d'you care?"

In his last phone conversation with Tiffany, she'd asked him how "his little marina adventure" was going. He could almost hear her mother's voice-over. Vicki's hesitation when he'd threatened legal action gave him some hope that this time she'd relent and let Tiffany come. If only it wasn't too late. He loved his daughter and wanted to make up for those times he'd missed birthdays, dance recitals, school conferences.

He rose wearily and brushed his teeth, turned out the lights and climbed into bed. God, he was tired. The dog hopped up and stretched out across his feet. "Small comfort, Bull, but Vicki sure cured any stupid ideas I had about Monahan."

CHAPTER FOUR

JERI PICKED UP the knife and whacked the head of lettuce into fourths. Then, with equal vengeance, she attacked an onion. Last night's humiliating gazebo scene had played through her mind all day. Who had she thought she was—starry-eyed Liesl in *The Sound of Music?*

Every time she believed she detected a glimmer of sensitivity in the Great Contini, he swiftly proved her wrong. She would not be toyed with like some impressionable—she fumed while searching for the right term—marina groupie! *You want a challenge, Chief, well, step right up. You haven't seen anything yet.* A large green pepper fell victim to her cutting blade.

Slicing and dicing, she reluctantly had to admit her own role in what she chose to call The Incident. She'd walked, like a lamb to slaughter, out of the crowded, well-lit community center into that never-never land of moonlight and stardust, leaving behind caution and common sense. The man did something to her. Maybe if he had warts or a weak chin or—

"Ouch!" She sucked the cut on her thumb. Okay, so she was strongly attracted to him. And the dancing and kiss *had* been...fun. But next time—what next time?— she'd resist.

She picked up the cheese grater and started in on a wedge of Monterey Jack. No need wasting valuable time and energy on the sexy fire chief. She had enough on her mind with Scotty and her father.

The screen door slammed and her brother threw his thermos and lunch sack down on the counter. "What's for dinner?" He leaned over her shoulder, picked up a hunk of cheese and crammed it into his mouth.

"Tacos." She eyed him accusingly. "Now with a lot less cheese."

"Dan wasn't a happy camper today. What'd you *do* to him last night?"

Jeri opened the refrigerator, extracted a pound of ground beef and slammed the door. "Just drop it, will you?"

Scotty's face clouded. "Pardon me for asking. I'm goin' to the shower." As he walked off, she heard him mumble, "Gee, Jeri, glad to see you, too."

Well, that left only Dad to alienate. She pulled out a skillet, turned on the burner and began browning the meat, stirring vigorously. She'd just added taco seasoning when the phone rang.

"Jeri? It's Dad. Sorry to call so late, but I won't be home for dinner."

"Oh?"

He stammered slightly. "Something's...come up."

This was the final straw. She wasn't a short-order cook. "Like what?"

"There's someone...a business acquaintance. I thought we'd eat at the River Inn."

"Wonderful." She couldn't keep the irritation out of her voice.

"Hope you haven't fixed anything that won't keep."

Just pheasant-under-glass. "No. Only tacos."

"I may be late. See you in the morning."

"Sure." She was being selfish. Her voice thawed.

"Have a nice evening, Dad." She hung up and began setting two places at the kitchen bar.

The sudden crackle of the two-way radio and the shrill tone of the emergency beeper caused her to drop a spoon. "Structure fire at 9 Sparrowhawk Trail. Report to the fire station." This was all she needed. A house fire! Well, here was her chance to prove to Contini she was as prepared as the next guy.

She turned off the stove, grabbed her keys and yelled downstairs to Scotty, "Fire call. Food's ready."

She hopped into the Explorer and roared down the drive, her nerves jangling. She hoped the occupants of the house were safe. In that case, the volunteers would do what they could to minimize property damage, handicapped as they were by the limits of their training and equipment. But if someone was inside... She tried not to think about that.

DAN'S JEEP SCREECHED to a halt beside the tanker truck. The red lights of both vehicles cast eerie shadows in the thickening dusk. The wail of sirens screamed in the distance. A plume of gray-black smoke poured from the roof louvers of the Hunnicutt cottage, and Dan could see tiny fingers of flame grabbing at the shingles. A quick look confirmed that at least he was dealing with a composition roof. That'd slow the fire down some. He raced the last few feet toward Smitty, who was attaching the hose Jeri and Carl Rojas were quickly uncoiling. Jeri! He didn't have time to think about her other than to hope she knew what the hell she was doing.

He turned to Smitty. "Where's Cora Hunnicutt? She still in there?"

Smitty nodded his head to the left, where Dan could

make out Ted Allison, the EMT, bent over someone. "She's okay, Dan. Scared to death, though."

"Carl, start at that worst point and try to get that roof watered down before the damn thing spreads."

Just then Earl Gunderman and Jay Simmons arrived with the other tanker truck. Dan motioned them to drive around to the right and attack the roof from the back of the house. The snapping and popping of the fire made Dan's gut twist. Once a fire had this big a head start, about all a volunteer unit could do was contain it so it didn't spread to outbuildings or the adjacent woods.

Three more firemen jumped from a pickup and came running toward him. Dan directed two of them to the back of the house to assist that crew and the third to help Smitty man the hose. The thrust of the water made the hose heavy and difficult to manage, but Smitty, with Jeri's help, was holding it steady. Out of the corner of his eye, Dan saw Cora being restrained by Ted Allison, and through the confusion he heard her high-pitched screams.

Dan lifted the hose out of Jeri's hands. She looked up indignantly, her hazel eyes alive with questions. "Go help Ted with Cora. He's got his hands full." She hesitated only a fraction of a second before taking off at a run.

Sparks flew off the roof and the two streams of water seemed puny weapons against the flames. Two more volunteers arrived, quickly scaled a hastily erected ladder and began chopping a hole in the roof. Tongues of fire licked the shingles. It would be only a matter of time before the main story caught. The ceiling could collapse at any time. Dan swore through gritted teeth. It was a helluva thing to watch someone's home burn to the ground. But this fire added insult to injury—it had been only a year since Cora had lost her husband.

He called over his shoulder to Smitty. "Check the gauges. See how the water's holding out." No convenient fire hydrants existed in his fire district. Pretty soon he'd have to dispatch one of the tankers for a refill, and that meant the fire would gain even more momentum.

"Roof's goin'!" Smitty hollered, readjusting his grip on the hose. Dan moved to get a better angle. He glanced up at the sky, relieved to see giant thunderheads racing toward them from the south. If only it would rain to beat hell. Sure would make their work easier. But he judged they were a good ten minutes away from so much as a drop. Ten minutes was a lifetime when you were fighting a fire.

Just as another spot on the roof erupted in flames, he caught a blur of motion in his peripheral vision. He aimed the nozzle at the new flames and then glanced to his left. One of the firemen was sprinting toward the house. What the hell?

"Get back!" he yelled at the top of his lungs. His voice was drowned out by the roar and whoosh of the fire. Dammit, the volunteers all knew you never went into a burning building if the occupants were accounted for.

He glanced around frantically for someone to hand the hose to. Miraculously Steadham appeared beside him, huffing and puffing. "I was in town. Just heard." Dan thrust the hose at him and took off after the idiot running toward the house. With a sickening lurch of his stomach and a white-hot fury so scalding it stopped his breath, he recognized the small figure. Hell, he should've known. *Monahan!*

CORA HAD BEEN beside herself. She'd clutched at Jeri's coat, screaming hysterically. "Fritz! Somebody, please! Get Fritz! In the utility room." Finally calming the woman down enough to learn her miniature Schnauzer was trapped inside, barricaded behind a pet gate, Jeri had assessed the condition of the fire. Surely, if the utility room was just beyond the kitchen...

She raced toward the house, taking a huge gulp of air before throwing her weight against the door.

Smoke, thick and swirling, momentarily blinded her as she fumbled toward the utility room. Staying low, she felt her way along the counter, barely able to hear the shrill yipping of the dog over the crackling of the flames. She bumped into something solid. Damn! The refrigerator. Her lungs begged for air. The smoke was thickening; overhead she heard the inferno crescendoing. With her insulated gloves, she scrabbled frantically until, with heat blistering around her, she felt the gate, felt something squirming against her hand. *Hurry!*

Sensing rather than seeing where the dog was, she scooped the wriggling creature up in her arms. Crouching low and turning around, she felt an eruption of pure terror rising in her bursting lungs and exploding in her brain. She couldn't see anything. Nothing at all. Where was the door? She had to move...*now!* But what if she guessed wrong? Panic unlike any she'd ever experienced immobilized her. A crash, thundering and immediate, appeared to doom them. She held the dog in a death grip, terrified of losing consciousness. With her last bit of strength, she thrust the dog under one arm and began crawling toward where she prayed the door was.

Air! I can't breathe! She dug her feet into the floor, clawing and pushing her way toward...what?

Suddenly, miraculously, she felt hands under her arms, dragging and lifting her. And then she felt it— air! She sucked great drafts of it into her lungs and found herself lying on the ground, Ted Allison looking down at her with concern. Someone gently took the frightened dog out from under her arm. She closed her eyes. Safe. She was safe.

EXHAUSTED, JERI HUNG her helmet on the hook and ran her fingers through her damp hair. Her clothes stank of smoke and sweat, and her lungs felt seared. Her shoulders sagged. She could hardly muster the energy to drive home. Even in her worst nightmare, she'd never imagined a more devastating experience than this house fire. Poor Cora.

She put her palms in the small of her back and stretched in a futile effort to relieve strained muscles. Well, no point standing here reliving it. Swallowing hard, her throat parched, she scooped up her purse and moved through the group of tired beaten men.

The door to the office opened. "You're not going anywhere yet, Monahan." A grim-faced Dan Contini stood in the doorway, his red-rimmed eyes boring holes through her. "Step inside." He stood ramrod stiff as she passed him. Then he closed the door with an ominous click.

She should've known she wouldn't get away without a Contini lecture. She *had* disobeyed department policy, but it had turned out all right, hadn't it? Deep down, though, she didn't want to face, much less talk about, the unbridled hysteria that had consumed her when she'd been unable to orient herself in that smoky darkness.

Dan gestured to the wooden chair. "Sit."

She perched on the edge of the seat. He remained standing by the door, staring at her, motionless except for the angry twitch in his jaw. Finally he moved to the front of his desk, leaning against it, his arms folded across his chest. He loomed over her, making her feel like a fourth grader sent to the principal's office. She leaned back in the chair and squared her shoulders.

"Okay," he said. "I'm a patient man. What've you got to say for yourself?"

Honesty seemed advisable. "I was terrified."

He waited. She heard the tick of the minute hand on the clock as it advanced one notch.

"And I'm beat. Can't this wait until tomorrow?"

"No."

Dammit, he was not going to make her feel like a defensive child. "I exercised the best judgment I could at the moment."

He moved behind the desk, running a hand over his head as if he couldn't believe what he was hearing. Then he leaned on the desk and faced her, his voice rasping. "If that's your best judgment, Jeri, this department can do without you."

Icy calm descended over her. "Aren't you even going to listen to the explanation?"

He sat in the desk chair, eased back and steepled his fingers under his chin. "I'm all ears."

"Did you notice Cora was hysterical?"

"Yes. That's not unusual in the situation. Your job was to help Ted calm her down."

"And I succeeded, didn't I?"

"At what potential cost? That ceiling fell only seconds after we made it out. You put at least two lives on the line—yours and mine. And for what? A damn dog!"

She stood up, fists clenched at her sides. "You don't get it, do you? It was a lot more than a 'damn dog,' as you so sensitively describe it. Fritz was the only thing in the world Cora had left."

Dan abruptly sat forward, elbows on the desk. "I don't care if Lassie, Bambi, Morris and friggin' Flipper were all in that house. Your job, Monahan, was to fight the fire, save *human* life where possible and minimize damage. We're not a sophisticated big-city outfit, so that's about all volunteers can do. I can't overlook the fact you acted in violation of department policy."

She crumpled back into the chair, biting her lower lip. She wouldn't give him the satisfaction of seeing her cry even if giant tears *were* oozing against her eyelids. "So... what's my punishment?" Even to her own ears she sounded maddeningly like that child she didn't want to be.

"Lord, Jeri, it's not a matter of punishment." She could hear the weariness in his voice. "I'm responsible for these men—and you. We can't have loose cannons rolling around the deck. What you did tonight, regardless of your motives, jeopardizes not only our discipline but our lives. I can't have it."

She looked up, lips quivering. She saw not the self-assured chief, but a man, equally exhausted, whose primary concern was the welfare of others. A job he took very seriously. "No," she murmured. "I suppose not." How many men would've followed her, at considerable risk, into the smoky room and gotten both her and the trembling dog out of the house before the first floor ignited?

"Of course the dog was important to Cora. I know you thought if you could just rescue her pet, she'd calm down. But my God, woman, did you realize the danger you were in? What a close call we had?"

She swallowed the lump in her throat. "I'm sorry. I thought I had time." It took a huge effort of will to utter the next words. "I was wrong." She hesitated. "Does this mean...you don't want me in the department anymore? That I'll never earn my boots?"

His eyes softened. "No, stupid and frightening as it was, it was a beginner's mistake. One I *never* want repeated." His face relaxed into a rueful smile. "Do you always have to learn things the hard way?"

The question was rhetorical, and she didn't answer. Dan got up, walked around the desk and picked up her hand, drawing her to her feet. "Don't do that to me ever again, Jeri." His voice thickened. "I thought we'd lost you."

She slowly raised her head and looked up into his weary eyes. Tension drained from her body.

"Dan..." She hesitated and then spoke in a small voice. "It won't happen again." She turned, opened the door and walked slowly through the now quiet garage and out into the cool summer rain.

In the parking lot she paused before opening the door of the Explorer and stood, head tilted back toward the dark cloud-filled sky, drinking in the rain and the pure clean smell of the night. Dan's position was understandable; the reality was they'd barely escaped. Yet Cora had been pathetically grateful. Knowing the danger, Jeri wondered if she'd do the same thing again. She sighed, praying she'd never have occasion to answer that question. She pulled herself together and reached for the door handle. Before she could climb in, she heard Dan calling to her. She turned and saw him jogging toward her.

He stopped a few feet away. "Are you okay? I was pretty tough on you in there."

"I deserved it."

Stepping closer, he appeared uncertain. "I need to keep the lines clear here, but they seem blurred."

Her brow furrowed in puzzlement. "What are you trying to say?"

Rain dampened his dark hair. "In the fire department we know our roles, but personally..." He chewed his lip. "I'd like to do something about that." He looked at her and waited.

She could hear raindrops, like miniature timpani, beating on the hood of the Explorer in time with her heart. She caught her breath. "I don't understand."

"Tomorrow's my day off. My last free time before the three-day Fourth of July weekend." He paused. "How does an afternoon on the lake sound?"

She hesitated. Was this a good idea?

"One-thirty?" he added.

Oh, why not? "Okay. I'll meet you at the marina."

He tilted her chin and, with his other hand, tenderly wiped the raindrops from her cheeks. Still holding her chin, he leaned toward her and kissed her lightly on the forehead. Then he backpedaled toward the station. "See you then."

She hoisted herself into the driver's seat and sat, more confused than ever. Was this the same man she'd been furious with only hours before?

A TAWNY BOXER, stub of a tail wagging excitedly, greeted Jeri at the marina the next afternoon. "Your dog?" Jeri asked Dan as she knelt to pet him.

He stood in front of the outdoor freezer, unloading a bag of ice. "Yep. He's one of the best things about being out of the navy. Meet Admiral 'Bull' Halsey. I just call him Bull.''

"I like the name." The boxer rubbed his muzzle against her cheek. "I wouldn't have figured you for a dog lover."

"You mean after my remarks last night?"

"I believe you said something to the effect of being unwilling to save even Lassie."

"Here." He handed her a six-pack of beer to put into the cooler. As he dumped ice around the cans, he said, "Not unwilling. I didn't like the situation any better than you did. But in a volunteer unit, you just can't take those chances."

She nodded, the defensiveness of last night replaced by guilt. She'd let her heart overrule the training he'd given her. She slowly rose to her feet and drew her sunglasses from the top of her head down over her eyes. "I talked with Cora this morning. She's staying with friends."

"How is she?"

"Okay, considering. Still shaky of course, but determined to stay and rebuild. Fritz is okay, too."

He closed the lid and picked up the cooler. "Ready?" He placed a hand at the small of her back and guided her in the direction of a sleek ski boat.

"Nice."

He set the cooler in the stern and held out his hand to assist her. "My toy. Boats have always been my passion."

She lounged in the bow seat, watching him check the engine, untie the lines, take his place at the center console. "How's that?"

"I grew up on the Massachusetts coast." He switched on the ignition and the engine purred to life.

"My father was a commercial fisherman. Three of my brothers still are."

"Three? Are there more?"

"Yeah, Larry. He's an accountant."

"No sisters?"

"Nope. Mom and the dog were the only females." He shifted into gear and steered the boat slowly past the dock and out beyond the no-wake buoys. "You ready?"

Jeri nodded and he throttled the powerful craft, planing it to a smooth level ride. The wind whipped her face and ruffled her hair. Removing her cover-up, she smoothed sunscreen on her cheeks, nose and shoulders, wondering why she'd agreed to this outing. Judging from the way her throat had suddenly gone dry when she'd first seen him at the marina this afternoon, she had no business here. If the lines of their relationship were already blurred, today could serve only to blur them further.

She was acutely aware she was fighting her attraction to him. Fighting it just as she always did with any man who was both interesting and sure of himself. Why? She mulled over the question as the boat skimmed over the waves. She needed someone to fill up the empty space inside her. Beyond merely the void left by her mother's death, beyond her shifting relationships with Dad and Scotty. No, someone to fill that aching part of her, the part that wanted taking care of.

But she also needed control—in fact, was terrified of feeling *out* of control. With Contini, she didn't think both were possible.

DAN RESTED one hand lightly on the steering wheel and stretched out his legs, enjoying the view. A few fluffy white clouds idled their way across the azure sky. Vivid forest green pines mingled with the lighter yellow-green of the oak and sycamore trees clustered on the distant hills. The water looked cool and inviting. It was one of those Ozark days that reminded him why he'd moved here. Then, too, there was the view of Jeri in the bow— her short glistening curls, her sun-burnished face, her high-cut swimsuit revealing gorgeous legs.

He'd spent the morning berating himself for suggesting this caper, but he couldn't quite forget that kiss in the gazebo, nor could he simply chalk it up to the music and the moonlight. He'd certainly never intended to give in to the stirrings aroused by dancing close to her, smelling her delicately floral-scented skin and feeling her body mesh with his.

For any number of reasons, including the difference in their ages and his position as fire chief, it was unwise to become further involved. Judging from her reckless dash into the Hunnicutt house, she wasn't one to follow orders. He should be furious; her impulsiveness could've gotten them both killed. Yet last night in the rain, she'd looked so small and vulnerable. So incredibly appealing. But, he reminded himself, she was usually headstrong and confrontational, hardly his kind of woman. He needed someone like his mother—gentle, loyal, adoring.

He could still hear his father's commanding tone when he'd lectured him for sassing his mother. *You're not to treat your mama, ever, with disrespect. She takes care of all of us, never complaining, and I expect my sons to treat her with love and consideration. You do, and you'll learn how to treat all women. You'd be darned lucky to find a wife like your mother.*

Right! Dan pushed the throttle forward. Vicki. Hardly

lucky. Loyalty and faithfulness were empty phrases to her. He was well out of that marriage, even if it *had* taken four long years. Tiffany, thank God, had been conceived on their honeymoon, weeks before he'd left for sea duty, so he knew she was his; but she was the one who'd borne the brunt of that unhappy alliance. An occasional dad and a mother who treated her more like a sister.

He swerved to avoid a jug line floating in the water. Maybe this outing with Jeri wasn't such a good idea. He rarely acted on impulse, but last night it had seemed important to correct the mixed signals he was undoubtedly sending her. But involvement? Forget it. A man needed only one Vicki in his life to vow never again to let a woman make him vulnerable. The world was full of Sissy Haywards, eager to satisfy with no strings attached.

Jeri tucked one leg beneath her and, shoving her sunglasses on top of her head, turned to look at him. "Are we in some kind of race?"

Sweat beaded his forehead. "Race?" He didn't lift his eyes from her lithe body turned in profile as he eased back on the throttle.

"Yeah, I feel like I'm going after the bad guys in a James Bond movie." She rubbed a hand over her thigh. "That's okay. I can certainly hold my own. I just thought this would be a leisurely outing."

Hold her own? He didn't doubt it. He'd learned enough to know that, if necessary, she'd prove it to him. "See there?" He pointed to a small island with a deserted strip of beach. "Looks like as good a place as any."

He aimed for the gravel bar, cut the engine and scrambled into the bow, picking up the line. When the boat reached the shallows, he jumped out and pulled it in close, tying the rope to a sapling. He stretched out his hands to Jeri, unprepared for the wave of protectiveness that swept over him as he helped her step into the water. Was he getting in over his head?

JERI LAY on her stomach, her head cradled on her forearm, feeling the sun bake her back. There was something soothingly self-indulgent about sunbathing. Under other circumstances she'd probably fall asleep. But not today. *All* her senses were most definitely alert.

Through half-closed eyes, she squinted at Dan, standing at the edge of the water, methodically skipping stones. His bronzed muscular back and shoulders rippled as he threw. He seemed totally absorbed in the task of selecting just the right stone, then throwing it with perfect form. She closed her eyes. The Incident had been a touch of moonlight madness. Those loathsome words—*You're a challenge*—still stung. But here she was. Yesterday evening, when he'd stood there in the rain outside the fire station, he'd seemed genuinely apologetic, even a little hesitant. She did have to work with the man. What could it hurt to get better acquainted? A harmless burying of the hatchet.

Harmless? What was harmless about that body silhouetted against the sun? About the sureness of those strong hands grasping hers? About that intense blue gaze holding hers?

She groaned and flopped onto her back, covering her eyes with her arm. She didn't know whether it was the sun, the water, the faint scent of coconut oil or all three, but she could feel every nerve in her body melting into an erotic torpor.

I thought we'd lost you. His words had stayed with

her, replaying in her head. What had he meant? That he'd feared she would perish in the fire? That he'd be one *man* short in the department? She smiled wryly. Or, on some level, did he care about her, about their tenuous personal relationship?

A few moments ago when she'd asked him to rub sunscreen lotion on her back, she'd been unnerved by the feel of his fingers smoothing her flesh, pausing to cup her shoulders before sliding down across her back. She had become slowly and deliciously aware of her sensual arousal. She'd rolled over quickly. He, too, had seemed suddenly uncomfortable. He'd set down the lotion and walked off to skip stones.

She moved her arm, turning her head to watch him. He was hunkered down now at the water's edge, his forearms and hands dangling between his legs. A man careful with his words, mature in a nice solid kind of way. Maybe that was what motivated an insane urge to get his goat. Bringing the mighty low—one source of humor, her college-lit teacher had said. And something about Contini begged to be brought low.

She stood and strolled toward him, scooping up a handful of flat stones. "You've practiced enough. Ready to take on the pro?"

Straightening, he turned toward her, a smile twitching his mustache. "Who might that be?"

Legs planted, hands on her hips, Jeri responded, "Monahan the Magnificent."

He looked down, cocking one eyebrow. "Why am I not surprised?" He leaned over and took his time selecting his stones. "What're we going for—distance or number of skips?"

"Definitely number of skips. Finesse over strength."

"You're on. Three throws, total number wins." He executed a perfect four-point skip.

"Not bad," she said, and then threw her own four-pointer.

Both flubbed their second tries, miserable two-pointers. Contini observed the stones left in his palm and carefully selected one, discarding the other. Jeri watched the narrowing of his eyes, the concentration in his face. *Plunk-plunk-plunk-plink-plink.* He pumped a fist. "Yes!"

Jeri willed her body to relax. Why was winning this silly game so important to her? She swallowed, braced her feet, rolled the stone in her palm, gauging the heft. Then she drew back her arm and let it fly. "Four, five—" the pebble gave a last tiny plop "—six!" She jumped up and down. "I won, I won!"

Dan put a hand on her shoulder to ground her. "I see that." He looked down at her. "Don't you know you're supposed to let the guy win?"

She hooted. "Fat chance."

He grinned, then turned her around and led her back to the beach towel. "I'm thirsty after all that exercise." He pulled out two beers, popped the tops and then sat, leaning back against the cooler, stretching out his legs and eyeing her with amusement.

Suddenly self-conscious, she pulled on her shapeless cover-up and sat on her knees, sipping the beer, buying time to steady her pounding heart.

"You always like to win?" he asked.

"Always."

"Why?" He propped one elbow on the cooler, letting the can dangle from his hand, the pronounced veins and sinews in his forearm riveting her attention.

"Huh?"

"Why is winning so important?"

She turned the can nervously between her palms and thought about the question. "Doing my best is always important. And growing up with my brothers...well, nothing in the whole world was as great as beating them."

"Brothers, plural?"

"Scotty's the baby. It was my older brothers, Chuck and Doug, who taught me everything I know—" she smiled fondly "—and they didn't make it easy."

"Like?"

"Like using me for their tackling dummy, like having me shag balls for them at batting practice. My 'prize' was getting a turn at bat myself. Like bribing me to clean fish by saying I could go along in the boat with them. Like making a big deal out of teaching me how to mow the lawn so they could get out of doing it."

He crossed his legs and sat up. "Sounds familiar. I was the middle of five brothers. There were the 'big boys' and the 'little guys.' I was the loner, just sorta stuck in the middle. But I know how big brothers can be. Tough." He paused. "So you sometimes won?"

"Yeah, though not often. But I can hold my own with them on the tennis court and golf course, and I always won more prizes than they did at the county-fair midway. Patience, strategy, knowing your opponent's weakness. That's the secret."

"What was my stone-skipping weakness?" There was a mischievous glint in his eyes.

She made a show of considering the question. "Too much practice breeds overconfidence."

"Ouch! Do I come across as overconfident?"

She felt her stomach shift uncomfortably. "Well..."

"Go ahead. I'm interested in your opinion."

"I don't know if I'd say overconfident so much as sure of yourself." She screwed up her face in concentration. "I suppose you're used to ordering people around—the navy and all."

"And being ordered around. Yeah, I like knowing the rules, the procedures—what's expected. I'm not happy about surprises."

"Like my rescuing Fritz?"

"You scared me spitless."

"And confirmed all the reasons you didn't want a woman in the fire department."

"Don't get me wrong." His expression turned serious. "I'm just a very traditional kind of guy. I was taught to protect women, not endanger them. And once..." He shook his head. "Nah, forget it."

Jeri leaned forward. "No, tell me."

"It's just—" he struggled for words "—once you've seen someone engulfed in flames, someone you worked with every day..." He shaded his eyes.

"A woman?"

He nodded. "Could we just leave it?"

Jeri had never expected to see such...sensitivity in him. "Sure."

He stood up and pulled her to her feet. Still holding her by the hands, he moved closer. Her face was only inches from his shoulder. She felt, suddenly, awfully small. He smelled of sunscreen and beer. He dropped one of her hands and she felt his fingers twine through her hair, then stray down her bare arm, raising gooseflesh. Her legs trembled as she looked up into his eyes.

Then abruptly, he turned away. "We'd better go."

A surge of disappointment coursed through her for reasons she didn't want to examine. This afternoon had suddenly turned far too serious. He piled the towel in her arms and picked up the cooler. "Okay, Monahan the Magnificent. You wanna race?" He started running. "Last one to the boat's a rotten egg!"

Feeling as if a burden had been lifted from her shoulders, she sprinted after him, laughing breathlessly. She felt the thigh-deep water against her thrashing legs just before her toe caught on a submerged rock and she fell facedown in the shallows, soaking the towel. As she scrambled to her feet, she felt firm hands around her waist, setting her upright. She blinked the water out of her eyes and found herself standing dangerously close to Dan, her blood rushing.

"Are you all right?"

She tossed him the wet towel, flopped on her back and floated away from him. "I'm fine. C'mon. The water's great!"

He stowed the cooler and the sopping beach towel in the boat and began swimming toward her.

She sculled out where the gravel bar fell away to deep water. Surprises. He didn't like them. She lowered her legs so that she was treading water, then chuckled and waited. When he swam up beside her, he began treading water, too. She squinted at him. "Remember what we were talking about earlier?"

He smiled lazily. "What was that?"

"You know. How too much practice leads to overconfidence? How patience and strategy are important?"

"Yeah, what about it?"

"This!" She thrust her body as high as she could out of the water, grabbed him by the shoulders and dunked him with all the force she possessed. Then she swam several feet away.

He came up sputtering, blew out a mouthful of water and threatened, "Oh, no, you don't!" He started after her with a powerful crawl, then ducked beneath the surface, grabbed her by the waist and pulled her under. When they came up again, he still had his arms around her. She tried to squirm away, unsuccessfully.

"So you wanna play rough, do you?" Streams of water trickled off his hair and mustache, and his eyes were playfully challenging. "I'll show you about practice. Try this on for size."

And suddenly his lips crushed hers in a way that felt like the first time she'd executed a header off the high diving board. Then he released her. "Now what do you say to that?"

She treaded water and cast about frantically for a comeback, but all she could think of was *Practice makes perfect,* and that would never do. Or would it?

CHAPTER FIVE

FOUR MORNINGS LATER Jeri perched on the stone wall outside the historic Carnegie public library awaiting the ten-o'clock start of the annual Fourth of July parade. Tourists, video cameras in hand, lined the sidewalks; small children darted daringly out into the street; and periodically a honeymoon couple, arms entwined, sauntered past, oblivious to anyone else. American flags hung from every lamppost, and a huge banner over Main Street read Welcome, Visitors, to River Falls' Independence Day Celebration.

Even in the midst of the crowd, Jeri felt lonely. Every July Fourth the family tradition had been to eat an early breakfast, then come to town to watch the parade together from this very vantage point. Her mother had always brought a thermos of lemonade, and her dad had always insisted on wearing his straw boater with the red-white-and-blue band and breaking into "Yankee Doodle Dandy" at the slightest provocation. This year, though, her father had a Cedarcrest parade entry, her older brothers and their families were halfway across the country, and Scotty, of course, was gassing boats.

The rough granite beneath her abraded her bare legs. The humidity was oppressive, not a breath of air stirred the flags, and the massive walnut tree behind her offered scant relief. The relentless sun was already baking the pavement. When the teenagers next to her made room on the wall for a latecomer, she found herself wedged uncomfortably between a hot body and a post.

"Hi, Jeri." Jeremy Mason, a freckle-faced lumpy friend of Scotty's known to everyone as Bubba, leaned forward and grinned.

"Hi, Bubba."

"Scott comin' to the party tonight?"

Jeri's smile faded. "Maybe." She shifted uncomfortably, feeling smothered by the hulk next to her.

A loud cannon report stilled the onlookers, who turned as one, all eyes fixed on the top of the street where the colors, carried by Boy Scouts, were just coming into view. Strains of "The Stars and Stripes Forever" grew louder as the high-school marching band crested the hill. Jeri eased gratefully to her feet and placed her hand over her heart as the flag passed. Bubba and his friends poked each other and made satisfying guttural noises when the scantily clad pom-pom girls strutted past.

Jeri hopped back up on the wall. Why did it seem aeons ago she'd been a teenager? Maybe because, like it or not, she'd been thrust into a decidedly parental role. Last night's argument with Scotty was a case in point. He'd told her about the Fourth of July party tonight at Bubba's lake house. "Might not make curfew," he'd added offhandedly.

"Think again," she'd retorted. "With this three-day weekend, you'll be working late tomorrow and then all day Saturday and Sunday."

"So?"

"You need your rest. Mr. Contini didn't hire a deadbeat."

In a low angry tone Scotty had said, "Leave me alone. I'll handle it."

"You'd better start by handling your curfew."

In answer he'd curled his lip and mumbled, "You're not my boss," then left the room.

As the Elks' Club float passed in a blur before her, Jeri sighed. She knew she'd sounded sanctimonious to Scotty, and sure, she understood he wanted to party with his friends, but he had an obligation to Dan. She wished she could count on her dad for help with discipline, but he was working most of the time, seemingly quite content to let her deal with Scotty. Her brother and father shared a stubborn streak. It was exhausting to be the one caught in the middle. Maybe if she stopped serving as a go-between, they'd have to communicate with each other. That would be a novelty!

At least communication with Dan was on the upswing. Their outing the other day had eased the tension between them. Although her defensiveness had dissipated, she certainly couldn't say the same about the powerful effect of his kisses.

Berouged and sequined little girls twirling batons pranced past, but Jeri found it hard to concentrate on the parade. The self-pitying mood she couldn't seem to shake hung like a pall between her and the festivities. Restless, she heaved herself off the wall and carefully threaded her way through the throngs toward her car, parked on a side street at the bottom of the hill. She felt dizzy, as if she couldn't catch a full breath of air.

She flattened herself against a storefront when a heavyset man in faded overalls shoved past her, making a beeline for a vacated park bench. Two boys on skateboards rattled by in the gutter and executed swooping stops at the bottom of the hill just as the county-fair queen's convertible motored past. Feeling hemmed in on all sides by the press of strangers' bodies, Jeri stepped over a discarded piece of funnel cake lying on the rutted walkway, then turned into the shady side street.

Above the sounds of the parade she heard a voice. "Jeri! Hey, Tag!" She looked around, but saw no one. "Up here!"

Lifting her head to the next tier of buildings above Main Street, she saw Mike Parsons standing on the front porch of the Victorian cottage that served as his brokerage office. "C'mon up. I've got a bird's-eye view."

She waved and smiled gratefully. Mike was just the tonic she needed. She hiked up the ancient limestone steps carved into the side of the hill and joined him. He hooked an arm around her waist. "Unless you want close-ups, this is a great vantage point."

She watched the parade wind down Main Street, turn at the bottom and break up in the riverside park. Halfway down the hill, near the tail end, she made out a shiny silver convertible with the Cedarcrest logo on the side. A blond woman drove the vehicle while her father walked alongside, distributing brochures to the crowd. He smiled and waved, pausing often to shake hands or throw an arm around a bystander's shoulder. "This *is* a choice spot. See Dad over there?" She pointed. "He's hustling business."

Mike turned to her. "How's that going?"

Jeri shrugged. "It's hard to generate a lot of interest until he has something concrete to show people. He needs some up-front customers."

The convertible passed out of sight behind the Lamplighter Bed and Breakfast. Mike squeezed her waist. "He's a super salesman. He'll do fine."

"Oh, Mike, I hope so. It's about the *only* thing he shows much interest in these days."

Mike found her eyes. "Hey, Tag, that bad?"

She sagged against him and sighed. "Well..."

He perched on the porch railing, facing her. "Wanna tell me about it?"

Jeri tried to collect herself. "It's no big deal, Mike. I thought by coming home I could make things better, help Dad and Scotty adjust. But Dad's a stone wall, and Scotty resents just about everything I say."

Mike waited. When she fell silent, he spoke. "Take-charge Jeri can't make it work all by herself?"

She smiled sadly. "Maybe not this time."

He feinted a left to her chin. "Where's the old fight? The Monahan spirit? Win one for the Gipper and all that?"

She faced him squarely. "It's still there, I think. You've just caught me on a blue day."

"Correction, a red-white-and-blue day. And we're gonna do something about this sad-sack mood of yours. You have plans for later?"

"Not really. Scotty's working at the marina, and Dad said he'd be at the site all day."

"Perfect. I'll pick you up at four-thirty."

"Mike, you don't have to—"

He placed a finger on her lips. "Shh. No arguments. I'll swing by the Lazy Pelican and get a picnic supper. We'll take the ski boat out to the island and stay on the lake to watch the fireworks. Whaddaya say?"

She put her hands on his shoulders and gave him a sisterly peck on the cheek. "You're the greatest."

He thrust his hands in his pockets, pretended to give her remark serious consideration and grinned smugly. "Yeah, you could be right. The greatest."

She swiped at him and then backed down the steps. "See you later." She paused. "And thanks, Mike."

"So long, Tag."

At the bottom of the steps she paused to let a family pass. She started toward her car, then froze in her tracks. Across the street the silver convertible with the Cedarcrest logo was double-parked, engine running. The blond driver she'd seen from a distance earlier was an exceedingly attractive middle-aged woman—and sitting beside her with his arm around her was Jeri's father.

Jeri shrank back behind a spruce tree. When she dared to take another look at the couple, she felt a tremor of shock. Her father had leaned closer to the woman and was kissing her in a way that clearly had little to do with sealing a business deal.

MIKE EASED the throttle into neutral, turned off the ignition and let the boat drift to a stop in a small cove. The insistent chirping of cicadas, the drone of distant motors and the soft lapping of the wake hitting the stern filled the quiet.

As he tied the bowline to a half-submerged tree trunk, Jeri stretched a beach towel over the rear seat and settled back, fixing her eyes across the lake to the ridge of the mountain from which the fireworks would be displayed. Though the evening star was out, the fading sun still etched coppery streaks across the darkening surface of the water, where several hundred boats bobbed, vying for advantageous views. Jeri preferred the seclusion of the cove, with the dense dogwoods, hickories, oaks and pines crowding upward from the boulder-rimmed shoreline.

The craft rocked gently as Mike moved to the stern, finding the seat beside her. "We may not get the whole panorama, but we'll be spared howling babies or barking dogs in nearby boats."

"It's perfect, Mike." After the emotional storm that had racked her since this morning's awful discovery, she needed the peacefulness.

But even so, she couldn't dispel the image that, like the afterglow of a flashbulb, had branded itself into her retina—her father and that woman.

She trembled, remembering how she'd stood there observing her father disentangle himself, get out of the car and watch the sleek convertible move off down the street.

For a while she hadn't been able to move. Then, tears streaking down her hot cheeks, she'd jumped into her car and raced home, taking the curves dangerously fast. The hollowness of the empty house had echoed mockingly. The very normalcy of the surroundings infuriated her. Her world had tilted on its axis, so how could the toaster still be sitting in its accustomed place, the clock ticking on unconcernedly, the family photograph on the end table still projecting smiling faces?

She'd ripped off her clothes, pulled on an old swimsuit and raced to the dock, where she'd thrown herself into the cool water and swum a furious crawl far out into the lake. Finally, gasping and sputtering, she'd stopped to tread water and wipe the droplets and tears from her face. How *could* he? How long had it been going on? Who was this woman? She'd brought one palm down on the surface of the water with a furious splat. It wasn't only the betrayal of her mother's memory, but the way her father had shut her and Scotty out of his life, as if they were, at best, conveniences and, at worst, nuisances. His aloofness had hurt, but this new development had cutting edges that slashed at the bedrock of her certainties.

Mike reached in the cooler and handed her a cold beer. "You okay?"

She nodded. "I think so." She took a long sip and leaned back, closing her eyes. She couldn't even talk to Mike about what she'd witnessed. In fact, this afternoon she'd made a decision not to share her knowledge with anyone, and certainly not with Scotty for whom such information might be the final wedge between him and his father. She knew she needed to think the situation through, to find some satisfactory explanation, though she couldn't imagine what.

In the distance a dove cooed and Jeri opened her eyes in time to see, off to her left, the brilliant sun sink, like a giant lead ball, into the dusky rim of the far hills, leaving behind fragile wisps of blue-pink clouds. From the other end of the cove, she heard a splash—a large fish breaking the surface and falling back into the water.

Mike chuckled. "Remember that night Doug and I brought you fishing and made you swim out to untangle a lure from a submerged log?"

She raised an eyebrow. "When you guys gunned the boat and left me stranded?"

"So you remember?"

"Remember? I'm still studying suitable revenge. I was mad as hell and determined not to let it show. I had the last laugh, though."

Mike sat up. "You did?"

"Yeah, I swam to the point, hiked up to the Dingles and Smitty drove me home. I arrived before you did, and as I recall, Mom grounded Doug for two weeks."

"Hey, we were watching you all the time. We wouldn't have let anything happen to you, Tag."

"You expect me to believe that? Most of the time, you couldn't wait to ditch me."

He took a swig from his beer. "The best, though, was the time—how old were you, seven, eight?—when we locked you in the storage shed."

Her mind snapped back, and remembered hysteria rose in her throat. The dark interior of the sun-baked windowless metal building, fumes of gasoline mixed with odors of potting soil and old tires, closed around her as if it were yesterday. They'd been playing cops and robbers and, as usual, she was the bad guy. They'd captured her and taken her to "jail"—the utility shed. She'd been willing, even eager, to play along until she heard the rasp of the padlock inserted into the hasp and then, with terrifying finality, the click of the lock engaging. She'd pounded frantically on the door, choking on labored breaths and hot salty tears, but to no avail. Finally, with a whimper, she'd crawled up on an old picnic table, gagging as a thick cobweb brushed her face. She'd clutched her knees and sat motionless in the impenetrable darkness, shuddering every time she heard a mouse scuttle among the old magazines stacked in the corner. After what seemed an eternity, the door had opened, a shaft of brilliant light nearly blinding her, and her mother had scooped her up, crooning soft words in her ear.

"You know, I still don't like to think about that time." Her voice was stuck somewhere in her throat and her hands were clammy. "Maybe that's why I panic in cramped elevators and packed theaters."

"You're claustrophobic and you owe it all to Chuck, Doug and me?"

She swallowed hard. "I guess."

He stowed his now empty beer can in a side pocket of the boat. "And here I thought you were absolutely fearless."

"I would be, if it hadn't been for you three jerks."

"Jerks? Give us some credit, lady. Without us, you'd have been way too soft to volunteer for the fire department."

Jeri reached into her tote bag for a baggy T-shirt and pulled it over her head. The fire department! Just when she'd actually passed nearly four whole hours without thinking of Dan. Unless she counted that brief moment earlier at the marina when he'd looked up from the boat he was gassing and smiled. She'd waved, but when he'd seen Mike, he'd acknowledged them with a brief nod before turning his full attention to the hose nozzle.

A boom resounded over the lake and Jeri looked up just in time to see a spray of red and white sparks arcing in the air high above the distant ridge. Varying pitches of marine horns sounded from the lake as the boat owners signaled their appreciation. Mike slipped an arm casually along the back of the seat. "They're starting. Just sit back and enjoy."

The fireworks lasted half an hour, ending with a loud multiple burst of red, white and blue sizzling into the dark sky. When the last spark had been swallowed up by the night, Mike opened two beers and handed one to her. "No hurry. We'll let the crowd thin out."

They waited, lulled into companionable silence by the gentle rocking of the boat as wave action kicked up by departing craft washed into the cove. Finally the surface calmed and only the occasional boat could be heard purring toward home. Mike shifted and tousled her hair. "Ready to go?"

She smiled. "It's been a good evening, Mike. Thanks."

He moved to untie the line, then settled at the console. "I've enjoyed it. You need to take some time off, pal. You don't have to manage the whole world, you know.''

"Just the Monahan part of it.''

He paused before switching on the ignition and looked at her, his face somber. "Not even that, Jeri. You don't have to win 'em all. Not by yourself.'' The motor roared to life and he backed the boat around until he could accelerate out of the cove.

As they passed the no-wake buoys of the marina, Jeri found herself wondering if she'd see Dan again, but as they quietly glided past the dock where the marina office sat, she could see the office was closed. The calming evening ended with an unexpected thud of disappointment.

DAN SLUMPED in the Adirondack chair on his darkened deck, nursing a beer and trying to muster the energy to brush his teeth and fall into bed. Bull lay at his feet snoring intermittently. The Fourth had been brutally busy and weather permitting, he faced two more days just like it. The bad news was, he and his help were worn to the nub. The good news was, this weekend's business was the financial shot in the arm the marina needed. He'd sold nearly twenty-five hundred gallons of gas, countless sodas and candy bars, and, most profitable of all, he'd rented every seaworthy craft in his inventory.

He reached for the portable phone he'd brought out with him. Even though it was an hour later in Virginia Beach, he wanted to wish Tiffany a great Fourth of July. If his last conversation with Vicki was any indication, he doubted Tiffany would be asleep. He squinted in the dim light and hit the "memo" and "1" buttons. He waited three rings; then someone picked up the receiver, but immediately dropped it. In the background Dan could hear loud voices, the din of rock music and then giggles followed by a husky male voice, "Hello?…Can't hear ya, man…. Can ya speak up?"

Dan gripped the phone more tightly. "Tiffany." He raised his voice. "May I speak to Tiffany?"

The phone clattered on a hard surface again, and Dan could hear shouting. "Tiffer! Tiffer! Some dude's on the phone for ya."

Bull sat up, yawned and watched as Dan leaned forward, head in his hand, waiting. Minutes passed. He ground his teeth in frustration. What the hell was happening?

"Stop it, Tony, you're tickling!" The voice sounded like Tiffany. *Who's this Tony?* "Hi! Who's calling?" she asked breezily.

"Tiffany, is that you?"

"I can't hear you."

Dan vaulted to his feet and raked his free hand through his hair. "It's Dad."

"Brad? Get your buns over here. Party's on."

"*Dad*, as in your father, Dan Contini." He began pacing the deck, Bull following. "What's going on? Where's your mother?"

"We're having a little celebration. Bunch of the kids are here."

He thought he heard her hiccup. "Tiffany, let me speak to your mother."

"She's not… She's busy. She can't come to the phone right now."

"Are you all right?"

"Sure, Dad. Why wouldn't I be?"

He could think of any number of reasons, all of them guaranteed to make any self-respecting father old before his time. But what was he supposed to do long-distance? "I don't know. I just called to wish you happy Fourth of July."

"Gee, thanks, same to you, but I gotta go."

"Wait a minute, honey. Have you given any more thought to visiting me this summer?"

"Visiting you? In *Arkansas?*" She made it sound like the far side of the moon.

"You might like it," he muttered dryly.

"Soooo-eey!" Her rendition of the University of Arkansas Razorback cheer communicated her opinion more effectively than any four-letter word.

"I miss you," he said. "Think about it."

An especially raucous musical selection nearly drowned out her last words. "Gotta go, Dad. Bye!"

Dan clicked off the dial tone and leaned dejectedly on the deck railing. Physical exhaustion was nothing compared to the rejection he'd just experienced. Sometimes, like now, it was tempting simply to give up and wait until she was older, until she decided he wasn't so bad, after all. But she was his daughter, dammit, and he loved her enough to fight for her. He felt Bull's warm body pressed protectively against his bare leg.

He reached down and scratched the boxer's pointed ears. "C'mon, Bull. Let's hit the sack." He trudged inside to brush his teeth and get ready for bed.

After finishing in the bathroom, he turned out the lights and stood in the bedroom, letting his eyes grow used to the darkness. He yanked the string of the overhead fan and tried to jimmy the window open wider.

A movement on the water caught his eye. It was a ski boat, and when the dock light glinted off a curly golden head, he realized who it was. Jeri—and Mike Parsons.

Dan frowned. Seeing her with the guy this afternoon had, for some reason, irritated him out of all proportion. Standing there in that high-cut swimsuit, her bronzed body and honey hair gleaming in the sun, she'd sent an electric shock through him the likes of which he hadn't experienced in years. He'd nearly dropped the damn nozzle.

Turn it off, Contini. Go to bed. Despite his exhaustion, though, he stood watching from the window until Jeri and Mike hauled their gear from the boat to the car and drove quietly off into the night. Then, bone-weary, he stretched out on the bed and stared sleeplessly at the shadows playing across the ceiling.

CHAPTER SIX

THE NEXT MORNING after Scotty left for work, Jeri set her coffee mug down on the kitchen table next to the Cedarcrest ledgers and invoices. Her eyes burned, her head felt like a sodden balloon, and the sun glared distractingly off the glass tabletop. She'd hardly slept a wink, and when she'd finally drifted off, she'd been almost immediately awakened by early-morning bass fishermen motoring to their honey holes. Now here she was facing bills from Bud's Hardware and Elmo's Backhoe Service. From the open window she could hear powerboats skimming across the lake and the occasional shrieks of water-skiers. It was only Saturday; Sunday still remained before the noisy weekend vacationers packed up and went home.

With a deep sigh, she wrapped her bare feet around the chair rungs and began sorting the bills into categories. She'd written checks for all the utilities and was starting on the vendors' checks when her father, still in his boxers and formless T-shirt, emerged from the master bedroom. "Morning, honey."

She glanced up briefly, stifling her rage, and watched him pour himself a cup of coffee. He rubbed a hand over his unshaven chin and ambled to the screened-in porch. She turned back to the checkbook. Soon she smelled tobacco. Not a morning person, Hank was almost subhuman until after his coffee and cigarette.

The questions that had kept her awake most of the night hammered in her head: *Who is that woman? What is she to you? How could you kiss her like that? What about Mom?*

She drew in a sharp breath, ragged edges of grief lacerating her. Could she yield to the overwhelming loneliness she deliberately steeled herself against? No. Something else, like this betrayal of Dad's and the questions she had to ask, always saved her from confronting her pain.

In disgust she tossed the pen aside, uncoiled her legs and sat, fingers gripping the edge of the table. Waiting. A sense of awful inevitability clamped her mouth shut. Did she really want answers? Happy children's voices carrying in from the lake sounded in counterpoint to her hurt and anger.

Finally her father walked back into the kitchen, pausing to check the thermostat. "Think we ought to close up and turn on the air conditioner?"

She folded her hands in her lap. "Please. It's supposed to get up near a hundred today."

"Okay, I've adjusted it here. Can I talk you into pouring me some cereal while I close the windows?"

"Yes." Jeri stood and moved to the cupboard, wondering if her indignation showed. Somehow she had to get through these next few minutes one at a time, just as she had to get through the upcoming hours and days.

"Done." Her father settled into the place she'd set for him across the table.

"Banana?" she asked as she sat down.

"No, this is fine."

She watched him ladle the cereal. He looked up over the spoon and raised his eyebrows. "Something wrong?"

She wasn't ready yet to confront the main issue. Instead, she asked, "Do you know what time Scotty came in last night?"

"Uh, no. I must've been asleep."

"I wasn't."

"And?"

"Doesn't he have a curfew?"

"Of course he does." Hank set down his spoon and looked, really looked, at Jeri for the first time that morning. "What are you driving at?"

"Either he has a curfew or he doesn't. And if he does, then somebody has to make him accountable. I don't think I'm that somebody."

Her father's shoulders sagged. "How late was he?"

"Try one-thirty."

"I'll talk to him." Hank picked up the spoon and twirled it idly between his fingers. "He won't like it, though. Me, either. What's with that kid, anyway?"

"He's seventeen. It's a power issue."

"Well, I guess I'll have to clarify who's top dog."

"Terrific," Jeri muttered with undisguised irony. "That'll cement family togetherness."

Her father scooted his chair back, threw his napkin on the table and stood. "Look, Jeri, I know you're trying to help, but I don't need your sarcasm first thing in the morning." He started toward the bedroom.

She knew she'd gone too far, but a spearhead of anger goaded her on. "Okay, I'll change the subject. Who's the woman?"

"Woman?" He stopped in his tracks and pivoted slowly.

Jerry watched him intently. "The silver convertible?"

"You mean Celeste?"

Wonderful. Celeste. Nobody was named Celeste. Unless, of course, you counted Babar's elephant wife. "Who is she?"

With contrived nonchalance, he strolled back to the table. "She's a new member of our sales force."

Jeri studied his face. "You didn't tell me about her."

"I planned to today. We need to set up her payroll records."

And now for the slam dunk. "Do you always kiss your employees goodbye?"

His body froze. A lone Wave Runner swooped past their dock, the whine of the acceleration breaking the sudden silence.

Hank sat down, back erect, and leaned his arms on the table, his palms outstretched as if in supplication. "What do you mean, Jeri?"

"I saw you with her after the parade." *Score two for me.* "Your farewell went far beyond business."

"Oh." He returned her stare, then lowered his eyes. "You're angry."

A gusher of retorts filled her brain. *Oh, no, I love it when my father betrays my mother's memory.* Or, *Angry, who me? Whatever for? I'm only your daughter.* Instead, she clenched her hands in her lap, bent her head and replied firmly, "I don't know what I feel. But yes, anger's part of it."

"You think I'm being unfaithful?"

"Something like that."

"And too soon?"

"It hasn't even been a year."

He reached for the pack of cigarettes he'd left on the table, withdrew one and tamped it softly. "Yeah, I know."

She looked up and saw his pain-filled eyes. "Then why?"

"I don't expect you to understand. I've just been so damned lonely." His voice had a raw edge. "She's not Pat. No one could ever be, but—" he paused "—she makes me laugh. There was a time not too long ago I thought I'd never laugh again."

Begrudgingly Jeri admitted the truth of his last statement. "When did this...this relationship start?"

"Celeste's a recent widow. She moved to River Falls to be near her son in Fayetteville. Johnny Current at the bank knew I was looking for somebody with a Realtor's license. He introduced us."

She held her breath, waiting for him to go on.

Sensing her implied question, he continued, "That was about three weeks ago. We've been out to dinner several times. I only hired her Tuesday." He struggled on lamely. "I don't know where this is heading. Maybe nowhere, but she understands what I'm going through. She's been there. She's somebody to talk to." His eyes begged Jeri.

And what about Scotty and me? she asked silently. *We've been there, too.*

Hank waited, his body tensed. When she didn't immediately respond, he stuck the cigarette in his mouth and lit it. "Jeri?"

She found her voice, thick with unshed tears. "Would you have told me? Scotty?"

He stood abruptly. "Yes, dammit, when and if there was something to tell. Does Scott know?"

"No."

"Are you going to tell him?"

She raised her eyes. "That's your responsibility. But don't wait too long."

He stubbed out the cigarette, then came and stood at her shoulder. "I loved your mother, Jeri. We had a great marriage, but somehow I've got to go on living, hard as it is, and right now Celeste is helping." He laid a gentle hand on Jeri's cheek, pulled her head against his waist and held it there quietly. "Try to understand."

Jeri sat very still, part of her longing to fling herself into the comfort of her father's embrace, the other part strangely detached, emotionless. She shrugged. "I can't promise anything."

"I'd like you to meet her."

She moved away. "I'm not ready, Dad. Not yet."

He let his hand drop to his side. "I won't force you." She heard resignation in his voice.

He walked slowly across the bare plank floors and disappeared down the hallway. The ledger book swam in her vision, and her throat was scratchy. She'd won this round, so why did it feel like such a hollow victory?

She got to her feet and walked out onto the porch, gazing across the lake to the far shoreline, lushly green. Mom! Jeri pressed her fists into her eyes, trying to evoke her mother's image. She sucked in her breath when she realized she couldn't. All that was left was the picture album of her mind—isolated snapshots, frozen in time. But not the flowing ongoing details of each particular day blending into days. She couldn't recall the sound of her voice, what she was wearing the last time she'd seen her. Oh, God, why couldn't she remember?

JUST AS JERI FINISHED the bill paying, Scotty called to say he'd forgotten his lunch. Small wonder. He'd had only four and a half hours of sleep. She resisted the impulse to light into him for breaking curfew. After all, she'd turned that chore over to her father.

She found a place to park in the marina lot, grabbed the sack and headed toward the office. At the end of the gas dock, craft circled three deep, waiting to be refueled. She spotted Scotty servicing a fancy cabin cruiser. Two other teenagers jockeyed boats against the dock. Although a faint breeze riffled the surface of the lake, the thermometer beside the office door read ninety-six. Inside, three barefoot little girls with wet stringy hair stood in front of the candy counter debating their selections. Two sunburned women huddled by the door impatiently waiting while their husbands argued over who would pay for the gas. Dan stood at the cash register, the phone propped against his shoulder, break- ing a roll of quarters into the cash drawer and looking uncharacteristically harried.

When Jeri waved, he looked up, gave a slight nod and turned to process the gas buyer's credit card. She moved past the display of fishing lures out to the gas dock, passing the brackish-smelling minnow tank. Scotty grinned when he saw her.

"Food?" he said. She held up the bag. He hooked the nozzle into the holder and walked toward her.

"Thanks, Jeri. I'm starving, but we're swamped. Could you put the lunch in the refrigerator?"

"Sure. Don't work too hard." She turned back and entered the office. Dan was off the phone, filling out a rental contract for a timid-looking man with a big paunch whose worried wife fluttered around him asking repeatedly if he was sure he'd driven a boat before.

"Refrigerator?" Jeri asked.

"Back there." Dan pointed behind the counter and went on writing while Jeri set the lunch on the shelf above the stacked pint containers of night crawlers. When the phone rang, Dan gestured helplessly. "Could you get that?"

Jeri picked up the receiver. "Eagle Point Marina.... A rental boat for late this afternoon?" She looked at Dan, who shook his head vigorously. "I'm sorry, sir. All our boats are spoken for.... Okay, then, thanks for calling us."

Dan gave her a thumbs-up. "You're a natural."

"The voice of experience. I worked several years for a florist. That's also where I learned to drive a truck."

He crossed to her and gripped her shoulders. "Then you're familiar with cash registers, credit-card procedures, dealing with the public?" She would've laughed at his earnestness except for the disconcerting feel of his fingers.

"Sure am."

"I don't suppose you have the rest of the afternoon free?"

"Are you offering me a job?"

He dropped his hands. "We're in a bind. One kid didn't show up, and another one goes home at two. Could you help out at the register? I'd be indebted."

She grinned. "You'd give a woman that kind of power?"

"Today I'd welcome Lizzie Borden if she could give me some relief."

"I'm supposed to be flattered?"

The three girls chose that moment to place their half-melted chocolate bars on the counter. Dan looked distractedly out the window. A fisherman with a bucket stood beside the minnow tank tapping his foot. "Look, take these kids' money, I'll attend to that guy and be back to give you a quick rundown. You help me out and there'll be a bonus in it for you.'' He departed on the run.

What else did she have to do? It was obvious Dan was understaffed. She chuckled. Not under*manned*.

She gathered up the sticky change, completed the sale and from then on fielded a steady stream of customers—some happy-go-lucky, some frazzled and a few on the downside of intoxication. Scotty came in briefly to inhale his lunch, and Dan managed, between customers, to instruct her. Every time the door opened, a blast of moist hot air triumphed over the feeble efforts of the ceiling fans. By five o'clock she'd wilted, but there was no letup. When Scotty's shift was over, he'd gone home, leaving only three of them on duty.

At dusk Dan was cleaning up a rental pontoon boat when Jeri heard the ominous crackling of the two-way radio. She leaned out the door. ''Dan, there's a call coming in.''

He dropped the broom he was using to sweep the boat's carpeting and came toward the office on the double. ''Damn, double damn,'' he muttered as he raced past her.

She had trouble making out the garbled message, but Dan was already heading back toward the dock and the marina-owned speedboat. Over his shoulder he said, ''Keep an eye on things. Sheriff got a call from somebody who'd spotted our fishing rig with the nagging wife and the fellow who couldn't drive. Seems they're broken down and drifting up by the dam. I'll have to tow 'em. See you later.''

Following him outside, she watched as he took off in the speedboat. As his wake rolled in gently against the dock, she picked up the broom to finish sweeping the pontoon boat. Then, gathering the garbage the customers had left behind, she stuffed it in the oversize trash can. Mark, one of the teenage employees, was busy cleaning up the other marina boats, readying them for the next day.

She realized that working here had been fun and helped keep her mind off her father's troubling behavior. Despite the frantic pace today, Dan had found time to joke with the customers, especially the regulars grousing about the weekenders.

Jeri had enjoyed watching his naturalness with the men. It figured, she supposed, growing up with four brothers and spending months at a time aboard ship. She wondered about the women in his life. Seriousness, with her at least, seemed to make him ill at ease. Like the other day when they'd gone out in the boat. The two of them had gotten along better when the mood was light. Even then there'd been a certain intensity beneath the teasing and playfulness. It was becoming increasingly important to her to chip through his self-imposed emotional reserve. Bottom line: he intrigued her. And she desperately needed to nail down at least one of the confusing relationships in her life.

DAN LOOPED the final hitch of the rope around the stern cleat, returned to his seat and slowly eased the speedboat forward, the fishing boat in tow. The hapless couple were quite a pair—she sat in the stern, arms folded huffily, wearing a long-suffering I-told-you-so look. He sat meekly in the bow, avoiding eye contact. Damn fool had run out of gas and had fouled up the engine trying to fix the imaginary problem.

Dan groaned. Some people! His boat labored slowly across the lake, bow high with the drag. It would be eight-thirty or nine before they made it back to the marina. The kid would already have gone home, leaving Jeri there by herself, except for Bull. He didn't like it. You never knew when some weirdo would wander into the office. He should never have put her in that position. Okay, maybe he was being overprotective. But that didn't explain the twinge of jealousy he'd experienced yesterday when he saw her with Mike Parsons.

When she'd appeared today, as if summoned by his daydreaming, he'd been drawn up short by the coincidence—and by his pleasure. She wore brief flowered shorts with a blue scoop-neck tank top that did little to conceal the thrust of her breasts; and every time she leaned over the credit-card machine, he'd had to restrain himself from reaching out and touching her. *Back to business, sailor.* He glanced over his shoulder. The happy duo still weren't on speaking terms.

He needed to think of some way to thank Jeri for pitching in today. He felt a quickening between his legs. *Not that way.* He tried to picture the sinuous creamy body of Sissy Hayward, instead, but only a fuzzy image materialized. At least the attempt cured what ailed him. And whatever developed with Jeri, he realized Sissy was a thing of the past.

At eight-forty-five he arrived at the dock, bid a relieved farewell to Mr. and Mrs. Milquetoast and went about securing the boats. Through the window, he could see Jeri, head bent over the desk. The light danced on the gold highlights of her hair. His throat went dry. This was ridiculous!

When he opened the door, she looked up tiredly. "You had a good day today."

Then he noticed the cash receipts and credit slips spread in front of her. "You didn't need to—"

She cut him off. "Wanted to keep busy, so I figured I might as well help with the day's tally."

He stood behind her, leaning over to look at the figures. The scent of orange blossoms and the heat from her body were more arresting by far than his cash position. He shifted uncomfortably. "You're good help. Wish I could keep you."

She swiveled in her chair. "Why can't you?"

He took a step back. "What do you mean?"

Looking adorable in her sudden confusion, the double entendre hanging between them, she turned back to the desk and stammered, "Nothing. I mean...I just thought maybe you could use some more help here."

"Here?"

"At the marina."

He stood stock-still, considering. He *did* need more help, no question. While his first thought was how great it would be to have her around, his second thought came in the form of a red flag. Trouble.

She flipped off the crookneck desk lamp and rose. "I guess it was a stupid idea."

Before he could think, he reached out and took hold of her arm. "Not at all. It's just...I mean, why would you want to?" He gestured helplessly around the merchandise-stuffed room and at the walls where glassy-eyed trophy fish stared unblinkingly at them.

She looked up at him and smiled. "To tell you the truth, I'm getting bored at home. I need something to do, at least part-time, until school starts. Why not here? It's close, I know quite a few of your customers and I'm a hard worker." She colored slightly. "Sometimes I even follow orders."

How do you argue with that? Especially when you don't want to. He needed time to think. "Let's walk over to the house. I promised you a bonus. Will you settle for peanuts and a beer while we discuss the idea?''

They strolled without speaking to the brown A-frame. Jeri waited on the deck while he retrieved a tin of nuts and two bottles of beer from the refrigerator. When he returned, she was sitting contentedly in one of the chairs, Bull stretched out at her feet.

"It feels good to unwind," she said.

He handed her a beer. "Long day." He leaned against the railing and looked at her.

"You've had two in a row," she said. "You were sure busy yesterday when Mike and I were here."

"You two youngsters have a good time?" He sounded churlish. He wanted to kick himself.

"Yesterday? Sure, we always do when we're together."

Well, that settled it. Just in time—before he'd let this go too far. "He's a good kid."

She straightened, amusement in her eyes. "'Kid'? 'Youngsters'? I beg your pardon. He's thirty years old. Contini, you sound like Methuselah—and a tad condescending."

If she hadn't just made her preference for Mike clear, he'd swear she was flirting. "All I meant was, it's good you're dating someone near your own age."

She got up and walked over to him, hips swaying. "As opposed to, say, you?"

He shrugged. "I feel maybe I came on too strong... you know, the other night in the gazebo. I didn't realize you and Mike were a couple." He had the distinct feeling she was toying with him.

"Let's start at the gazebo. Wasn't it kind of like this?" She moved between his legs, captured his face in her hands and kissed him, deeply. He nearly toppled over the railing in surprise. Before he could recover, she whispered in his ear, "Or was it more like the rock skipping?" And she counted slowly to six, punctuating the numbers with a trail of kisses from just beneath his ear to the base of his neck.

Confused, he set her away, holding her by the shoulders. "I thought *I* was the one giving the bonus. What was that all about?"

She wriggled out of his hold and hopped up on the railing beside him, smiling mischievously. "Surprise! That was about an impulsive fireperson who forces herself on reluctant fire chiefs and rushes into burning buildings and who wants the *ancient*—" she drawled out the word "—marina operator to know Mike Parsons is an old friend, not a date. Anyway, she's much more attracted to—" she grinned wickedly "—even *challenged by* more mature men like, say—" she picked up his hand and slowly began caressing each finger "—a certain moody fire chief."

He was dumbstruck. She'd seen right through him, and damned if it didn't feel like all the fireworks he'd missed last night. He had no intention of standing there openmouthed and flat-footed. "Jeri, wait..."

If he made the next move, would there be any turning back? Before he could come up with a firm response, stop this conversation *now*, she reached up, pulled his head down and gave him the kind of kiss that proved he was no old man and she was definitely no kid.

JERI PULLED her lips away first, pressing against him, savoring the soft brush of his mustache on her forehead as he held her tightly against his solid chest. Then he tensed, pushed her to arm's length and looked at her with troubled eyes. His breathing was ragged "Jeri, I... Do you know what you're doing?"

Some part of him was withdrawing. She couldn't let that happen. She'd risked too much. She laid one hand on his chest, feeling his rapid heartbeat beneath her palm. "I think so. Don't you feel it, too?"

He dropped his hands. "This has to stop right here, much as I might enjoy it."

She put her arms around his waist and snuggled against him. "Why? Why does it have to stop?"

She felt his arms close around her again. "It's complicated. You don't know what you're getting into."

"And what might that be?"

His fingers played through her hair. "I'm not looking for a relationship. I wouldn't want to hurt you."

"And you think you would?"

He released her and paced to the other side of the deck, as if needing to put distance between them. "I *know* I would."

She gathered her pride and let out a deep sigh. To retreat now would give him control. And his words had been powerfully contradicted by his body. "How about another beer while you give me all the reasons?"

He shrugged, held the door open for her and led the way toward the counter that divided the small kitchen from the living room. Only one lamp was on, creating an intimate circle of light. She sat on a bar stool and waited while he opened a bottle and handed it to her. He stayed in the kitchen, keeping a barrier between them. She took a long sip and set the beer down decisively. "All right, Chief, let's have it. Reason number one."

"I'm thirty-six. Too old for you."

"So you think eight years' difference makes me a

kid, huh?'' She put her elbows on the counter and rested her chin in her hands. Something in his eyes flickered at the word ''kid.'' ''Contini, that's one big smoke screen. I'll give you maturity, but thirty-six is not old.''

She could swear she saw a faint hint of red creeping up his neck. ''Next reason?''

He cleared his throat. ''I could string you along. You're damned attractive, but I guarantee there's no future in it, so why waste your time?''

She set down her beer and slithered off the bar stool, then ambled around the end of the divider, took him by the hand and led him to the living-room sofa. She pushed him gently down and sat facing him, one leg crooked on the sofa between them.

''Future? Who's worried about the future? I just know I find you interesting. And sexy.'' She grabbed his hands. ''Look, I've got no expectations. I'm going to be working here. We'll be spending some time together. Couldn't we just see where it goes?''

He disengaged his hands and stood up, crossing to the bookshelf against the far wall, his back to her. ''It's not that simple.''

She got to her feet, too, and walked up behind him. This wasn't going well. Instead of clearing the air, she'd muddied the water. Yet there was something vulnerable, almost painful, about the tension in his back. Slowly she placed her hands on his shoulders and began kneading. ''Why not?''

He turned slowly and handed her a framed photograph of a young girl, maybe nine or ten years old, wearing a *Lion King* T-shirt. ''Here's one reason. My daughter.''

Jeri's head spun. ''You've been married?''

''Not for a long time.''

"She's adorable—" she waved the photograph "—but why should she make any difference?"

He sighed. "Jeri, my marriage was not a good one. My priority is my daughter, Tiffany. I think maybe you're looking for somebody... and I just happen to be convenient. It'll be a whole lot simpler if we agree you'll be an employee at the marina and a volunteer at the fire department—period."

Tears welled in Jeri's eyes as she carefully set the photograph back on the shelf. She'd made a mess of this; but if she could overcome her humiliation and focus on his evident pain, surely she could salvage something.

She turned back to him, picked up his hands and looked squarely into his eyes. "You're saying all the right words, Dan, but can you deny how strongly we react to one another? You've given me the full-blown Contini alert. I'm a big girl, okay? And I'm walking in with my eyes wide open."

She dropped his hands and reached up to frame his face. Standing on tiptoe, she kissed him, nudging his lips with hers, then exploring his mouth with her tongue until she heard a low moan and found herself gripped by his strong arms. "Jeri, what're you doing to me?"

"Kissing you, Contini," she murmured, "you stubborn fool!"

THE TUESDAY AFTER the Fourth of July weekend, Tiffany Contini perched on the kitchen table of her mother's apartment, her kinky dishwater-blond hair hanging in her face. She cocked the portable phone under one ear while she laboriously applied black polish to the nails of her left hand. "I don't know how long, Tony."

"This really sucks, Tiffer. You and me were starting to really get it on."

"You think I wanna go?" Her voice crescendoed. "I'd rather be put in a foster home. At least it'd be in Virginia someplace."

"Yeah, Arkansas's gotta be the pits. You'll hafta hang out with all them hillbilly dudes." He chortled. "Guess I don't have to worry about you with some ol' Festus redneck, right, baby?"

"Gimme a break."

"How long's this for?"

"Supposedly—" she rolled her eyes "—only a month. But with Mother, who's to say?"

"Y'think it could be longer?"

She pursed her lips and blew on her nails. "Not if I can help it."

"What's the problem, then?"

"Mom has herself a new 'relationship,' as she chooses to call what she's got going with this creep Purd Fields. Mr. Big Bucks. Seems ol' Purd the Turd wants to take her on a long trip in his palatial new motor home. And for some reason I'm not exactly welcome on this excursion." She mimicked a falsetto voice. "Whatever can we do with her? I've got it! Arkansas." Tiffany bonked herself on the forehead with her fist. "Duh. Like I was born yesterday or somethin'."

"When're you leavin'?"

"Who knows? To use navy lingo, I'm on standby."

"What's your old man like?"

"How would I know?" She screwed the lid back on the nail-polish bottle. "I haven't exactly spent much time with him lately. He's okay, I guess. But Arkansas? Yuck."

Before he hung up, Tony promised a big going-away

party. That would be the last fun she'd have for weeks. Mother couldn't wait to dump her on Dad and ride off into the sunset in that portable passion pit of Purd's.

Had anybody asked *her* what she wanted to do? That'd be a cold day! Dad would probably make all these wow-it'll-be-good-to-be-together noises like this was some Brady Bunch family reunion. Mom was only letting her stay with him because otherwise she'd be in the way, big time. Did either of her parents stop to think how it felt to be shuttled back and forth like some pet going to a boarding kennel? She swiped back her long mop of hair and slid off the table. And the media wondered what was wrong with kids today. Get a clue.

CHAPTER SEVEN

ON WEDNESDAY MORNING Dan stood in the office doorway watching solid sheets of rain swab the landscape gray. Distant thunder had awakened him about five o'clock. By seven the front had moved through, the wind had died and the storm had stalled in a steady downpour. Not even Fred, the fanatic of the fishing guides, had launched.

According to old-timers, this July was starting out the wettest in years. On Sunday two and a half inches had fallen in a matter of hours, effectively putting an end to the holiday traffic by noon. Except for yesterday afternoon and evening, it had rained ever since.

"Frustrating, isn't it, Bull?" He turned back into the office, trailed by the boxer, who flopped down on the floor by the battered desk. "Guess we've gotta expect days like this, but it sure cuts into profits." Dan settled into the desk chair and studied his inventory sheets. If the weather didn't clear, maybe he'd get Mark or Scott to come work while he went to town for supplies. He'd told the kids to stay home until he called—no point paying them to stand around. And Jeri wasn't scheduled until tomorrow. She'd agreed to work Thursdays, Saturdays and Sundays.

He set his pen down and rocked back in the chair. On Sunday she'd reported for work at eight and efficiently set about her business. And, except for the knowing little smile playing around her lips and the light dancing in her hazel eyes, you'd have sworn nothing had happened between them Saturday night. Ordinarily such assertiveness from a woman would've been a real turnoff. Instead, it had struck him as just right—just, well, Jeri-ish. Her up-front approach had none of the flirtatious overtones of, say, a Sissy or...a Vicki. There was something clean, like this summer rain, about her candor, her risk taking.

He laced his hands behind his head, smiling at the recollection of her determined mouth moving over his lips. She'd been gutsy, all right. Even as he'd tried to erect his defenses and restore reason to the conversation, her warm yielding body had provided a powerful counterargument. He was fooling himself if he thought he didn't need a woman.

He let the chair legs fall to the floor with a thump. Bull raised his head at the sudden sound. Turning back to his inventory, Dan tallied the stock on hand and made out his shopping list. The rain still thrummed on the roof. Only one customer had called. He walked out onto the covered dock and scanned the sky. No sign of a letup. Might as well go to town. He called Mark, who agreed to cover for him.

No sooner had he hung up than the phone rang. Vicki! She wanted him to know he'd "won," and Tiffany would be coming for a visit.

"When?"

"Sometime soon." When he asked her to be more specific, she responded in that patronizing sweetie-pie voice he hated. "Our plans are a bit vague. We're driving in your direction, leaving sometime in the next week or so. We'll drop Tiffany off with you for your four weeks while we do some traveling."

Who the hell was "we"? he wondered. No point stewing over that—the answer was obvious. Another poor sucker Vicki had reeled in.

As he drove along the winding highway toward town, remembering the conversation and Vicki's nonchalance about specifics, Dan's hold on the steering wheel was like a death grip. The Jeep sloshed through a huge puddle, splatting the windshield with a curtain of water, and he accelerated the wiper speed and tried to relax his hands. He didn't give a damn about Vicki and her plans. The important thing was that Tiffany would be coming. What did it really matter when? He wasn't going anywhere. Maybe they'd actually have enough time to repair some of the damage in their relationship.

He smiled wryly. In a matter of days he'd gone from having no females to worry about to having two—Tiffany and Jeri. So much for the notion of peace and quiet.

On Thursday when Jeri reported for work, the trees were still dripping from the all-night rain, and the sun was fighting a losing battle with the cloud cover. She tried, unsuccessfully, to quell the thrill she felt at seeing Dan again. He greeted her pleasantly, poured her a cup of coffee and settled at the desk, gazing thoughtfully at her. She hadn't talked with him since Sunday, and then, mainly about work; so his frank appraisal this morning, though agreeable, was unsettling.

She'd replayed Saturday night over and over in her mind. Had she pushed too hard? Worn her heart too obviously on her sleeve? She cast about for something to say. "Any word yet from the dive party? Have they canceled?" Eagle Lake drew numerous scuba divers who accounted for a solid share of the marina business.

"Yes. They rescheduled for the end of the month."
He swirled the coffee in his mug. "You ever been scuba
diving?"

Her voice echoed hollowly. "Once."

"You ought to try it again sometime."

She took a sip of the hot coffee to calm the sudden
gut-wrenching riot of nerves. "I don't think so." She
could feel perspiration breaking out on her forehead. "I
didn't like it." The memory of the face mask fogging
over and of the desperate terrifying sense of entrapment
she'd experienced caused her throat to constrict.

"Some people don't. I used to do quite a bit in the
Caribbean. I guess we'll have to stick to water-skiing
and sailing."

The panic subsided and she felt comforted by the
"we."

"You coming to the fire-department meeting tonight?"

"Of course."

"Would you have time afterward for a drink in town
with a 'stubborn fool'?" His expression was hard to
read. "We need to set some things straight."

Was his tone teasing or serious? "I'd like that."

He finished his coffee and stood. "Good. I've decided it's time I seized the initiative." Before leaving
the office, he turned at the door and gave her a jaunty
two-finger salute.

Tonight, no matter how hard it might be, she needed
to let the ball rest in his court.

THE RAIN BEGAN again in earnest during the fire-
department meeting, and Jeri and Dan had to make a
dash for his Jeep after the crowd cleared out. He started

the engine, switched on the wipers and headed toward town. "Where to? The Lazy Pelican or Dottie's?"

"I think Dottie's." Was it calculating to pick the place with the more intimate atmosphere?

They had just crossed the dam when the strident voice of the dispatcher broke in on the two-way radio. "Emergency at Bender's farm. Line cut out on me. Don't know the exact nature of the problem. Something medical. Lives way up in the hills beyond the dam. You take Martin Road and then wander off to the north somewhere after you cross Coyote Creek."

Dan reached for the microphone. "This is Contini. Monahan and I are close. We'll take a look. Better call an ambulance out just in case." He replaced the mike and shrugged. "So much for Dottie's."

She smiled grimly.

He sped along the dam road, the rotating red light casting grotesque shadows on the damp pavement. "Do you know how to get there? Those directions were pretty vague." He leaned over to tune in the emergency-radio band, barely making out the dispatcher's voice through the static.

"I think so, but it's been years since I've been that far up in the hills. Turn left off Martin at the Corey Mountain Road and go to the old logging camp, and then hope to God I recognize something or we get clearer directions from the dispatcher." Jeri leaned forward in an effort to make out landmarks through the persistent rain. "Do you have a medical kit?"

"Yeah." He nodded toward the back seat.

"Sounds like we'll need it."

He picked up her hand, icy with tension. "Some evening, huh?"

"At least it's not dull."

She hung on for dear life as he turned off the asphalt pavement onto a gravel road. Before they reached the logging camp, the storm accelerated, beating straight down from the sky. Suddenly at the edge of the lighted triangle made by the headlights, Jeri saw rushing water.

"The stream, Dan, watch out!" Normally dry, Coyote Creek was running a torrent of water. The Jeep lurched and ground through the ford and struggled up the bank.

"I hope the ambulance can make it," Dan muttered as he controlled the vehicle, now bucking over rocks, ruts and fallen limbs.

"Okay, there's the logging camp." Jeri strained to see. A lightning bolt briefly illuminated the clearing. "Veer right on that old utility easement road. If I'm not mistaken, his house is at the very end."

"I sure hope so," Dan said. "Time could be vital."

Her feistiness surfaced. She set her mouth firmly. "We'll make it."

The wind picked up, and the rain swirling around the Jeep created a phantasm of roiling trees, evanescent mist and eerie shafts of lightning. Finally Jeri spotted a pinprick of light in the distance. "There, Dan. There's the house."

As they rolled into the weed-infested littered yard, they again heard the dispatcher's voice. "Eagle Point Mobile Unit One—the ambulance is a few minutes behind you. Head your vehicle toward them and leave your lights on."

Jeri reached for the medical kit and jumped clear of the Jeep before Dan quickly turned it around. She ran to the shack and pounded on the door. "Mr. Bender!" She heard a muffled groan, turned the knob and entered, Dan right behind her now. The room was illuminated only by a single bulb suspended from the ceiling. The acrid odor of burned bacon assaulted her nostrils, and crumpled newspapers covered the soiled furniture. On the divan a grizzled old man with rheumy eyes and filthy gray skin lay on his side gasping for air and clutching his left arm.

"Get me some light, Dan!" She checked the man's pulse, then his pupils. He struggled to speak. She bent over him, reassuring him as she loosened the collar of his shirt and affixed the blood-pressure cuff to his arm. Dan held a flashlight above the man's body. She worked efficiently and calmly, oblivious to her surroundings.

To her relief, the paramedics burst into the room and knelt beside her. She quietly explained the situation. "Thank you, miss, we'll take over now." After quickly assessing his condition and tentatively diagnosing a heart attack, they carefully moved the old-timer onto the gurney.

Dan and Jeri followed them to the ambulance, using a frayed quilt to shield Bender from the pelting rain. One paramedic jumped into the back before the driver slowly pulled away. Jeri shuddered. Encircling her with his arm, Dan led her toward the house.

"Come on. Let's dry out for a few minutes. We need to turn off that hot plate and toss out the bacon. Whew!" He held his nose. Jeri watched from the doorway as Dan turned off the burner and passed her, holding the skillet high.

"Be right back. I'm gonna dump this mess outside. Maybe a desperate raccoon will eat it."

When he came back, he paused and searched her face. "You okay?"

She took a deep breath. "Now I am."

"I'm glad you knew where this place was. It's not

easy to find.'' Dan's eyes reflected admiration. "You did a good job, trooper.''

At last! Genuine praise from the fire chief. Wet hair hanging in ringlets, Jeri allowed herself a surge of satisfaction.

DAN SECURED the house as best he could before closing and locking the door. He and Jeri were drenched by the time they reached the Jeep and started down the mountain.

In four-wheel drive, the vehicle slipped on the wet grass and lurched over the mud holes. Jeri jumped when a jagged fork of lightning was accompanied by a gigantic thunderclap. The storm was right on top of them. The wind howled through the trees, causing the swaying branches jutting into the narrow roadway to scrape the windows.

Visibility was practically nil. Dan reached forward to wipe the condensation from the windshield, struggling to steer the Jeep over and around the obstacles.

"There's the turn, Dan. On the left.'' Jeri pointed to the logging-camp road. He saw it just in time to execute the maneuver. Rivers of water, eroding the thin gravel top layer, made the descent torturous. He was afraid of what he'd find when they reached Coyote Creek, notorious for flash flooding. He hoped to hell the ambulance had made it out, but he wasn't optimistic about his and Jeri's chances.

"You okay?'' He reached over and squeezed her hand.

"My teeth are still in my mouth—'' the Jeep scraped and bounced over a large rock "—barely.''

"This is some storm. I hate to say this, but I'm not sure—''

"—that we'll make it across the creek?"

"You got it."

"The ambulance…?"

"Yeah. I've been thinking the same thing." He picked up the radio. "Eagle Point Mobile One to base, come in." A garble of sound cutting in and out was the only answer. Damn. He tried again. This time he could make out a response. "Mobile One to base. Can you give us the condition of Coyote Creek? Over."

Through the static came the dispatcher's words. "Flash floods. Ambulance barely made it. Don't…the ford. Wait…morning." Dan stared disconsolately at Jeri, then shrugged. "Roger, base. Let Hank Monahan know we're okay. Out."

Just then the Jeep's headlights illuminated the torrent that was Coyote Creek. Dan leaped from the vehicle and ran closer for a good look. A tree trunk floated past and wedged against a rock outcropping. Rain cascaded off his ball cap. Dashing back to the Jeep, he slammed in behind the wheel, water dribbling on the floorboards and seat. "Dammit to hell!"

"Did you think you were going to cross somehow? Pull a Moses?"

He threw his drenched cap into the back seat and ran a hand exasperatedly through his hair. "Just making certain."

"Chief, I think we're stuck."

"See? This is the kind of thing that happens to firemen."

"Uh-huh. So?" Jeri's level gaze locked with his.

"So…it's no place for a woman."

"Good grief! Here I am marooned in a storm with you, and we're going to spend the night debating the role of women?" Her voice rose. "Did it make a difference back there before the ambulance came that I'm a woman? And as for our current situation, I've been wet before, and I've been cold before."

He had to hand it to her. Not only was she not complaining, she even sounded logical. But just as he'd never forget Virginia Adams's voice muffled by burn dressings, he'd never forget the avalanche in his gut when he'd seen Jeri streak toward the Hunnicutt house. He drew a deep breath before he spoke. "I've seen enough of you in danger to last me a good long while."

"Look, I'm through trying to prove anything. I just want to help."

"I know. Sometimes, though, in this job, we lose people we care about."

She looked up at him, her face illuminated by a streak of lightning, her eyes swimming with sudden tears. "It's not just this job. Sometimes we lose people we care about, anyway."

He reached for her then, pulling her closer, feeling her icy hands dwarfed by his. "Your mother?"

She stared down at their clasped hands and nodded. He heard her inhale sharply in an effort to stifle a sob.

"That was a tough one." He hesitated, wondering whether to say more. "You had no warning at all, did you?"

"No. I'm glad she didn't suffer, but none of us was prepared. She was too young."

That he could understand; it was the same with war. Young men—and women now, too—dying in their prime. "It may be none of my business, but how are you, Scotty and your dad dealing with it?"

She drew her fingers back into her lap. "Dad keeps busy with work, and Scotty...he's hard to figure. Neither one of them talks about feelings."

"And you?"

"Sometimes it overwhelms me, but keeping busy helps. It's like anything else—you simply have to pick up and go on."

He put his arm around her and pulled her against his wet shoulder. "You never stop fighting, do you?"

She hesitated a beat, then, "No. I can't." She laid a palm against his chest and pushed up, shivering.

"Cold?"

"And wet."

"I have a blanket in the back. Since we seem to be spending the night here, we'd be more comfortable there." Then protectiveness—desire?—overcame caution. "Anyway, I could at least warm you up without this damn gearshift getting in our way."

In the back seat, Jeri shuddered as she settled against him. He could feel warmth slowly creeping back into her hands. Gradually she relaxed, clasping her arms around his waist and cuddling closer. He rested his chin on her damp curls, aware of how snugly she fit into him. He gathered the blanket over her legs and sat quietly, lulled by the sound of the rain drumming on the metal roof.

On some level he knew if he wanted to preserve his peaceful life, he must detach himself from the surge of emotions he was experiencing—tenderness, connectedness and—time for honesty—need. Not just sexual. That, too, but this urging went beyond that, attacking an emptiness he'd ignored for years.

She sighed just then, a small sound like a contented kitten, and kissed the hollow at the base of his throat. His heart stopped. That small gesture aroused him more powerfully than all of Sissy's posturing. As sheets of lightning lit the sky, he looked into Jeri's eyes, limpid with desire. He leaned down, his lips brushing the corners of her mouth in slow tantalizing anticipation. Then he wound his fingers into her hair and crushed her mouth with his, unleashing his tongue and feeling a surge of exultation when she responded with matching ardor.

He shifted in pleasant startled reaction when he felt her palms move up under his shirt, exploring his chest, brushing his nipples. "Come here, woman." He turned her on her back across his lap and bent to kiss her eyelids, her mouth, the soft place on her neck where he could feel her pulse with his lips.

Her tiny moan urged him on, and slowly, his eyes never leaving hers, he began undoing the buttons of her blouse, certain that, with each gesture, he was moving irrevocably into the danger zone.

Suddenly she drew back. "What about...?"

He gently rubbed his forefinger over her lips. "Shh, it's okay. I'm prepared."

His last bit of control gone, he succumbed to his urgent need. As he feathered her soft skin with his mustache and slipped his hand beneath the lace of her bikini briefs, he felt her fingers clutching at his arms. He knew then he was beyond retreat; steaming full speed ahead was the only course....

When she trembled convulsively and pulled him closer, he whispered, "Jeri, like I said before...you'll never be one of the boys."

THE LAST DRIPS of rain filtered through the soggy branches as the gray eastern horizon gradually took on an orange tint. Jeri felt Dan's hands cup her face. "Wake up, sleepyhead. The creek's going down."

She unwound her cramped body from his and shed

the old navy blanket. Groggily she recalled the won-
drous night—the frenzied exploring, the playful
"shower" in the rain, the sweet reprise and the dream-
less sleep. She'd never imagined lovemaking could be
so varied, so totally satisfying. As she shrugged into her
shorts, she giggled, then laughed outright. "You know,
I don't think I *want* to be one of the boys!"

He tickled her playfully. "That's a relief!"

"But I *am* going to be one of the girls who's a proud
member of the Eagle Point Volunteer Fire Department."

He kissed the nape of her neck. "You win. If I've
learned one thing about you, it's that you're one persistent woman. But I have to admit it's part of your
charm."

She turned, grinning delightedly. "You're not so bad
yourself." She threw her arms around him. "And,
Chief, the fireworks have only begun!"

They sat, arms entwined, sated and content, in no
hurry.

As the sun burst over the line of far hills, they heard
the rumble of a vehicle, tires churning over muddy
ground. Dan gave a couple of toots on the horn. "I
kinda hate to see this night end," he said, sighing.

Jeri looked impishly at him. "Got any plans for
breakfast?"

Just then Smitty's black pickup lumbered to the far
bank. Surveying the creek, Smitty shook his head, then
yelled to them, "You can probably make it now, but I
thought you might need help. I brought food and coffee,
too."

He stood outside his truck, watching as Dan started
the Jeep, inched forward and lumbered slowly through
the receding water. When they'd achieved the crossing,

Smitty handed Dan a thermos and some sandwiches. Leaning on the open window of the Jeep, Smitty raised one eyebrow and asked, "You two get along all right out here? It was a helluva storm."

Dan squeezed Jeri's hand. "All in a day's work, Smitty. Just two firefighters doing our duty."

As Smitty moved away to climb back into his own vehicle, Jeri thought she heard him mutter, "This is one fire I damn sure don't need to put out."

CHAPTER EIGHT

THE FOLLOWING MONDAY evening Dan draped an arm around Jeri's shoulder and pulled her closer to him in the dim booth at Dottie's. Because the weekend weather, hot and sticky, had drawn hordes of visitors to the lake, heavy marina activity had left little time to explore his reactions to Thursday night's adventure. He did, however, know two things for sure—he'd never forget that night, and his feelings for Jeri, though still confusing, ran deep.

He gazed at her, her honey-tipped hair brushed back from her high forehead, her lips pursed as she perused the menu. He grinned self-consciously. He couldn't take his eyes off her.

She looked up with a whimsical smile. "What are you staring at?"

He leaned over and brushed her forehead with his lips. "You. Sexy you."

She rubbed a hand along his thigh. "I like the way you talk, Chief."

After they ordered, he shifted away from her slightly. "I told you last week I needed to set some things straight. About my marriage, about Tiffany."

"It's not necessary."

"Yes, it is." He raised his eyes to the ceiling in an effort to collect his thoughts. "My marriage to Vicki, my divorce...well, both were disillusioning. The end result has made me...gun-shy. With women."

Jeri toyed with her spoon. "She must've hurt you badly."

"Initially, yes. For a hotshot navy man, few things are as humiliating as an unfaithful wife."

Jeri looked up, startled. "Unfaithful? She must've been blind or stupid."

"In fairness, being a navy wife is tough. It takes a special kind of woman, one with patience and staying power. Qualities Vicki lacked. One thing she didn't lack, though..." His voice trailed off.

"What's that?"

"An indiscriminate sex drive."

"Oh." Jeri's voice sounded small and faraway.

Dan's jaw twitched. "Hell. Let me just get this over with. Our marriage probably wouldn't have lasted, anyway. We weren't suited. We were just two horny kids with unrealistic notions. It's what she's done with Tiffany that hurts."

"What's that?"

"Turned her against me. I'd have sued for custody if I'd had any way to take care of Tiffany. But I was gone too much. It wouldn't have been fair."

"It doesn't sound like Vicki's been very fair."

He snorted. "'Fair' isn't in her vocabulary, and she's pretty manipulative." He swiveled to face her. "My daughter's coming for a visit soon. It could...make matters difficult for us."

"It needn't. I understand you'll want to give her lots of attention."

Jeri had hit the nail on the head. "She's only going to be here a month. I just hope it's long enough."

"For?"

"For trying to make up for being an absentee father. For, I don't know, bonding. Partly from growing up with brothers, spending most of my life with men, I don't know how to treat her. Girls, women, they've never been my strong suit." Jeri raised one eyebrow as if to question that last statement. The implied compliment felt good. He rushed on. "No mission was ever as crucial to me as this one. I just hope I can show her how important she is to me."

"When's she arriving?"

He let out a sardonic laugh. "Good question. I don't know."

"Why not?"

"Vicki's vagueness is just one more way to show me she's in charge." He paused as the waiter set down their platters of fried catfish, french fries and coleslaw. "Enough of that. I wanted you to know, that's all."

She smiled at him, relieving his dour mood. "Thank you."

After dinner they sat nursing brandy ices, listening to the lone guitar player sitting on the small stage playing old Simon and Garfunkel tunes. Dan was keenly aware of the honeysuckle scent of Jeri's hair, of her breast pressed against his arm, of the warmth in her eyes every time she looked at him, which was often. He could hardly wait to have her all to himself to love the daylights out of her.

Suddenly she clenched his hand, nearly cutting off the circulation. He looked at her. Her face had turned pale and she was sitting at attention.

"What's the matter?"

He followed her gaze, which was riveted on the entry. He recognized Hank Monahan talking to the hostess. Standing slightly behind Hank was a stylishly dressed blonde. He watched as the woman moved up next to him and slid her arm possessively through his.

"Jeri, what—"

"It's them!" She seemed to shrivel beside him. Her eyes were bright with unshed tears and her lips were set in a grim line. "It's my father and his—" she choked out the next word "—date!" She cringed. "Damn, they've seen us."

Dan looked up to see the couple threading through the packed tables toward them. He leaned over and whispered in Jeri's ear, "I don't know what's going on, but I'll help get you through it." He rose to his feet as the twosome approached.

Hank shook his hand and then put his arm around the woman. "Celeste, this is my daughter, Jeri, and her friend Dan Contini." He nodded at his date. "Celeste Ives." He fixed his eyes imploringly on Jeri.

Jeri glanced at him, then back at Celeste. Slowly she pulled her hand from her lap and shook Celeste's. "How do you do."

Celeste smiled. "I'm delighted to meet you, Jeri. Your father thinks the world of you."

Jeri withdrew her hand. "Thank you."

An awkward silence followed. Dan finally spoke. "We'd ask you to join us—" Jeri kicked him under the table "—but we were about to leave. Maybe some other time."

Hank's shoulders sagged. "Yes, some other time. We'd like that. Have a good evening." He steered Celeste to a nearby table.

Dan signaled the waiter for their bill before easing back into the booth. "What was that all about?"

Jeri sighed. "A difference of opinion about what constitutes a suitable mourning period."

"Oh." Dan wasn't about to touch that subject. He threw down some bills and drew her to her feet. "Let's get out of here."

"Gladly."

He propelled her to the door and out into the parking lot. There he pulled her into his arms and held her for a long time, combing the fingers of one hand through her hair. "You seem so upset."

She looked up. "Oh, it's just...Dad seeing another woman...." She shuddered. "Everything's different. Dad. Scotty."

"Let's see if we can get your mind on something else, then." He framed her face with his hands and kissed her with all the tenderness at his disposal. Her lips tasted like brandy and cream.

She moved against him, deepening the kiss, thrusting her tongue into his mouth. He reacted spontaneously, grabbing her to him and grinding his hips into hers. She could get him hot just like that!

"Dan—" somewhere above the pounding of his blood, he heard her tiny voice "—please...take me home with you."

FROM THE KITCHEN the next morning Jeri could hear the clatter of utensils, cupboard doors opening and shutting. Scotty must be fixing a bowl of cereal or his lunch. She should get up, but lassitude drained her energy, leached away her will. Normally an early riser, she huddled under the sheet, letting the ceiling fan play over her as the sun rose higher and higher.

Dan's tender lovemaking last night had been a soothing balm. He'd sensed intuitively how much she needed to be held, comforted. He hadn't pressed her to talk about her father and Celeste. Somehow he'd read the situation and had known exactly what kind of remedy to apply. Her body still throbbed with the memory of his carefully applied kisses and expert hands.

But for all his sensitivity, the wound of seeing her father and Celeste still festered. She rolled onto her side, staring vacantly at the dogwood tree just outside her window. To be fair, it wasn't Celeste's fault. And admittedly her own curtness had caused the hurt in her father's eyes. She knew she should face the facts like an adult. Her father was lonely, he'd met an attractive woman, he deserved to go on with his life. So what besides the timing rankled? She sat up on the edge of the bed. She knew. She'd always thought of her mother and father as an inseparable pair, one's actions defining the other. And now there was only one. Who was this man she called Dad?

She placed her hands on her knees and drew in a deep breath. That was it, all right. She stood up, grabbed her robe and ran a brush through her tangled curls. But what could she do about it? The answer? Meet him halfway—if she could.

Scotty was just leaving when she wandered into the kitchen. He paused in the doorway, leering at her. "Have fun last night?"

She grabbed a cup off the mug tree. "MYOB, bud."

"Little late getting in, weren't you?"

She picked up the coffeepot and glared at him. "Who're you to talk?"

He shot her a scorching look. "At least our absentee father won't ground *you*." He walked out, slamming the door behind him.

Shakily she poured the coffee. Things were obviously no better on that front. She popped two pieces of bread in the toaster and sat on a stool. Her problems lodged in her chest like shards of broken glass.

The phone interrupted her daze. It was her father calling from his office. She hadn't seen him this morning because she'd slept late.

"You looked like you were enjoying Dan's company last night," was the first thing her father said.

He must've seen her before she saw them. She couldn't have looked like she was enjoying anything after she'd spotted Celeste. "Yes."

He seemed taken aback by her monosyllabic answer. "I'm glad Celeste was able to meet you."

"It was bound to happen sooner or later."

"Jeri, I—" she could hear the sharp intake of his breath "— I hope you'll make an effort to understand. Celeste is really a very fine person."

Jeri let the phone drop below her chin as she tried to formulate an answer. With sudden clarity, she realized she didn't want to lose her father. But she *did* want to know what was going on with him, and that knowledge inevitably involved Celeste. "She seemed lovely. I'm the one with the problem, Dad, but I'll try. I really will. Give me a little time. Then maybe the three of us can get together."

"Oh, honey—" she heard the lilt in his voice "—I'd like that." He paused. "I do understand this isn't easy for you."

"No, it isn't. Change is painful, but I guess it has to be lived through. Will you be home for supper?"

"Yes. I realize I haven't been very attentive to you or Scott."

That, at least, was a step in the right direction. "Okay. I'll see how badly I can screw up a pot roast."

His laughter defused the tension, and she hung up on a more optimistic note. It was a beginning.

LATE THURSDAY AFTERNOON Tiffany sat cross-legged on the bench in the rear of the motor home, flicking the TV remote control. "Jeopardy"—oh, there was a good one. All those nerdy contestants gave her a pain. "Looney Tunes"—kid stuff. Finally, "Oprah"—something halfway interesting, anyway. Sure beat looking out the window at dumb scenery like the muddy waters of the Mississippi. After the ocean, she was supposed to be impressed? They'd spent the morning in Memphis. Purd the Turd was a big Elvis fan and nearly peed his pants when he stepped onto the sacred grounds of Graceland. Totally boring!

Her mother was sitting up front next to Purd. He had on this gross Hawaiian shirt that looked like vomit walking. And with his thick gold chain nestled in that mat of gray chest fur, he probably thought he looked like a real stud. *Think again, bozo.* Mother seemed taken with him—or more likely his bank account.

The motor home began to weave and lurch around curves. Up and down. Back and forth. Tiffany thought she might puke. Where the hell were they? She stood up and made her way to the front. The two-lane highway wove in front of her in distressing zigs and zags. Her mother turned around when she approached.

"Look, sweetie, isn't this just gorgeous?"

Just gorgeous. Nothing but trees, hills and stationary mobile homes with crap all over the front yards. She figured when they crossed the Mississippi, she'd experienced the last of civilization, but nothing had prepared her for...Arkansas. She'd seen these big signs—Welcome to Arkansas, the Natural State. That was dumb. *Natural,* as opposed to what? Artificial?

Just then the motor home swooped down a steep incline and across a bridge. Tiffany felt the corn chips she'd been munching all afternoon rise to her throat. "Can you slow down or something?"

"Sure, sugar." Purd tapped the brake. "You just hang on. Only a few more miles to Harrison. We'll stop there for the night."

Tiffany negotiated her way back to the rear, holding on to the fixtures as she went. How could her father have come to a barbaric place like this? She'd only just crossed the state line, and already she couldn't imagine how she could stand this backward place for a whole month. She stared out the window, blinking back tears. It wasn't fair. Other kids had real homes with mothers and fathers who cared about them. Her mom and dad cared about her in their own way maybe, but something else was always more important—like Purd and this trip or the navy, or now the stupid marina. She'd never come first with either of them. Not really.

Oh, crap! If things weren't bad enough already, there was a billboard advertising—she made retching noises—Hillbilly Heaven Café.

JERI SWIPED her moist forehead with the back of her hand. Not a breath of air stirred the surface of the lake. Bull lay beside the cooler, panting. The noisy overhead fan served only to stir up the sultry air. Not for the first time today she wondered what had ever possessed her to volunteer her services here when she could be home luxuriating in frigid air-conditioned comfort.

Was it cooler outside? She strolled onto the dock and observed Dan gassing a boat full of college students.

His ball cap pulled low on his forehead, he moved efficiently, economically, his muscular legs and broad back glistening. Even in his most abandoned lovemaking there was that same precision born of the desire to make every gesture, every caress, count. She rubbed her arms, shivering with the sudden recollection of those splayed fingers moving intimately over her inner thighs, inciting her to a fever pitch. Dan Contini. He was why she worked at the marina.

Dan straightened, caught sight of her and smiled. He collected a bill from one of the students, gave the hull a gentle push away from the dock and headed toward her. When he reached her, he used a finger to flick away the drops of perspiration pebbling her skin at the crevice of her halter top. "Hot enough for you?" He stood very close, eyeing her breasts and gently tracing that same finger up her breastbone. There was no mistaking his double meaning. The heat, the sudden quiet, his heady proximity, all merged to send a shudder of desire through her.

What she wanted was to strip that T-shirt and those gym shorts from him, take his hand, jump into the cool water and, like a shimmering fish, slip and slide against him until her need could be satisfied. Instead, she ran one hand up his arm and smiled at him. "Not half enough." She stood on tiptoe and whispered huskily, "Wait until I get you alone tonight."

He chuckled. "You're playing with fire, you know."

She flipped the bill of his hat with her index finger and looked straight into his eyes. "Lucky you taught me how, then, isn't it?"

Just then her brother, astraddle a Wave Runner, rounded the first set of slips and nuzzled up to the gas dock. "Here's the five-o'clock rental, gassed and ready to go."

As Scotty secured the rope, Dan eyed the sky. "Clouding up a bit. Maybe we'll get some relief."

"At least a little breeze." Jeri pointed to the flagpole before reentering the office. The listless Stars and Stripes fluttered halfheartedly. "See you guys later."

Inside she pulled a bottle of lemonade from the cooler and forced herself to sit in the wooden desk chair, her thighs sticking to the seat, and tackle the day's receipts. She pressed the cool bottle to her hot temple as she riffled through the slips of paper. She was interrupted once by the "five o'clock"—a thirty-something preppy-type eager to prove his manhood aboard the Wave Runner.

Just as she was finishing the accounting, Dan and Scotty came in and flopped into two vinyl-covered chairs. "I don't like the looks of things," Dan said. "Have you had the radio on?"

Jeri moved to the small refrigerator, fixed two glasses of iced tea and handed them to Dan and Scotty. "What do you think? A storm?" She dialed in the radio weather band.

"That'd cool things off," Scotty offered.

Dan hunched his shoulders and threw his ball cap on the table. "Maybe, but it's too damned oppressive. When are the rental boats due back?"

"One at six, the other two at seven."

The detached voice of the National Weather Service forecaster said, "Storm watch for northeastern Oklahoma and the four northwestern counties of Arkansas."

Dan swigged the tea and stood up. He moved nervously to the door and peered out. "Think I'll check the moorings. Be sure everything's shipshape just in case.'' He opened the door and walked toward the rental slips.

The sky visible from inside was still blue, with only the occasional small cloud. Scotty looked at Jeri. ''What's his problem? It doesn't even look like rain.''

Jeri settled in the vacated chair, blowing at the damp curls clinging to her forehead. ''Summer storms don't give much notice.''

Scotty ambled to the door. ''Oh, great. Well, I just hope those idiots on the rental boats have enough sense either to come back before the storm or to lay anchor in some cove. But no, they'll probably come right at the height of the storm and expect yours truly to get drenched.''

''Maybe it'll miss us.''

Scotty shot her a skeptical look. ''Not with my luck.''He shoved open the screen door. ''Guess I better go help Dan.''

Jeri went to the front door and looked at the hill blocking the western view. Storms had a way of swooping down over the Ozarks with little warning. As if to emphasize her thought, there was a faint rumbling of faraway thunder, too distant to accurately locate the direction. The flag straightened and flapped against itself with a smart crack. The approaching hum of motors drew her attention to the buoy line. The Wave Runner and rental fishing boat were coming in. She glanced at her watch. Right on time. Six o'clock.

While Dan and Scotty gassed both and secured them in their slips, she handled the paperwork for the renters. One of them, a frequent local customer with weathered skin and a scrawny body, removed his cap and scratched his head. ''Storm comin'.''

The thirty-something preppy agreed. "Waves were churning in the main channel." He grinned confidently. "I gave 'em a helluva ride."

Jeri bit her tongue. *I'll just bet..* She turned to the fisherman. "See anything of our pontoon boats out there?"

"Only the eighteen-footer. Up by the dam."

She put the bills in the cash drawer. "Thanks." Wave Runner Man picked up his credit slip and the two left together. The hairs on the back of Jeri's neck prickled. The swaying of the dock, on which the office sat, grew more pronounced. A sudden loud rumbling reverberated from the mountains across the lake. Bull scrabbled across the floor and cowered beneath the counter.

She stepped outside just as Dan finished hauling down the flag, gathering up the life jackets and stowing them in the compartment under the roof overhang. As clouds massed, the skies darkened to a putty color and the surface of the lake seethed.

He put his arm around her. "Hang on. I think we're in for it." He scanned the lake. "Dammit, I hope those jerks know enough to get the boats off." She shuddered, considering the investment he had in rental units.

The wind picked up, blowing out of the northwest. The cove was still somewhat protected, but she could see the main body of the lake rising and falling as the white-tipped waves picked up height. She felt Dan's grip tighten on her shoulder as he pointed in the distance. "There's one!"

Dipping and cresting across the surface of the lake was the eighteen-foot pontoon boat, the four passengers huddled near the console. As the boat drew near, she could see their anxious faces. Scotty ran to the end of the dock waving them in on the lee side. Dan grabbed the bow, looping the line around the dock cleat. The two men tried to appear calm, but their wives were clearly terrified. Just as Scotty was assisting the first woman onto the dock, the wind violently shifted straight out of the north, blowing the woman's straw hat into the now crashing waves.

Jeri held the office door open as the two women scurried for shelter. "Oh," one gasped, "I thought we was goners. Myrtle here don't swim. And, hon, there's whitecaps *that* high!" She held her hand at waist level. Jeri didn't doubt her. The office was rolling beneath her feet and she experienced a sudden spasm of vertigo. When the four men burst into the office, a violent gust of wind wailed through and tore the door from Scotty's hand.

Gunmetal waves, topped with dingy foam, beat relentlessly against the dock. The boardwalks creaked and buckled with the force of the onslaught. Before Jeri could say anything, Dan dashed out the other door, his voice drowned by the wind. Something about gas tanks. The four hapless boaters made a mad dash for their car. Just then a jagged streak of lightning split the sky, too close for comfort, followed immediately by a gigantic thunderclap. Within seconds large drops of rain pelted the roof like BBs, then a rushing curtain of water beat against the windows.

Jeri grabbed the edge of the counter for support. "Scotty, where's Dan?"

"Turning off the gas lines to the dock so if they rupture, they won't spill."

The idea of Dan out there in the dark, with all that lightning, fiddling with metal valves, was unsesttling. The office lurched and the bottles in the cooler clanked. "I don't like this," she said in a small voice.

With an attempt at bravado, Scotty answered, "It'll blow over soon." But his eyes glanced warily from the door to the window.

The fan stopped whirring and the lights flickered and went out before slowly coming on again. "Oh, no, not a power outage," she implored.

The door flung open and they both looked up, startled at the whoosh of cooler air. Dan stood there drenched, rivulets running down his face, water puddling at his feet. With effort, he pushed the door shut behind him. Jeri handed him a towel from behind the counter.

He rubbed his face and hair. "It's nasty out there. I hope that fella in the twenty-four footer had the sense to hole up somewhere." Worry lines creased his face.

"No such luck!" Scotty, who'd moved to the window, pointed. "Here he comes."

Dan threw down the towel. "Son of a bitch! That dummy'll ram the boat right onto us."

The three of them ran into the dark slashing rain, maintaining their footholds with difficulty on the slippery surface. The marina, pounded by waves, plunged and reared like a thing alive. It was impossible to gauge distance or motion. Jeri felt her skin crosshatch with goose bumps and within seconds she was soaking wet. She clung to a wooden post, slick with moisture, and watched as Scotty and Dan, grotesquely outlined by a furious lightning fork, struggled to the end of the dock. The pontoon boat was moving toward them too rapidly, and in the dark, the driver seemed unaware of the frantic motions both Scotty and Dan were making to direct him to the lee side. Instead, with inexorable power, the bow was making straight for the storm-lashed weather side.

A powerful pitch lifted the boat atop an incoming wave. For an instant Jeri thought the pointed fronts of the pontoons would cleave the dock in two. She caught only snatches of what Dan was shouting. "No! Circle wider. Over here!" His voice was impotent against the roar of wind and water.

At the last moment the driver tried to correct his error, but the wave action picked up the stern and savagely pushed the craft broadside toward the dock. Jeri moved quickly to help as Dan and Scotty, in an effort to prevent damage, tried to hold off the heavy boat. At every lurch and roll, the vessel, battered by the relentless waves, moved at counter purposes.

Meanwhile the frantic occupants—a man and two young boys—left the motor running and clambered off the boat, clutching at Dan and Scotty in their haste to abandon ship.

Jeri heaved all her strength against the hull, aware that it would take only one implacable wave to crunch the metal sides. She saw Scotty leap from the dock onto the stern and make his way to the console. He gestured frantically for her to shove him off so he could move the craft to the leeward side of the dock. Dan clutched the bow, his body arced over the water in a Herculean effort to keep the boat from ramming the dock.

When Scotty shifted into reverse, Jeri gave a mighty shove into the wind. At that same moment she heard a dull thud to her left. She turned and stared with horror at the empty space where, just a moment before, Dan had been.

She screamed his name, then rushed to the spot and peered into the inky roiling waters. God! Where was he? She flattened herself on the wet planks, groping frantically in the water. With glazed eyes, she saw the pontoon boat moving like a shadow through the storm.

She hollered for help, her cry lost in the din of the storm. She slashed the water with her arms. Nothing!

She jumped into the lake, furiously searching underwater, her palms spread out before her. Just when she thought her lungs would explode, she felt something—an arm! She grabbed it and dragged the heavy body with her to the surface, then yelled into the maelstrom. "Help me! *Please!*"

Miraculously she felt her burden lightened as someone leaning over the dock helped her heave Dan's unconscious body to the surface. Through the rain she recognized the man who'd been on the pontoon boat. She felt a flash of anger. If it hadn't been for him and his stupidity... But then, if it hadn't been for him now... She shut her eyes. She couldn't think about it.

The man grabbed Dan beneath his armpits and pulled as Jeri pushed from below. When Dan was safely out of the water, with her last shred of energy, Jeri scaled the ladder and knelt over Dan's outstretched body. His eyes fluttered and he coughed as he tried to speak. She leaned closer. "Boat okay?" he got out.

That was all he was worried about? The stupid boat? When he'd scared her half to death? She wiped his face gently in a futile effort to keep the rain off.

"Miss, hadn't we better get him inside?" The customer stood at Dan's feet, gesturing helplessly.

"Just a minute." She did her best to give Dan a quick examination. "Where do you hurt?"

He tried to lift his hand. "Shoulder. Head."

"What's your name?"

He was alert enough to raise one eyebrow in exasperation. "Dan Contini."

She held up three fingers before his eyes. "How many?"

"Three."

Jeri turned to the man. "I think we can move him. But be very careful."

Cautiously they half-carried, half-slid him into the office. Jeri dashed for the phone.

Dan groaned. "Not 911. Just Ted."

She paused, the phone in her hand. He repeated, this time more forcefully, "Dammit, just Ted!"

It made sense. The fire department EMT, only minutes away, could decide if they needed an ambulance.

Scotty burst into the office. "Jeri, what..." His eyes widened at the sight of Dan on the floor. "Is he...?"

Dan tried to sit up. "I'm fine. Just hit my head on the boat." He faltered and lay back down. "Damn." He moaned and clutched his shoulder.

The two little boys, eyes bulging, huddled by the counter while their father stammered his apologies.

Jeri hung up the phone and hurried to Dan's side. "Ted'll be right here. You just stay quiet." She glanced up at the nervous father and, biting back her still-present anger, said, "Thanks for your help, but I think it would be better if you left now."

Just after the trio bade their ashamed goodbyes, Ted arrived, and Jeri sat back on her heels, dizzy with exhaustion.

Ted made his examination. "Sorry, buddy, but you've got to go to the emergency room."

Dan tried to rear up, restrained by the flat of Ted's hand. "No arguments."

"*No* ambulance, you got that?" Dan's lips clenched with determination.

Ted shrugged. "You're one stubborn cuss. You've got a bump on your head, maybe a slight concussion, and your shoulder's probably dislocated, but I can get you there if you insist."

This time Dan successfully struggled to a sitting position. "I do." He glanced around fuzzily, and his eyes alighted on Scotty. "The boat?"

Scotty grinned. "Safe and sound in her own slip."

"Good."

Jeri quickly rubbed her hair with the towel, then grabbed her purse. "Scotty, call Raymond and see if he can get over here and help you close down. I'm going with Ted."

Holding one shoulder and supported by Ted, Dan stood up, face grimacing with pain. "No."

"No?" Jeri moved to tuck her arm under his elbow. "Is that any way to treat the woman who saved your life?" And with a wink at Ted, she helped escort Dan through the rain toward the waiting vehicle.

JERI WAS ACUTELY AWARE of a kink in her neck. She flexed the fingers of her left hand—asleep. She opened her eyes slowly and squinted at her surroundings. Something was wrong.

She pushed herself up on her elbows. Where was she? Then it all came back. The storm, the accident, the emergency room. The Spartan simplicity of Dan's guest bedroom came into sharper focus, and she remembered. The trip to the hospital, with Dan complaining all the way. A mild concussion and a dislocated shoulder, the doctor had said. Iron Man Contini wouldn't even consider staying overnight at the hospital. So here she was, Nurse Jeri. Because of the concussion, seizures were a possible side effect, and so somebody had to wake him periodically.

She threw her legs over the edge of the bed and

righted herself. Her clothes were wrinkled beyond repair and her hair felt grungy. Events swam in circles in her mind. She'd been so pumped with adrenaline last night that only in the quiet hours after midnight had she come face-to-face with her terror. He could've drowned. The mere thought of it jolted her.

She staggered to the window and parted the blinds. The morning was Edenesque, such a contrast to the night before. The calm water glinted with sunlight. On the dock she spotted Scotty and Raymond, who'd agreed to handle things today.

She tiptoed into the hall, heading for Dan's room. He'd had a restless night. Because of his concern about the concussion, the doctor had provided only minimal medication for the shoulder pain. She entered Dan's room and stood over his bed. He was still asleep, but every so often his lips twitched and he uttered a guttural moan. The doctor had cut Dan's shirt off to get at his shoulder. Now his bare chest rose and fell evenly. A sheet loosely draped his lower body.

Jeri sat on the side of the bed, observing. One hand lay on his torso, fingers spread, the veins standing out in relief. His thick lashes rested against his tanned skin, and she could see the individual hairs of his blue-black mustache. She brushed the backs of her knuckles over his temple. Asleep he seemed boylike and helpless and——her eyes drifted to the sheet tangled around his hips——so sexy! He shifted in his sleep, and the sling encasing his arm and shoulder grabbed. Groaning, he resettled more comfortably. She glanced at the clock on the bedside table. Eight-thirty. She'd last awakened him at six. Surely she had time to grab a quick shower and freshen up before rousing him again.

In the bathroom she shed her soiled clothes, located

the shampoo and stepped into the shower. She dug her fingers into her matted scalp and massaged until her head was fully lathered. The hot water served to revive her; and when she finally rinsed her hair and stepped out, she felt halfway human again. She rubbed herself down with a man-size Turkish towel emblazoned with USN. She considered her clothes briefly. She couldn't bear the thought of donning the wrinkled shorts and shirt just yet. Maybe Dan had a T-shirt she could put on over her briefs.

She wrapped the big towel around her body, gathered up her dirty clothes and stepped into the hall, then into Dan's room.

He groaned feebly. "Jeri? That you?"

She set her clothes down on a chair, gathered the towel more tightly over her breasts and made her way to the bed. She beamed down at him. "Morning, sailor. How're you feeling?"

He winced as he shoved himself up against the pillow. "Awful. My head's pounding and this damn shoulder feels like a road grader mangled it."

She giggled. "You must be getting better."

"How's that?"

"Your complaints are more specific. And for your information, you nearly *were* mangled—between the dock and the boat."

He moaned. "I remember." He struggled to sit up. "I can't lie around here all day. The marina—"

"Hush! Raymond and Scotty have things under control."

She felt a tingle as his warm hand stroked her forearm. "I like your outfit." He tugged on her arm until she was sitting close to him on the bed. He fumbled with the sarong fold just above her breasts. "But you don't need it."

For a moment she savored the rush of blood to the surface of her skin, but then trapped his straying hand in hers. "You're not *that* well yet."

He tried to sit up but collapsed against the pillow. "Damn. I guess you're right. But couldn't you at least spare a guy some TLC?"

She leaned forward and gently touched her lips to his, feeling the titillating brush of his mustache on her upper lip. As his mouth moved beneath hers, she felt his good arm trail tantalizingly across her bare shoulders.

Suddenly he stopped, withdrew his mouth and lay with his head facing the door. "What's that?"

"What?" she murmured, kissing the vulnerable spot just above his Adam's apple.

"Didn't you hear it?"

"*What?*"

"The front door." The house was suddenly quiet as a tomb, and then she, too, heard something—footsteps in the hall.

Jeri sprang guiltily to her feet, frantically retucking the loosened fold of towel. Dan propped up on his good elbow and called out. "Who's there?"

"Just me."

Jeri stood, immobilized by the sight she faced. In the doorway, one hip cocked defiantly, stood a skinny teenager with long kinky dishwater blond hair dressed in combat boots, black leggings and an oversize Grateful Dead T-shirt.

Her eyes, agate blue, bored holes through Jeri. She glanced quickly at Dan who had somehow managed to struggle to a sitting position. "Hello, Dad. I guess you weren't expecting me, huh?" She turned back to Jeri, her lips curled in a sneer. "Just who the hell are you?"

CHAPTER NINE

THE MINUTE she got home, Jeri skinned off her dirty clothes, threw on a drab gray T-shirt and an old pair of cutoffs. Then she attacked the kitchen floor with soapy water as if the effort could erase the stain of being discovered half-naked in Dan's bedroom by his daughter. She'd never been so humiliated in her life!

She squeezed her eyes shut to blot out that cold assessing look on Tiffany's face when Dan, ashen beneath his tan, had introduced them. Tiffany, taking in the scene, had apparently drawn her own conclusions. The words still bit into Jeri's brain: *Excu-use me all to heck, but, Dad, this is one little detail*—she nodded at Jeri—*you forgot to mention on the phone.*

One little detail! Right, like the one other little detail Dan had failed to mention. Contrary to the photograph he'd shown her, his daughter was no ten-year-old.

Jeri sat back on her heels and furiously twisted the sponge over the pail, watching the stream of dirty water spatter into the suds. She'd like to wring his neck. Or Tiffany's. Or her own, for being so stupid in the first place.

She took another vicious swipe at the floor. But it hadn't ended there, oh, no. Before she'd had time to beat a retreat, they'd heard the clackety-clack of high-heeled mules headed for the bedroom. "Dan, yoo-hoo, here we..."

The voice had trailed off. Tiffany had stepped aside and, with the flourish of a P.T. Barnum, ushered her mother into the bedroom. Vicki, eyebrows raised, had scrutinized Jeri from head to toe. "Why, Tiffany, I do believe we've interrupted something."

Jeri could scarcely remember how she'd made her escape except for sputtering her excuses, dressing hastily and bolting from the house as Dan attempted to explain. To justify her humiliation, she almost wished something *had* been going on between them at that moment.

And Tiffany—now there was a piece of work! She'd actually seemed to take malicious delight in the drama unfolding in front of her. Jeri recognized the same cynicism she'd seen on the faces of some of her more world-weary students, those pseudosophisticated nymphets whose ideas of weekend fun would rival those of the inhabitants of Melrose Place and whose attitudes toward adults were marked by disdain.

She wrung out the sponge, placed a hand on the counter to lever herself upright and picked up the pail. Nothing Dan had said about Tiffany had prepared her for the actuality. Since he hadn't seen his daughter in a while, maybe he couldn't recognize trouble when it stood in front of him. For Dan's sake, she hoped her first impression was wrong.

She slowly poured the ammoniated wash water down the sink. Well, the good news was, she didn't have to work at the marina today. Dan would have time to adjust, Tiffany could get settled in, and maybe, just maybe, he'd offered a satisfactory explanation for that awful bedroom scene, and work tomorrow wouldn't be too awkward. She drew in a deep breath and exhaled slowly. At least the floor was clean and she'd taken out the worst of her anger and humiliation on something inanimate.

The phone interrupted her thoughts. It was Dan. She collapsed on a chair.

"You okay?" he asked.

"Still a little shaky and embarrassed. Tiffany isn't what I expected." She tried to keep her voice light. "No doubt, I wasn't what she expected, either."

She sat very still while he offered a rambling explanation, ending with Vicki's show of reluctance to leave Tiffany in such a "questionable environment." Jeri recognized the edge in his voice. "Like she's got room to talk."

"How's the shoulder?" Anything to change the subject.

He grunted. "Hurts like hell."

"Have you taken your pill?"

"What pill?"

"The pain pill."

"Don't need one."

Masculine logic. She spoke as if to a small child. "Your shoulder 'hurts like hell,' I believe you said. But you won't take the pain pill the doctor prescribed?"

"You got it."

"In that case, I don't want to hear about pain."

"No sympathy from this quarter?"

She relented. "Maybe a smidgen. You looked kinda cute held captive under that sheet by three women."

"Cute? I felt like a damn fool."

She paused. "That makes two of us."

"I'm sorry you were put in that position."

"So am I."

There was silence on the line. "Jeri?" His voice was tentative. "I think...I'm going to need your help."

"With your shoulder?"

"No. With Tiffany." She could tell how difficult it was for him to make this admission. "I don't know what I expected exactly. I mean, I know she's fifteen, but I wasn't quite ready for...you know..."

"An independent young woman with definite opinions of her own?"

He sounded miserable. "Something like that. She hates the house, says the place smells like fish. She's sitting in her room with the blinds pulled and her boom box turned up full bore. I don't even know how to talk to her."

Oh, boy. "You'll have to be patient, get acquainted all over again."

"I want her to have a good time here. For the two of us to connect. For her—this sounds stupid—to *like* me."

"You can't rush it. The more you push for a father-daughter moment, the more she'll resist."

"Yeah, well, thanks. I'll see you tomorrow."

She started to hang up but heard him say something else. "What?"

His voice sounded more relaxed. "That was a becoming shade of red you were wearing with that towel." He managed a chuckle. "Bye."

She slowly cradled the receiver. Help with Tiffany? If she did, indeed, have Miss Contini's number, she and Dan would both learn the meaning of "challenge" all over again!

ON SUNDAY MORNING Tiffany, with Bull at her side, sat at the end of the farthest pier dangling her feet in the water and picking at her cuticles. Every now and then a grotesque mud-colored fish with rubbery floating whiskers would glide out from under the dock, totally grossing her out. Only twenty-seven more days of exile. This place made detention at school seem like a holiday. At least there she knew somebody. The only good thing here was Bull. She'd always wanted a dog. She laid her face along his back, hugging him.

Off to her left her dad was filling air tanks for a group of scuba divers who looked like a displaced "Hee Haw" audience. So far it was clear her father didn't have a clue what to do with her. Even though he hadn't said anything, she could tell he didn't approve of her music. Worse yet, he treated her like a kid, always hovering around asking if she needed anything. At supper last night they'd pretty much had nothing to say to each other. He'd asked the typical grown-up questions, and she'd answered as briefly as possible.

What right had he to barge into her life now when he hadn't cared enough to stick around before? The navy, his ship, his men. That was what had been important to him. And now this dumb marina!

If he expected her to hang around this sorry place all day every day, he had another think coming. Being only fifteen was the pits; he wouldn't even let her drive. Stuck! Somehow she had to get wheels. If not wheels, maybe he'd let her learn to drive a boat. You didn't need a license to do that. She studied the sleek speedboat in the nearest slip. Might be kind of fun. How fast would it go?

Then there was Jeri. She and her father had undoubtedly been *doing* it. Yuck. Must've been tough to manage with that sore shoulder. Her mouth curled in distaste. The thought of people her parents' age doing it was enough to make her throw up. She didn't know which was worse—visualizing her mother with Purd the Turd or her dad with Gidget Monahan.

She withdrew her toes from the water and crossed her legs. She and Tony had talked about it. He'd promised to use a condom and all that, and they'd come close a couple of times, but something at the last minute always held her back. He'd wanted her to do it before she left, to prove her love, he'd said; but she couldn't see what the big deal was. If Tony was like the men she'd seen parade past her mother, they couldn't care less about feelings. She didn't know whether she believed in love or not, but she was never going to be dependent on men like her mother was.

However... She watched one of the guys working at the marina ease a rental Wave Runner into the gas dock. His white-blond hair glistened in the sun, in stunning contrast to his deeply tanned face, back and shoulders. He wore faded red swim trunks and deck shoes and had a body that made her look twice. Sort of innocent-looking, but possible. Definitely possible, especially if he had a car. He just might be her ticket out of this dump.

"C'mon, Bull." She jumped up, took time to fling her long hair back from her face and to straighten the T-shirt over her small breasts before ambling toward the gas dock where the hunk was working. As she passed the office, Jeri spotted her and stuck her head out the door.

"Tiffany, how about helping me stock the cooler?"

Oh, yeah, like I'd like to get a tetanus shot or take a quiz in geometry. She kept right on walking. "Not now." Gidget was out of her mind if she expected to sucker her into working. This was, after all, her vacation, such as it was. She felt Gidget's eyes boring into her back as she sauntered on toward the blond guy.

When she reached the first gas pump, she leaned up against it, crossed her arms and stared at the stud. When he turned around, he seemed surprised.

"Hi," she drawled, raking his body with her eyes. She noticed his face coloring. "I'm Tiffany Contini. Who're you?"

He stood in front of her, his chest gleaming with a sheen of sweat. "Scott Monahan."

Monahan? "Any relation to..." She jerked her head in the direction of the office.

"Yeah. Brother." He nudged Tiffany aside to hang up the hose nozzle. "And you're Dan's daughter?"

"Yeah." She studied his face. "Whaddaya do around here for fun?"

He looked at the lake, considering the question. "Water-ski, fish, sail."

She stood erect and dug her hands deep in the pockets of her baggy shorts. "No, I mean fun, like—" she cocked her head "—*fun*."

He looked nonplussed. "Are you talkin' about parties and stuff like that?"

A knowing smile creased her lips. "Yeah, stuff like that. Where's the action?"

A bass boat approached the dock. "This is a small place. There's not much to do. A few parties, but mostly we just hang out." He caught the prow of the incoming boat with his foot and leaned over to fasten the rope to the cleat.

Terrific. Arkansas is every bit as bad as I thought. She started back toward the house, calling over her shoulder, "Lemme know next time something's happening, okay?"

Dullsville. But maybe ol' Scott Monahan would liven things up. At the very least, he'd be a way to stick it to Gidget.

"WELL, WHAT DO YOU think?" Dan sat in the office that same evening cradling a can of root beer.

Jeri glanced up from the calculator. "About what?"

"Tiffany."

She sucked in her breath and took her time arranging the paperwork on the desk. She stood and leaned on the counter looking at him, searching for the right words. "She's going to need time. This has to be very different from Virginia Beach."

"I don't know what to do with her." He sounded defeated. "She doesn't want to help out here or at the house. But I can't just leave this place—" he gestured helplessly around the room "—to entertain her."

"She's old enough not to need constant entertaining. What about tomorrow? It's your day off."

"I'm taking her into town, showing her the sights. But that's just one day a week. What then?"

"Maybe she'd like to learn to water-ski or sail."

"When I mentioned that, she turned up her nose and looked at me as if I'd suggested she join a...a clog-dancing troupe."

Jeri came around the counter and stood over Dan, resting one hand lightly on his good shoulder. "It's a typical reaction. She's bound and determined not to like anything, not to try anything."

"Why?"

"She's punishing you—and her mother. She has a few legitimate reasons to be mad at the world, you know."

"I'm afraid you're right." He looked up plaintively. "What do I do?"

She sat down beside him and took his warm hand in hers. Chief Contini, leader of men, floored by a fifteen-year-old? "Exercise some patience and, more important, some firmness. Earn her respect and love."

He looked up quizzically. "Firmness?"

"Yes. Who's calling the shots here?"

His lips thinned.

"It's not just adults who are into power trips," she explained. "Some of the most challenging kids in my classes were the ones daring an adult to set them some boundaries. To prove their love by telling them no." She paused. "Would it be so bad to insist that Tiffany help at the house and here at the marina? Work won't kill her."

He sat slumped for several moments. "Insist? I don't think I can. I thought you understood—I don't have much time with her. I can't risk screwing this up, turning her even more against me."

Jeri released his hand and rose to her feet. "It's your life and you have to run it, but somehow I doubt you screwed up too many enlisted men by insisting, by being firm." She forged on. "The kindest thing you could do for your daughter is to set some limits, give her some responsibilities."

Dan tossed the empty beverage can into the trash and stood up, wincing slightly as he adjusted the sling. He came over and stood so close to Jeri she could feel the heat radiating off his body. He ran his fingers through her curls. "I don't know. I just don't know." He paused. "Maybe you and I are having our first disagreement."

She shrugged. "Unless you count the one about female firefighters."

He put his good arm around her and pulled her tight against his chest. "And I don't know when we'll find time to work this through. Right now Tiffany comes first, and I've gotta do what I've gotta do." She could sense him withdrawing emotionally. He nudged her forehead with his chin, compelling her to look into his troubled eyes. "I guess I have to ask you to be patient, too."

She knew it was childish, but she felt set aside. "Not my long suit."

He brushed her cheek with his lips. "Please try. And—" she could tell the next words were difficult for him "—please give Tiffany a chance."

She stepped back, allowing her open palm to graze his cheek as she did so. "Maybe Scotty can help. He could get her acquainted with some of the local kids, interest her in sailing or something."

Dan's face relaxed into a smile. "That'd be great."

Jeri had no idea how Scotty would react; she hoped she wouldn't regret the suggestion. Contini sure had a thing or two to learn about teenagers.

THE NEXT EVENING Jeri stood at the kitchen counter stirring ingredients for potato salad and considering how to approach Scotty about Tiffany. The subject had to be handled carefully. Through the window she could see her father putting hamburgers on the grill. The three Monahans were actually going to eat dinner together.

She tasted the potato salad for the umpteenth time. Mother had told her the secret ingredient, but she couldn't remember. Pickle juice? Vinegar? She reached in the refrigerator. Maybe a dash of bottled French dressing. She added a dollop, blended it and tasted a spoonful. Still not right. She banged the spoon on the side of the bowl, dislodging a blob of salad. For better or worse—done. She covered the dish with plastic wrap, put it away and turned to check the baked beans in the oven. Pretty hard to ruin them, at least.

"How long till dinner?" Scotty hollered from the lower level. Had she been this noisy and demanding as a teenager? Suddenly, plain as day, she could hear her mother's patient voice: *If you want to talk to me, come where I am. I will not shout.*

Jeri walked to the top of the stairs and looked down at her brother. "Come up here and I'll tell you."

He made a grand salaam. "Yes, Your Highness. May I approach?"

She laughed and made a regal gesture as if bestowing a much-sought-after favor. "Certainly. The queen awaits you in the kitchen." She went to the silverware drawer and pulled out knives, forks and spoons, relieved to see a flash of the old Scotty and his humor.

Behind her she heard him clumping up the steps. "I'm starving. How long?" He reached over the counter, tore open a bag of chips and stuffed a handful into his mouth.

Jeri decided not to spoil his mood by chastising him. "As soon as Dad finishes cooking the burgers. Here, make yourself useful." She handed him the napkins and silverware. Then, steeling herself, she plunged in. "I have a favor to ask."

He paused, gripping one place setting. "Yeah?"

"Dan Contini's been a pretty good boss, hasn't he?"

He plunked down the fork. "Uh-huh. I like working there." He grinned. "And it's kinda fun watching my sister moon over him. 'Dan, oh Dan,'" he mimicked in a falsetto voice. He wrapped his skinny arms around his shoulders in a mock embrace. "So, is it love?" he asked.

Somehow this conversation had taken an awkward turn. She found herself stammering. "I...we...I like him a lot."

Scotty shot her a disbelieving look. "Right. Like." He snorted.

She shrugged and a smile softened her features. "Well, maybe a little more than like."

He perched on a stool and leaned his elbows on the counter. "You could do a lot worse. He's a cool guy."

"I'm glad you approve." She turned away to retrieve the condiments from the refrigerator. "The favor has something to do with Dan. And Tiffany."

He sat up straight. "Tiffany?"

She set the mustard and catsup on the counter and faced him. "Yes. She doesn't know a soul here. And Dan's pretty tied down at the marina. We were hoping you'd be willing to spend a little time with her, introduce her to your friends, you know, help her get acquainted."

He slid off the stool with a thump, holding up his hands, palms forward, in front of his chest. "Oh, no, you don't. No, ma'am, not me." His voice rose in a howl. "She's a creep, Jeri. No way!"

Jeri raised her eyes imploringly to the ceiling. "I already said you would."

"Oh, that's terrific, just terrific. Now my big sister's single-handedly ruining my social life."

"Please?" she asked in a small voice. "It won't hurt to be nice to her."

"Ha! Won't hurt *you*, maybe."

"You'll be working around her for nearly a month.

You could at least make the best of it. Dan would really appreciate it.''

"Have you looked at her, Jeri? She's an East Coast grunge with an attitude. What'll my friends think?"

"Imagine how you'd feel if you went somewhere where you didn't know anybody." She looked at him hopefully. "Try it, for my sake."

"Jeesh!" He shoved a hand through his hair, turned away and continued setting the table.

"Do the best you can, okay?"

He shrugged. "Just don't expect much."

"So you'll try?"

"*Yes!* Are you satisfied?" He banged down a spoon.

Any hint of the humor that had surfaced earlier was gone. A glum silence fell over the room as she got out the plates, removed the beans from the oven and set out the potato salad.

Hank Monahan backed through the door, holding a tray of hamburgers. The aroma of sizzling beef filled the kitchen. "Here they are. Get 'em while they're hot."

Jeri stood aside while her father and brother heaped their plates. Her appetite was gone.

"Looks good, honey," her father said as she took her place at the table.

"What's this supposed to be?" Scotty asked, holding up a lumpy forkful of potato salad.

In her lap, Jeri clenched her hands. "Mom's potato salad," she mumbled.

Her father, chewing tentatively, looked up in surprise. "No kidding?"

"I guess I didn't quite get it right."

"No matter," her father said. "It's really...tasty."

Scotty was carefully hiding his portion under a leaf of lettuce.

Hank wiped his mouth and cleared his throat. "Since we're all together, I'd like to talk about something. Jeri already knows about this, son, but I need to let you in on it."

No, Dad. Bad timing. Not now.

Scotty, the hand holding his hamburger frozen half-way to his mouth, eyed his father. "Sounds serious."

"It is. And to tell you the truth, I don't quite know how to start."

Oh, Mom, I don't know if I can stand what's about to happen. Dread, like gorge, rose in her throat.

Scotty, eyes wary, slowly lowered his sandwich to his plate. "Just say it." He glared at Jeri as if questioning her complicity.

"I guess there's no gentle way. Scotty, your mother's been gone awhile, and…"

Jeri saw Scotty's jaw tighten and a shutter fall over his expression. She couldn't breathe. "…I'm seeing someone."

Scotty sat stunned, staring at his father. Finally he stammered, "*Seeing* someone?"

Her father had the grace to look discomfited. "Her name is—"

Scotty knocked over the chair as he sprang to his feet. "A woman? You're seeing a woman?"

Hank rose and tried to place a placating hand on his son's shoulder. "Please, son, let me explain."

Scotty shoved his father aside. "You son of a bitch! That's sick. How could you?" Then he whirled on Jeri. "You *knew* about this?" He flung his arms about in frustration. "What do you both think I am? Some baby?" He zeroed in on his father. "Explain? No way!'' He dug frantically in his jeans pocket and pulled out his car keys. Jeri placed a restraining hand on his arm. ''Don't touch me. I'm outta here.'' He moved toward the door.

''Son, get back here!'' Hank barked.

''You can't stop me.'' Scotty slammed the door and Jeri stood, graven, watching her father run after him. Her ears rang with the noise of an engine revving and gravel spattering from tires gripping the road as Scotty's Toyota accelerated away from the house.

After several minutes, her father reentered the kitchen and stood shaking his head. ''I sure made a mess of that. I didn't know he'd...take it so hard.''

Jeri didn't feel like being conciliatory, yet Dad looked so drained, so defeated. ''What did you expect?'' she asked softly.

''I dunno. I just dunno.'' He pulled a pack of cigarettes from his pocket. ''I'll be out on the porch.''

He left her standing in the middle of the kitchen, her stomach coiling and recoiling in anger and...something else. Maybe fear.

She contemplated the mess left on the table. Then with a savage swoop, she picked up the bowl of potato salad and, with tears trickling down her cheeks, chunked the whole mess into the garbage disposal, taking masochistic pleasure from the grinding, grating, sucking action of the appliance.

DAN SAT on his deck steps Monday evening, elbows dangling between his knees, trying to figure out how to get through to Tiffany.

He'd assumed spending his day off showing her the sights would somehow improve their relationship, help bridge the gap. He'd started out this morning with high hopes. A leisurely stroll through the quaint village center with its ice-cream parlors, boutiques, galleries and gift shops had resulted in Tiffany's scorn when she'd discovered, to her horror, that River Falls had neither a movie theater nor a video arcade.

As they'd walked, he'd attempted to put his arm around her, but she'd jerked away. A leisurely—and expensive—lunch on the flower-bedecked terrace of the Ozarks Inn was compared, unfavorably, with a thick-crust pizza from a well-known national franchise. In an attempt to improve on the morning's activities, he'd taken her to see one of the area's many spectacular caves. She'd announced in no uncertain terms that she'd rather be "laying out" on the smelly dock than creeping about in a musty old cavern.

Dan rubbed his mustache with his forefinger and wondered what he could do for an encore. He'd moved here in an attempt to secure for himself peace, tranquillity, simplicity. Because he found this place soothing, he'd hoped Tiffany would, too, and that this location, which held no prior associations for either of them, would help build a bond. *Dream on.*

Then there was Jeri. Okay, he'd asked her for help, but what did she know about being a parent? Somehow he didn't think teaching was quite in the same league with diaper changing, chicken pox and puberty, but that hadn't stopped Jeri from being convinced she was right. And her advice sounded like a surefire way to make Tiffany even more miserable.

He slumped with weariness, feeling like an old man, and a helpless one at that. He was on the downhill run to forty and couldn't manage one fifteen-year-old girl.

He stood up and whistled for Bull. Even the dog was disloyal. He'd hardly left Tiffany's side since she'd arrived. At least she'd warmed to something. Bull didn't appear. The fickle boxer must have developed a passion for Hootie and the Blowfish and holed up with Tiffany in the bedroom she'd already turned into a disaster area.

Gazing absently out over the marina, he stiffened as he watched a speedboat gunning toward the no-wake buoy. Damn, that idiot should know better. He took two steps toward the marina, then paused. Bow high in the air, wake churning behind the motor, the boat stopped suddenly and idled in toward the marina.

Scott Monahan! He'd noticed him heading out in a fury about an hour ago. Young punk. If he hadn't killed that motor before creating havoc with the dock, he could've kissed his job goodbye.

Dan sat back down, watching as Scott glided into his slip and secured the dock lines. When the teen finished, he walked across the gangplank, hesitated at his Toyota, then turned and looked toward Dan's house. In the dusk Scott seemed to blend into the shadows. From a distance and just for a moment, Dan thought he looked lost. Then, as if coming to a decision, Scott waved at Dan and walked toward the house.

"Tiffany here?" he asked as he approached.

Dan squelched his surprise. "Yeah."

Scott stared awkwardly at the ground, tracing a semicircle with the toe of his worn deck shoe. "Think she'd wanna go into town with me?"

Dan felt the tightness in his chest easing. "Why don't you ask her? I'll get her." He disappeared into the house and came back a few moments later, trailed by Tiffany and Bull.

"I'm goin' into town, Tiffany," Scott said. "Wanna come?"

Dan thought she came close to smiling, but he

couldn't be sure in the dim light. "Might as well. I'll get my purse."

When they'd left, even with Bull's relenting and sitting beside him, Dan suddenly felt very alone. The quiet should've been comforting, peaceful. Instead, it was empty, yawning, gnawing. What the hell? Couldn't he ever be satisfied? Maybe he'd call Jeri. But what could they do? Where could they go? He had no privacy. He was either working or with Tiffany most of the time. How were he and Jeri supposed to figure out anything about their relationship? *What relationship? Did you honestly presume, Contini, that you could have a relationship with a twenty-eight-year-old woman who wants to fight fires? Who thinks she knows how you should rear your own child? You? With a feisty meddling younger woman? Ha!*

It wasn't just kids whose hormones were out of whack. If he did want another woman, he'd always told himself she'd be a nurturing, passive, doting type—like his mother. What in hell had happened to that idea?

TIFFANY HUDDLED silently against the passenger door as Scott took the dangerous curves at stomach-lurching speeds. He didn't look particularly happy, and she wasn't about to bother with small talk. The main thing was, he'd sprung her from the marina. Freddy Krueger or Scott Monahan, it didn't matter to her.

The windows were all wide open, and her hair whipped around her face. Finally she reached up and gathered it in a hank and held it with one hand.

"Too fast for you?" Scott asked without looking at her.

"I like fast."

"Good." He pressed the accelerator to the floor and

passed a 1983 Buick Roadmaster. He seemed familiar with the roads and had control of the vehicle; otherwise, she might've been scared. But this was the most excitement she'd had in a week. When he hit the city limits, he slammed on the brakes and slowed to a crawl.

"Run out of gas?" she quipped.

He gave her a long-suffering look. "You're not used to small towns, are you?"

"No, thank God."

"It's like this. Every one of our four cops knows us. Believe me, you don't want to tangle with them. Especially Shooter."

"Shooter?"

"Big guy with acne. Hates kids and doesn't mind lettin' you know."

"Thanks for the tip." Did River Falls roll up the carpet after dark? Except for a couple of bars and restaurants, the town looked dead. "Where're we going?"

"You care?"

"Gee, you're a regular Prince Charming, aren't you?"

"Bunch of us are meeting in the supermarket parking lot. We hang out there. You can get acquainted."

"That's it?" she shrieked incredulously. "That's what you do for fun? Sit on car hoods and count the trucks going by?"

"We can't all be big East Coast party animals, can we?" His tone was sarcastic.

"You wish." She shrugged and folded her arms firmly across her chest as the neon lights of the supermarket came into view. The closer they got, the more grim-faced Scott became. She studied him. "You're not happy about this, are you?"

He looked at her blankly. "What do you mean?"

"Did your sister make you bring me?"

"Not exactly."

"I see." She felt a sudden hole in her stomach where her self-confidence used to be. He was embarrassed. Probably didn't want his friends to see her. She tossed her head defiantly. Well, to hell with them. She didn't care whether they liked her or not. She hated everything about this place. Might as well hate the kids, too.

"Look, I'm sorry," he said. "I'm just in a bad mood tonight."

"You could've spared me."

He eased the Toyota between a VW bug convertible and a Jeep. He pointed halfheartedly to a group of teenagers a few yards away. "There're my friends. I'll introduce you." But he didn't immediately climb out of the car. After a few moments he turned to her and his eyes softened. "I'm really not usually like this. I had a fight with my dad. I guess I don't need to take it out on you."

Fights with parents. *That* she could understand. Maybe this evening wouldn't be so bad, after all, even though she could tell at a glance her grunge look didn't fit in with the shorts and blouses of the clean-cut girls posing for the guys lolling on the hood of a mammoth vintage Cadillac limousine. Not one of them remotely resembled Tony or any of the kids back home. She took in the defeated slump of Scott's shoulders and hesitated. He appeared more hurt than sullen. "Wanna talk about it?"

"Not now. Maybe later. C'mon, let's go."

River Falls, get ready. The Tiffer's here.

CHAPTER TEN

JERI WROTE the date, Monday August fourth, on the final check and leaned back with satisfaction. Cedarcrest was showing more promise with each passing month, causing her father cautious optimism. Celeste had proved to be an asset—at least in real-estate sales. Judging from her father's general mellowing, Celeste's charm was obviously working with him, too. After a couple of business-related phone conversations with her, Jeri begrudgingly admitted the woman had done nothing to merit active dislike.

Scotty was another story. He'd told Jeri flat out he didn't intend to hang around and listen to his father try to justify his rotten behavior. Dad's admission about Celeste had been a near fatal blow to his already fragile relationship with Scotty, who'd also made it clear Jeri was damned by association. In fact, his exact words were, "Thanks for your confidence in me. Keeping dumb Scotty in the dark, right?"

She carefully stacked all the outgoing checks and clipped the bills inside the ledger book. Too bad life couldn't be reconciled as easily as the neat columns of the spreadsheet.

She fixed herself a glass of iced tea and strolled onto the porch. The lake shimmered blue-silver in the strong afternoon sunlight and was so calm you could see in it a nearly perfect mirror image of the opposite shoreline.

Only the occasional boat distorted the glassy surface. Jeri settled into the hammock-swing and pushed herself gently back and forth, soothed by the repetitive motion.

True to his word, Scotty hadn't stuck around. When he wasn't working, he escaped to his room and turned the stereo speakers to the "annihilate" setting. More often, however, he joined his friends—fishing, shooting hoops or just hanging out. To her dismay, in the past week he'd been spending more and more time with Tiffany.

Tiffany. Now there was another problem.

When Jeri worked at the marina, she found herself the number-one target of the girl's resentment. Tiffany lazed around watching soap operas on the office TV, a practice that had intensified when she'd learned Jeri had no use for them. Whenever she suggested Tiffany lend a hand, the girl would part the hair that obscured her face like a curtain and mutter her standard answer. "This is my vacation."

Jeri didn't question that the girl was unhappy and the marina wasn't exactly an amusement park, but that didn't excuse laziness or surliness. She needed a good swift kick in her skinny posterior!

So, despite her best intentions, Jeri was finding it increasingly difficult to muster sympathy for the teenager, who, no doubt, had good reason to feel defensive and bitter. However, as a teacher, she'd seen other kids with worse problems rise above them. Tiffany, by contrast, seemed committed to wallowing in hers.

Dan, nearly recovered from his accident, continued to permit his daughter to buffalo him, seemingly unaware of her moodiness. His pathetic attempts to cater to her every whim bugged Jeri, and he remained unmoved by her repeated suggestion that he was doing his daughter more harm than good, that what the girl needed most as proof of his love was structure.

Dan had taught his daughter to water-ski and drive the speedboat, both of which she did with reckless abandon. And, distressingly, her moves on Scotty this past weekend had been particularly overt. Tiffany had spent yesterday sunbathing near the gas dock in a tiny fuchsia bikini that left little to the imagination. Every time she stood up, she'd leaned over to adjust her bra top in such a way that her small breasts were almost completely bared. Jeri had had to resist the urge to throw a beach towel over her. And whenever the boat traffic had fallen off, Tiffany had lounged against the pump flirting with Scotty. Once Jeri tried to intervene, but Scotty had shot her such a scathing look she'd backed off.

She jiggled her glass, making the ice clink, then took a sip. Jeri wasn't so naive she believed Scotty was an innocent, but she'd seen enough of teenagers to know he'd met his match with Miss Contini. Jeri needed to talk to someone about it. But who? Not Scotty himself, not Dad and certainly not the doting father. What would Mom have done?

Two crows landed on a nearby tree, their raucous cries providing an appropriate background chorus for her dark thoughts. And Dan? She scowled. The magic was difficult to sustain when they hadn't had time alone with each other, not really, in more than two weeks. When he *could* get away from the marina, it was to take Tiffany someplace; and when they'd tried to find some privacy at the marina, Tiffany had always found a way to insinuate herself into the scene.

Jeri rotated the seat, twisting the support ropes tighter and tighter, then at last gave a shove with her feet and let the swing twirl dizzily until it finally came to rest.

She felt frustrated with Dan's permitting Tiffany to call the shots. She knew she should be big about it, try harder to understand Tiffany's hurt and Dan's desire to please his daughter. Still...

She stood up decisively. Enough negative thinking. Tonight she and Dan were actually having a kind of date. Tiffany and Scotty, along with Bubba and his girl-friend, were taking the boat to a barbecue some of the kids were having over at the cliffs on the south shore of the lake near the abandoned Rakestraw cabin. The attached springhouse, carved cavelike out of the side of the cliff with its pool of cold water, was perfect for icing down beverages. Even in her day, the cabin had been party headquarters—not a particularly reassuring memory.

The upside? Dan had suggested a barbecue of their own at his house. High time!

DAN DRAGGED the small drop-leaf kitchen table out onto the deck and set it with two cracked plastic place mats. He'd even located a chipped glass candlestick and a half-burned green Christmas candle. Definitely not the Ritz, but the best he could do to create the mood of intimate al fresco dining. Being around Jeri at the marina without being able to talk, really talk, or to touch had been hell.

He glanced around. Bull dozed by the steps; the sun had just set, leaving the eastern mountains in dark blue-green shadow; and the chicken was grilling to perfection. The kids had left an hour ago with a cooler and enough chips to provision a battleship. Scott's attention to Tiffany had been a godsend, and although she still didn't seem thrilled with life at the marina, she'd shown some evidence of adapting.

Last night, for example, she'd attempted to fix dinner—boxed macaroni and cheese, a rubbery gelatin salad and canned corn. A start. And after Vicki's only phone call so far to her daughter, he'd noticed Tiffany thawing further. Progress or a signal that right now he was the lesser of two evils? He hated this self-pitying attitude. Jeri would cure that, he hoped.

As if on cue, she strolled up the path from the parking lot. Bull roused himself and ran out to greet her, with Dan following. Her off-white gauze slacks and matching scoop-neck blouse made her look like ice cream walking. He grinned at his uncharacteristically poetic image and at his next thought—*I'd like to take a lick.* Clearly they were long overdue for some time alone.

Later, after dinner, Dan sat back in his chair, more relaxed and satisfied than he'd been since before the night of the accident. Except for the glow of the sputtering candle and the full moon cresting over the cove, they were shrouded in companionable shadow. Jeri sat, smiling face turned in profile, watching the moon rise. Her enthusiasm for simple pleasures was one of the things he liked best about her.

As if sensing his thoughts, she turned to look at him. "This is nice, Dan."

He scooted back his chair, stood and held out his hand to her. "Yeah, it is. But I know something even nicer."

He pulled her into his arms, cradling her head with one palm and curling her tight against him. The familiar honeysuckle fragrance of her hair filled his nostrils as he bent his head to her. She met his kiss hungrily— and, in the effort to encircle his neck, pressed against him invitingly. Through her filmy blouse, he could feel her breasts thrusting into his chest. He tore his mouth away from hers to look into her eyes, dazed with desire. "I've missed you," he whispered.

She ran her hands seductively down his back. "I know the feeling."

"Care to demonstrate how much?"

She cocked her head and gave him that I-dare-you look he'd come to recognize. A wide grin split her face. "Yeah, c'mon."

She grabbed him by the hand and raced toward the dock. "Hey!" he said. "What do you think—"

"No thinking allowed." Still holding his hand, she laughed in delight as she pulled him to the farthest of the rental docks, where moonlight painted the weathered boards with a silvery patina. She threw her arms around him. "Don't look so solemn. This is playtime!" Then, to the accompaniment of tiny swells washing against boat hulls, she pulled away, stepped out of her shoes and, looking straight into his eyes, started shucking her slacks.

"Whoa. Wait a minute." He glanced around, concerned someone might see them—a late fisherman berthing his boat or kids from the nearby campground hunting for frogs. But no one was in sight. When he turned back, she stood there, silhouetted against the shimmering water, in only her lacy bra and tiny briefs. He sucked in his breath, then felt her nuzzle against him and begin unbuttoning his shirt.

"Where's your sense of adventure?" She giggled and pulled his shirttail out, then eased the shirt off his shoulders. He felt her lips on his nipples, her fingers fumbling with his belt buckle. A steam piston took up residence between his legs.

"Jeri, we can't—" he began lamely.

"Watch us." She stepped back, legs spread, and, in

silent challenge, unsnapped her bra and let it fall. He scarcely had time to take in the moonlit fullness of her breasts before, in one smooth motion, she stepped out of her panties, cried, "Last one in's a..." and dived into the water.

He followed her, plunging in shorts and all. When he surfaced, he sputtered and looked around. Where was she? He treaded water and thought, dammit, this wasn't funny!

Then he felt hands sliding his shorts down over his buttocks. He floated helplessly, caught in the delicious sensation of fingers flicking over his legs. Finally her head broke the surface right beside the dock and she heaved the sodden clothing up on it. As she breast-stroked toward him, her eyes never left his.

"Now isn't this better?" she said, then turned on her back, arms outspread, the mounds of her breasts and pubis just visible. The cold water, which had temporarily taken the wind out of his sails, now had no effect on his arousal. Lord, she was gorgeous—and shameless. He felt positively pagan.

She'd reached him now and treaded water only inches away. Her eyes were closed and a contented smile curled her lips. He ran a fingertip over one nipple and watched as her eyes fluttered open.

She sighed and said, "God, I love skinny-dipping. Don't you?

"I've never done it before."

She splashed him playfully. "You're kidding!"

"I'm not. But it feels great."

She swam close, so close they were treading water nose to nose. "This next part I've never done, either," she breathed against him. And she took his hands and placed them on her breasts, then kissed him, open-mouthed.

He lowered his hands and reached for her buttocks, as her arms slid around his neck. When her legs straddled his hips, only his energetic kicking, which interfered damnably with his total enjoyment of her, kept them from going under. Finally, gasping, they separated. He took her head in his hands, clutching her tightly, feeling her damp curls between his fingers. "Mmm! I had no idea what I've been missing."

She ran one hand up his thigh and captured his erection. "There's just one slight problem."

He laughed ruefully. "Yeah, I know. Mechanics. It's over our heads here."

She released him and trailed her fingers up over his navel to his chest. "We could move to shallower water."

The idea of making love waist-deep in water home to turtles, frogs and snakes with rocks cutting into his feet—not to mention risking discovery by anyone out for a nocturnal stroll along the shore—suddenly didn't seem nearly as appealing as a comfortable bed.

"Jeri, I—"

"Ah! The voice of reason speaks."

He caressed her shoulders. "Something like that. The kids could be—"

A faint chill accompanied her words. "—coming home?" She turned away and swam to the dock. Hanging on to the ladder, she faced him. "They're having a good time and, knowing kids, they won't be back before midnight."

He swam to the dock, watching her pull herself up, her delicious round bottom highlighted by the moon. *Knowing kids?* A sudden disturbing image of himself as a high-school senior in the back seat of a convertible with Annie Watson destroyed his last vestige of calm. "What do you think they're doing?"

"Well, I'm sure they're having fun."

"Yeah, but what kind of fun?

She stepped into her briefs. "Oh, Dan, sometimes you just have to trust them."

"Maybe—but I'm worried."

"You're sounding like a parent."

He hung on to the ladder. "It can't have escaped your notice that I *am* a parent."

Disregarding her wet skin, she shoved her arms into her bra straps and efficiently fastened the band. "Believe me, I've noticed." There was a distinct edge to her voice.

He hoisted himself up on the dock and reached for his wet shorts. "What's that supposed to mean?"

"Nothing." She shook out her slacks and stepped into them.

He rolled his eyes. "Uh-oh. A man's always in trouble when a woman clams up." He stood, hands on his hips. "Okay, lay it on me."

She tucked her blouse into the waist of her slacks, raked her fingers through her wet hair and shook her head to settle the curls. "Well, it seems to me you're trying to be Superparent, to the exclusion of anything else."

"Like what?"

"Like taking time for—" she hesitated "—me."

"Jeri, I thought you understood." He could feel his chest tightening. "Tiffany is only here for a short time, and while she is, she deserves my attention."

"Your attention or your pampering?"

He felt ridiculous standing there in dripping shorts

debating the obvious. "That's not fair. And if it *is* pampering, what the hell is wrong with that?"

Jeri flung his shirt at him. "Nothing, if you'd treat her like a normal kid, instead of like a prima donna."

"Dammit, Jeri. I get so few chances."

"To what? Spoil her rotten? Indulge her laziness and rudeness?

He felt himself go cold. "You'd better stop right now."

"Stop? You asked. You're gonna hear the answer. I suspect somewhere in that narcissistic little body of hers there's a decent human being. But Vicki's self-centeredness coupled with your admitted neglect hasn't produced one yet. And if you keep letting her manipulate you and—" she flapped her arms in frustration "—abuse everyone she comes in contact with, then what'll you have? A carbon copy of your ex-wife, that's what!"

"Are you finished?"

She pounded her fists against her thighs a couple of times. "Yes."

He started walking down the dock. She hurried after him. "Aren't you going to say anything?" she asked.

"No." He paused and looked at her. She suddenly appeared small and defeated. "Except good night. I'll see you Thursday at work." He strode angrily toward the house.

Moments later, he heard her car engine roar to life.

TIFFANY LEANED BACK against a rock outcropping high above the lake, clutching her knees to her chest. *Whoop-deedoo!* Scott was making a Boy Scout production of stoking the bonfire, Bubba—jeez, get a name!—and that giggly LaFaye had picked up a blanket and shuffled off into the trees, fooling no one about their intentions. Personally she couldn't think of anything less appealing than making out on a nest of scratchy pine needles with the bulky Bubba. Most of the other kids had either paired off in the darkness or were down below on the thin strip of beach, swimming. In the distance she could hear an owl hooting. She studied the nearby deserted mountain cabin that the locals thought of as Party Central. To her, it looked like the original residence of the Beverly Hillbillies, the hicks in that old show she'd seen on TV reruns.

How much longer did they have to wait for Bubba and LaFaye to do the deed so they could go home? Scott had been about as entertaining as a ventriloquist's dummy, and the other kids...well, they hadn't exactly voted her Miss Popularity.

Lost in her thoughts, she didn't hear Scott come up behind her. "Want another brew?"

She shrugged. "Sure, why not?"

"I'll get us a couple."

She watched him disappear into the cabin, emerging a few moments later with two ice-cold beers. He snapped off the tab tops before sitting down beside her and handing her a can. "What keeps them so cold?" she asked.

"A natural spring runs underground and comes out inside the springhouse, forming a pool. The water's pretty cold. The Ozarks are full of caves and springs. This whole area is nothing but one big limestone sponge."

"Are you some kind of science nerd?"

"Well, excu-use me. I was just trying to answer your question." He stretched out his legs, took a swig and stared at the fire.

"How much longer do we have to stay here?"

He frowned. "Having fun, are you?"

"What do you think? The prom queens and jocks are frolicking in the woods or water, Bubba and LaFaye are doing who knows what, and I'm sitting here on a rock ledge watching you avoid me."

"It's your boat. We can leave anytime."

"Right. Like I can't wait to get home."

"You could try to get along, you know."

She tossed down a third of her beer. "Why would I wanna do that?"

He sighed disgustedly. "Were you born with that giant chip on your shoulder or do you wear it just for me?"

His question gave her pause. "Am I really that bitchy?"

He searched her face. "You want the truth?"

She gulped. "Shoot."

"Big time. I know life may not be a picnic for you, but you're not the only one who ever had to deal with crap. Believe me, you haven't got the market cornered."

She set her beer aside and looked at him. There was no mistaking the bitterness in his voice. His eyes were fixed on a point beyond the fire. Despite stirrings of reluctant sympathy, she couldn't help blurting, "What would *you* know about problems?"

He shot her an incredulous look and jumped up so suddenly he knocked over her beer. "Jeesh! You really are about the most self-centered person I ever met. Clue in, Tiffany. There *are* other people in the world and we don't all win the friggin' lottery!"

He stamped off toward the fire and stood, hands

jammed in his pockets, gazing down at the swimmers, whose laughter floated up fron the lake.

She felt the sticky wetness of the beer soak into her shorts and rose to her feet, feeling suddenly lonely and defenseless. His words stung. The one possible friend she had in the entire state of Arkansas and he thought she was a bitch. *Wonderful. What now?* For some screwy reason, she felt an overpowering urge to cry. She swallowed hard and smoothed her eyelids with her fingers. She didn't need him, or anybody else, either.

He turned toward her. "Tiff?" His shoulders sagged. "I'm sorry. That was the beer talking."

She walked slowly toward him, stopping two feet away, and tried to read the expression on his face. "I don't think so." She paused. "You got problems, too?"

He laughed sardonically. "Try a bossy sister, a dead mother and a creep of a father. Happy family, huh?" He leaned over, picked up a twig and threw it onto the blaze.

"Uh, do you wanna, like, sit down and talk about it?" she offered.

"What're you—Ann Landers?"

She picked up his hand. "No, but I guess I have acted pretty crappy since I came here."

He allowed her to lead him to the rock she'd been leaning against earlier. She cradled his hand in her palm and laid their entwined hands on her knee. "I know about your bossy sister, but what about your parents?"

"Jeri's not so bad, really. She's just trying to help." He drew a ragged breath. "Nothing's been right since Mom..." He faltered. She squeezed his hand gently and waited. "...since Mom died. Like that. Just like that." His voice faded.

"When? How?"

The fire crackled and popped. The night air carried a suggestive giggle from the woods. Scott's chin rested on his chest. Finally he lifted his head and cleared his throat. "October. It hasn't even been a year." His voice rose in protest. "I came home from basketball practice. Mom was raking leaves. She started to joke about how I oughtta be an all-American leaf raker, instead of...instead of a basketball player, and then..." He bit his lip and turned, his expression haunted, to look at Tiffany. "...she laughed, but suddenly her eyes got real big. She grabbed the rake tight and staggered toward me."

He stopped, his Adam's apple working. "I stepped forward to catch her, but she still fell. I tried CPR, but it was too late. I couldn't... I'd never seen a dead person before, but I knew. I knew." He jerked his hand from Tiffany's grasp, covered his face and bent over his knees, racked with sobs.

Tiffany froze. *God, how awful!* She couldn't imagine it, couldn't even begin to sort out how you'd feel, how you'd ever erase that picture from your brain. She'd had no idea. He'd seemed so privileged, so carefree, so different from her.

Tentatively she reached out and laid a hand on his shoulder. When he didn't react, she moved closer. She didn't know what to say.

Finally his heaving shoulders stilled, and she heard him draw a ragged breath and whisper, "Shit!"

Oh, God, he must feel embarrassed about crying in front of her. She began gently massaging his back. Then she spoke softly. "'Self-centered' doesn't begin to say it."

"Huh?"

"I'm sorry. I didn't know. I just thought I was the only one with a screwed-up family."

He snorted. "You might as well hear it all. My father's already got the hots for another woman." The disgust in his voice sent a chill down her spine. She waited. "I thought he loved my mother. Some love!"

She tried to imagine how Scott felt, but it was hard. Her mother always had the hots for somebody. Oh, she tried to be discreet, but Tiffany wasn't born yesterday. Vicki needed a man like a plant needs sun. From the pain in Scott's voice, she guessed he really loved his father. She supposed that kind of screwing around would disappoint most kids big time. She didn't know how she felt about her own father.

Well, that wasn't exactly true. She resented the vibes that flew around any time Dad and Gidget were in the same room. You could cut the lust with a knife. "That must be tough," she finally mumbled.

"Yeah, tough. I hate him!"

"Parents are the pits. Mine don't exactly thrill me, either."

Scott struggled to his feet. "So help me God, I hope I never treat my kids like that." He reached down and helped her up. "Tiffany, I don't...that is, I mean, I never talk about stuff like this."

"Me, either. But maybe I could." She looked up at him wistfully and saw sympathy in his eyes.

"It's only fair," he said. "I dumped on you." When he put two big hands on her shoulders, she felt warmth creeping all the way to her toes.

She stepped closer, maintaining eye contact. "I know. I'm...I'm glad."

"Uh, me, too," and his arms slid down her back. The next thing she knew, he was kissing her far more tenderly than Tony ever had. Before she had time to deal with these new unexpected feelings, she heard a thrashing noise coming from the woods. She pulled away and cocked her head. "What's that? A bear?"

Scott chuckled. "Not hardly, unless Bubba qualifies."

Just then Bubba and LaFaye stumbled onto the ledge and stood by the fire, their hands still pawing each other. Tiffany grimaced. LaFaye had lipstick smeared all over her face and Bubba wore a smug self-satisfied look.

"Hey, Monahan," sneered Bubba. "You gettin' a little Eastern action?"

Tiffany felt Scott tense. "Shut up, Bubba."

Bubba turned to LaFaye. "I think they wanna be alone." He picked up the cooler. "We'll meet you at the boat, lover boy. By the way, there's a few old mattresses in the cabin. Kinda convenient, if you catch my drift."

Scott scowled fiercely as the couple made their way down the steep path toward the lake. "Sometimes I wonder why we're friends. Son of a bitch!"

Then he looked at Tiffany uncertainly, with a kind of wonder, as if he'd never seen her before. He pulled her to him. "Forget Bubba. He can be gross. I've got ideas of my own...."

He pulled her close and kissed her again. It felt good, very good. Maybe, Tiffany thought, things were looking up. Maybe she could get used to Arkansas, after all. If only—Scott's lips momentarily chased the thought away—if only Daddy would love her the way she'd always wanted him to. She surfaced from the kiss. If only Gidget wasn't throwing a big monkey wrench into that plan. Gidget's brother, though, he was another story!

AFTER JERI'S DEPARTURE, Dan wandered aimlessly through the house fuming about her insulting accusations. He ended up standing in the doorway of Tiffany's room, his hands hanging limply at his sides. He didn't know what he was looking for really, maybe some evidence that would give him a clue to what made his daughter tick.

Dirty clothes were piled in the small wooden rocker, and the bed could hardly be called made—the burgundy comforter had been pulled up hastily and the pillow wedged against the headboard. Covering the scarred wooden dresser were an assortment of cosmetics, rubber bands and ribbons, and a fluorescent pink hairbrush with dark blond hair caught in the bristles. From the poster over the bed Brad Pitt fixed him with a sultry look.

Bull lunged past him and leaped up on the bed, then stared at him. "I know," Dan said. "I'm invading your territory, fella. Thanks a lot for abandoning me. You're a sucker for a pretty blonde, I guess."

The words, meant in jest, hit home. "Hell!" He slapped the doorjamb with his hand. Bull wasn't the only one. He himself had been knocked for a loop by a pretty blonde, one with hair like spun honey. Right now, though, he was in no mood to think beautiful thoughts about Ms. Jeri Monahan. How had he deluded himself into thinking he could fool around with her? From the very beginning common sense had argued against it—he was the fire chief, not some guy on the prowl; she was hell on wheels, not the even-tempered partner his mother had been; he had responsibilities concerning Tiffany, and Jeri had a mouthful of plati-tudes based on...experience? Hell, no, on her own smug belief in the infallibility of her opinions.

Besides that, she came on too strong. What was that striptease on the dock all about? Not that he hadn't en-joyed the scenery and the wild aching it had aroused in his groin, but her sexuality carried a challenge with it. Look at Vicki. Apparently he'd never been man enough to satisfy her. No way would he set himself up again!

He shrugged and returned to the living room, picked up a catalog from a marine supplier and sprawled on the worn couch. He flipped through a few pages before throwing the pamphlet down in disgust. *Did* he let Tif-fany manipulate him? Jeri's words echoed in his head—*a carbon copy of your ex-wife.*

But what right did Jeri have to pass judgment? Tiffany had had a rough life and damn little nurturing. These few weeks were his chance with her—maybe his last chance—and he wasn't going to let Jeri screw things up. He'd concentrate on his daughter, on showing her how much he cared, how he'd do anything to protect her from further rejection.

From the parking lot, he heard Tiffany's high-pitched laugh. He glanced at his watch. *About time!* He went to the window and looked out just as his daughter melted into somebody's arms. Scott? Damn punk. Why, he had a good mind to...

Before he could react, Tiffany began walking toward the house, pivoting every now and then to watch the car exiting the lot. Under the porch lamp, she paused, one strap of her tank top slipping over her shoulder, a wistful smile playing over her lips. At last she opened the screen door and tiptoed across the floor, stopping in her tracks when she became aware of him.

"Dad?" A giggle surfaced. "What're you doing up?"

He turned away from the window. "Waiting for you. I was getting worried. It's easy to get lost on the lake at night."

"Dad, we were fine. Anyway, I let Scott drive the boat back."

He cleared his throat. "Looks like you and Scott are getting along okay."

She giggled again. "Yeah." She pulled the strap back up on her shoulder and then ran both palms through her hair, fluffing it out. She stumbled slightly and steadied herself against the kitchen counter.

"What about the other kids?"

"You mean the Arkies?" She hiccupped softly.

Dan clenched his fists. That patronizing bored tone of voice reminded him too much of Vicki.

"Surely you can find something positive to say."

She hooted. "I should live so long."

"Honey, you've gotta start looking for the good in people."

Her eyes suddenly glinted steel. "Easy for you to say. You didn't find much good in Mom."

Oh, boy, get ready. "Nor she in me, I guess."

"You should've thought of that before I came along."

Dan sighed. "Hindsight is easy. Your mother and I probably never should've been married. She didn't bargain for the navy life."

He crossed to his daughter, put an arm around her shoulders and, despite her initial resistance, drew her close. "But I wouldn't trade you for anything. You're the best thing that ever happened to me." She stared at the floor. His words apparently hadn't touched her.

She squirmed away and lurched against the counter. He barely made out her words. "Whatever. I don't care."

He grabbed her and twirled her around, anger coursing through him. "What does it take to get through to you, anyhow? Are you gonna punish me the rest of my life because I'm only human?"

"Leave me alone." Ice was where her pupils used to be, and he could smell the faint sweet smell of beer. She tried to turn away, but he gripped her arms.

"Have you been drinking?" he demanded.

She struggled. "Let me go."

"Answer the question."

"None of your business."

He tightened his fingers. "It's very much my business, young lady."

"It's no big deal."

"You're underage. It's illegal, not to mention dangerous to operate a boat under the influence."

She turned a how-did-you-get-so-stupid look on him. "Whoopdeedoo." She twirled an index finger in the air. "Chill out, Dad. Nobody was 'under the influence.' Besides, it was only a couple of beers."

White-hot anger choked out reason. Damn Scott Monahan. Then, with sudden insight, he realized that the person he was furious with was Tiffany—furious about the drinking, furious about her barely disguised tolerance of this place, furious about the way she coldly and deliberately set about to cut him out of her life. Hell. He hadn't known helplessness like this—ever.

Shaking, he removed his hands from her arms, shocked to see the pale imprint of his fingers. She stood, her head cocked to one side, her mouth curved in a sneer. "That it for tonight's lecture?"

Where had he lost control of the situation? How could his own child make him feel so powerless, turn on him with such devastating effect?

He shoved both fists into his pockets. "All for tonight. But we're not through with this discussion. I'm not giving up on us." For a moment she held his gaze, then shrugged and sauntered down the hall to her bedroom.

He expelled a pent-up sigh. He'd screwed up royally. Was he expecting too much? Were there too many obstacles between them? Tiffany seemed determined to resist his overtures. Was it too late for a satisfying father-daughter relationship? With blinding clarity, a new thought struck him. Had Jeri been right, after all? Maybe firmness *was* called for.

He flipped off the lamp and sagged onto the couch, fingers laced behind his head, staring into the darkness. *Firmness? Nah.* Look where it had gotten him tonight—farther behind the eight ball than ever.

CHAPTER ELEVEN

SCOTTY STOOD at the kitchen counter Thursday evening, fingering his car keys and glaring at his sister with barely concealed loathing.

"Quit tellin' me what to do."

Jeri bit her lip to keep from lashing out. Today had been her first shift at the marina since Monday night's debacle with Dan. Exhausted from the beastly heat, Tiffany's hostility and Dan's aloofness, she resented having to scrape herself together for tonight's fire-department meeting.

"I merely said I don't think you have any business staying out after midnight every night of the week." *Especially not with Tiffany.*

"I'm old enough to do what I want. Besides, you're not my parent." His eyes narrowed. "In fact, I don't seem to have one."

"Scotty, that's an awful thing to say."

"It's the truth."

"But Dad—"

His expression sent shivers through her body. "Right, good ol' Dad. I don't see what difference it makes when I come in. He's never here. Warming the sheets with what's-her-name. Some example!"

"Scotty, we don't know that. Besides, Celeste may be a very fine person."

He rolled his eyes. "I suppose you believe in the tooth fairy, too."

She swallowed hard, feeling desperate. "Scotty, what's happening to us?"

"Happening? I dunno about you, but I'm growing up fast, and I don't like the facts of life."

She struggled to find words to reach him. "We used to be such a close family."

"Yeah. That was...before."

"Mom wouldn't want us to be like this."

For a moment his features relaxed, then just as quickly hardened. "Don't talk to me about her." He picked up his ball cap and slammed it on his head. "I'm leaving." Scooping up his keys, he headed for the door.

"When will you be back?"

"Dunno."

Tears of frustration threatened her fragile composure. She and Scotty were cruising for a showdown. It had to happen, but she couldn't face it tonight. She would not cry. Crying accomplished nothing. Besides, she needed every shred of composure to carry her through tonight's meeting with the Great Contini. Damn his hide! If only she didn't care so much.

"YOU GOTTA WATCH your live wire when you're making a rescue. Sumbitch might curl or roll on the ground. You gotta pin that wire down, mebbe throw two heavy objects on it, till the linemen git thar."

Jeri bit her lips to keep from yawning. The visiting trainer, a fireman from a nearby town, pronounced "wire" as "wahr," and his monotone bass was soporific. She squirmed in her seat and tried to listen to his description of hot-line cutters. Out of the corner of her eye, she could see Dan, sitting spike straight and rigid-jawed. She'd arrived as late as possible, and it was her intention to slip out immediately at the conclusion of the training. She'd seen quite enough of Dan for one day.

She felt a sharp poke in her ribs. Smitty Dingle, sitting next to her, nodded his head in Earl Gunderman's direction. Earl's chin had fallen onto his chest, and periodically his lips fluttered with an expelled snore. Jeri tried not to giggle, but the longer she watched, the more tickled she became. She stared at the floor, praying for a merciful conclusion to the talk. Just then Earl's head lolled off to one side and he righted himself with a carthorse snort.

It was too much. She clamped a hand over her mouth to imprison the explosion of giggles, her shoulders heaving, tears streaming down her face. Beside her, Smitty was rocking in mirth. She covered her eyes with her fingers.

"If y'gotta git that wahr off a body, pull the wahr t'ard you, backin' away the while…"

She peered through the slit between her index and middle fingers. Earl was at it again. She forced down an audible hiccup of laughter. In the distance, Contini turned ever so slightly in his chair and glared in her direction. That did it! She bolted from her chair and scuttled to the rest room where, with relief, she erupted.

She collapsed against the sink, laughing uncontrollably. At last, gasping, she wet a paper towel and held it to her hot tear-stained face. God, the laughter had felt good, but she'd been way out of line. Another involuntary titter escaped. She sagged against the wall, aware suddenly that she was absolutely wiped out and had come to the brink of a monumental crying jag. She sobered. *No wonder*. A family in shambles and Monday night's disaster on the dock with Contini.

She cracked open the door and saw that the meeting was breaking up. With any luck, she could leave without being noticed. Turning off the light and closing the rest-room door, she threaded her way through the firemen milling around the coffee urn. She had just evaded the long-winded Carl Rojas when she heard the chief's voice. "Monahan!"

Monahan. So it's come to that. She paused, her hand on the exit door. "Yes, *sir?*"

"I'd like to see you in my office."

She could read nothing in the drawn lines of his face. Was she going to be reprimanded for her unprofessional behavior tonight? She let her hand slip off the doorknob. "Whatever you say."

DAN DREW a deep breath and strode into his office, his decision made. Jeri sat huddled in the wooden office chair, defiance shooting from those damn brown-sugar eyes, watching him as he skirted the desk and settled into his seat. He felt self-conscious. What was he doing—establishing his territory, his ank? Or was he keeping a solid object between them so he wouldn't reconsider?

He leaned forward, his hands clasped on the desk. This was going to be more difficult than he'd thought, but it had to be done. "Jeri, I—"

"Don't say it. I know, it was unforgivably rude, even childish."

He frowned. Was she talking about Monday night? She'd led him right into his subject. He took a stab. "I know we don't agree about Tiffany, but—"

"Tiffany? What's *she* got to do with it? I'm talking

about my, er, lapse of manners tonight. Isn't that what you wanted to talk about?''

He averted his eyes. "Partly."

"Whatever, I apologize. It won't happen again." She started to rise. "Are you satisfied?"

"Sit down, Jeri."

She paused, then sat back down, crossing her arms. He tried to avoid looking at the way her breasts were pushed up.

She waited.

He stood and began to pace behind the desk. "What I want to talk about is us."

She raised an eyebrow, but said nothing.

He leaned on the chair back. "It's not going to work."

"Not going to work?" she echoed.

"You and me." His words rolled out faster. "You're a terrific person, but we don't see eye to eye on things. I have to put my obligations as a father ahead of my own nee— ahead of anything else. Regardless of what you may think of Tiffany, she's all I've got, and I intend to devote whatever time and energy I have to making her happy." He paused to collect himself. "Furthermore I have to be the kind of parent I am, not the kind anyone else thinks I should be."

Jeri flushed and started to speak, but he raised his hand. "I'm not criticizing you. Hell, you very well may know what's best, but it's not me. I can be hard as nails with the men under my command, but when it comes to my only daughter, well, I just can't hurt her."

This time Jeri stood and searched his face. "That's it? Just like that?"

He could see her struggling for control. He nodded.

"That's it. I'm sorry." One stray curl stuck to her forehead and he resisted the urge to reach out and touch it.

"I'm sorry, too." Her eyes filmed over. She paused. "What about work?"

His voice sounded gruff in his ears. "I still need you." He winced at the unintended irony.

"Very well. I'll be there Saturday." With that she sailed out of the room, leaving him feeling like a gutless wonder.

SHE COULDN'T COVER the parking lot fast enough to reach the sanctuary of the Explorer. The nerve of him! Of course, she'd made a big mistake; the subject of Tiffany was obviously sacred, and she'd ridden roughshod over his feelings with her remarks Monday. But she'd thought their relationship was solid enough to withstand one ill-considered incident. Ye gods, she'd made him a pretty strong commitment. If he thought she slept with just anyone, well...

She stopped dead in her tracks a few feet from her vehicle, and said, "That's *it?* It's been fun, but..." She felt her heart race and her face redden. *Down twenty points at halftime and you're gonna concede the game?*

She whirled, stomped back to the community hall and stormed into Chief Contini's office. "I can't believe what you said! Just 'That's it'?"

He struggled to his feet, but she rounded the desk and poked an index finger into his chest. "And I'm a 'terrific person, but we don't see eye to eye'?"

He placed his hands on her shoulders. "For God's sake, Jeri, listen—"

"No, you listen to me." She put the flat of her palm against his chest, pushed him down in his chair and stood over him, glowering. "I don't give up this easily.

You're worth fighting for. *We're* worth fighting for."
She perched on the edge of his desk, crossing her arms.
"And what's more, Chief, I thought we cared quite a
bit for each other. I know I did...do."

She paused for a breath. "Look. Tiffany is a concern
and an important one. You and I were getting along fine
until she arrived. Of course you want a solid relationship with her. You think I don't *understand* that? And
yes, maybe I've been a little jealous of her, but it's not
an insurmountable problem."

Dan shoved his chair back against the wall and
looked at her doubtfully. "It's more complicated than
that. You're not making this easy—"

"And another thing. You act so damn patronizing
sometimes. I'm not seventeen, you know. Are you trying to make yourself old before your time? What's eight
years' difference? Can't you get it through your thick
skull that I find you virile, manly, sexy as hell?" She
plopped down on his lap and wove the fingers of one
hand through his hair.

His hands flailed at his sides. "This isn't going to
solve anything."

"Oh, no?" She picked up one of his hands and
placed it on her hip. "Well, what is?" She felt his other
arm circling her waist.

"We're past that, Jeri. Didn't you hear what I said
earlier?"

"Sure, I heard. You had that pretty speech down pat.
What I didn't hear was conviction."

"But Tiffany needs—"

She found his mouth and smothered his words with
a long tender kiss. Slowly she withdrew her lips. "What
Tiffany needs—" she cupped his face and looked
straight into his eyes "—is a happy father, one who

loves her enough to take care of himself. And, Contini, in your case, like it or not, I think that involves me.''

She felt him shudder as he expelled a deep sigh. ''Don't make this harder than it already is, Jeri.'' He carefully lifted her off his lap and stood up in front of her, holding her by the elbows. ''This is not a choice I can make.''

She flared. ''Why does it have to be a choice?''

''I am a father first.''

''I understand that.'' Her voice was beginning to sound strident.

''If we can't agree on something so basic as child rearing, what kind of future—''

She shook her head regretfully. ''Silly me. I thought love might have something to do with it.''

''Jeri, I never said...'' He looked forlorn.

She retucked her blouse into her shorts and retreated to the far side of the desk. ''I know you didn't. Wishful thinking on my part, I guess.'' She opened the door and then paused. ''It could've worked, Dan. Tiffany and all. It really could've.'' She sighed. ''I guess we're both too stubborn.''

Her footsteps echoed hollowly through the deserted meeting room, and her heart felt like a dull lead weight. *Three strikes and you're out—Dad, Scotty and, oh God, Dan.*

She made it to the Explorer just before the tears came.

SUNDAY AFTERNOON Tiffany dipped the paintbrush into the white paint, wiped it back and forth on the lip of the can and made a preliminary swipe across the weathered gray boards of the floating fish-cleaning shed.

Things had never been hunky-dory here, but ever

since Thursday tension ruled at the marina. Gidget was avoiding Dad, Dad was stalking around in a grand funk, and they spoke to each other only if they had to. She almost felt sorry for her father—he seemed kind of lost. Meanwhile, Scott stayed out by the pumps, even eating his lunch on the dock. At least he was still speaking civilly to her, if not to anybody else. They'd been out several nights this week, and she knew he was really steamed at his sister. Only Bull, stretched out sunning nearby, seemed the same.

Maybe there'd been a lovers' quarrel. Well, that was fine with her. Now she'd have her father all to herself. She'd about had it with Gidget's schoolteacher voice: *Would it hurt you to help me?...Tiffany, would you mind turning off the TV?...I'd really appreciate it if you'd latch the screen door when you come in and out.* She saw right through all that—Gidget was pissed off big time that she, Tiffany, wasn't pulling her weight. But she hadn't come to Arkansas to bust her butt for anybody, least of all the hired help.

She dipped the brush again and slapped on more white. Boring. The only reason she'd agreed to do this painting was to get out of the office—that, and because Dad had asked her. She was finding it harder and harder to resent him. He wasn't such a bad guy. She'd really expected him to be a bigger jerk, to smother her or try to con her about the past. But he hadn't. He'd come right out and called his marriage a mistake. It kind of hurt to think your parents didn't have, like, the love of the century or something. She'd thought about that, though. The more she was around him, the harder it was to imagine him married to her mother. He seemed too...dull? No, that wasn't it. Solid? Stable? But if he was so stable, how come she'd grown up basically without him?

She couldn't blame the navy for all of it. Other kids' fathers had sea duty. They adjusted. But Mom hadn't ever been welcoming to him. Once she was divorced it was like she didn't care if she ever saw Dan Contini again, and she sure didn't make visitation easy. Tiffany could remember the impressions she'd gotten about him from her mother—the tapping of the foot, the exasperated sigh and always the accusations. Maybe there was stuff she didn't know; maybe her father had tried harder than she knew.

Suddenly an idea occurred to her. She set down the brush and dashed into the office for a pencil. Returning, she began sketching fish on the bare wall. What if she made a mural? The shed was so ugly and drab. People around here had no imagination. As long as she had to do this, she might as well make the job as fun as possible, and after all, art class *had* been her favorite.

Tomorrow was Dad's day off. Maybe he'd take her to the hardware store to buy some colored paint. She could make an underwater scene, put in some seaweed, maybe even a gross catfish, and then a shoreline above it. She stepped back, visualizing. Yeah, it just might work. And it'd sure as heck be more interesting than plain white. "Whaddaya think, Bull?"

The dog opened his mouth and yawned. "Beats the work Gidget thinks I oughtta do. And it could take quite a while to get this just right."

She smiled and began sketching in the tree-rimmed shoreline. She might just have time to finish the project. Dear old Mom must be having the time of her life with Purd, because she'd called to say they were extending their trip. Pooh! Just when she thought she'd be out of here in another week.

She eyed Scott at the gas dock. Actually the news hadn't been the end of the world. Ever since that first kiss, well, she and Scott had developed a sort of "thing." She liked spending time with him, and she especially liked the tingly warm way he made her feel. He wasn't a phony like so many kids were. She would never have guessed, though, about his problems. That father of his must be a real dork.

She hunkered down to outline an underwater rock formation. She remembered the question he'd asked her last night as they sat parked above the dam: "Do you think there's any such thing as a happy marriage?"

She hadn't had much of an answer to that. Her experience was the pits.

He'd gone on, "I used to think my parents had one, but I don't know anymore."

Distracted by the memory, she laid down her pencil. Scott's feelings had really been stomped on. Maybe that was even worse than knowing your parents had never been happy. Sure didn't inspire a whole lot of confidence in the future. But what did? Scott's folks, Purd and Mom, Gidget and Dad? Not exactly candidates for the Romance Hall of Fame!

CHAPTER TWELVE

By Sunday evening Jeri didn't see how things could get much worse. After Thursday night, being around Dan at the marina was not only awkward but humiliating. How could she have totally misread their relationship and thrown herself at him like that?

She tossed her purse on the kitchen table, opened the refrigerator and inspected the contents. As usual she was eating alone—both Scotty and Dad had said they'd be late. Indifferently she pulled out a cucumber, a tomato, half a head of lettuce and a bottle of ranch dressing.

She prepared a tossed salad, poured herself a glass of iced tea and strolled out to the porch. The sun was just setting in the cloudless sky, and long shadows played across the steep lawn sloping to the water. In the trees bordering the yard two does grazed. She chewed half-heartedly, reviewing the past several days. Disaster. Total disaster.

She hadn't changed her mind about Tiffany; if anything, her opinion had been substantiated by the teenager's subtly gloating behavior since she'd realized her father and "Gidget" had cooled it. The girl knew how to turn the knife.

Jeri searched her soul. She'd come on strong with Dan. Even if it was the truth, comparing his daughter to his former wife, who had obviously hurt him badly, was the height of insensitivity. Damn. Why did she always let her mouth run away with her?

A piece of tomato lodged in her throat. The whole summer was disintegrating around her. Both she and Scotty were miserable, and Dad was an enigma. Why had she ever thought she could arrive in River Falls and restore normalcy? She swallowed hard. She wasn't used to failure. But that was exactly what had happened—she'd failed with the family, she'd failed with Tiffany, and she'd certainly failed with Dan.

And it hurt. Until Dan, she hadn't known how much a relationship could mean to her, how complete her emotional investment could be. She'd thought he wanted her as much as she wanted him. Behind his carefully controlled features, she'd read yearning. In his lovemaking there was more than playfulness, more than desire. There was need. The planes of his face had relaxed, his eyes had shone clear and trouble-free. How could she have so completely shattered that peacefulness?

And yet the issue of Tiffany couldn't be overlooked, either. *Can I simply ignore her spiteful behavior, look the other way, feign acceptance?* She set aside her salad plate and massaged her temples with her fingertips. If she'd been any good at pretense, the situation wouldn't have come to this. No, it wasn't in her nature to be hypocritical. Good old Jeri—nothing subtle about her, just in your face!

She stood, picked up the plate and carried it into the kitchen. Speculation was useless. It was over with Dan. The only legitimate issue was how much longer she could endure working at the marina, seeing him, wanting him.

She barely heard the rap on the door over the clatter

of loading the dishwasher. She cocked her ear. "Jeri, you home?"

Mike. She hurried to the screen door, a delighted smile on her face. "Hey, stranger, come on in. Where've you been lately? I've missed you."

Mike dropped an arm loosely around her shoulder as they walked toward the great room. "Two-week investment seminar in San Francisco."

"Tough duty. Fresh fish, all the sourdough bread you can eat and Napa Valley wines."

He flopped on the sofa. "Tough, but somebody had to do it. Might as well be me."

"Can I interest you in a beer?"

"Ever known me to refuse?"

Jeri poured a cold beer into a tall glass, refilled her iced tea and settled at the other end of the sofa. She eyed his swim trunks and floppy T-shirt. "I didn't see you at the marina today."

"Nah, I just ran down this evening to check on the boat."

"I'd have been sorry to miss you, so I'm glad you stopped by."

"The little blonde in the office there isn't winning too many friends."

Jeri's heart sank. "Oh?"

"Yeah, I had one of those excuse-me-for-asking experiences. Who is she, anyway?"

"Dan's daughter."

He lifted his glass in a toast. "Well, here's to Dan. Looks like he's got his hands full."

"That's not all."

He raised an eyebrow.

"She has Scotty wrapped around her little finger. I'm

surprised she was still at the marina. The two of them planned to drive into town for ice cream.''

''You look worried.''

''Tiffany has created a few problems,'' she said glumly.

''Like?''

Jeri set her tea down and sat cross-legged facing Mike. ''Like? Where do I begin? Jeez, Mike, this is going to sound petty.''

''Petty's okay. Spill it.''

''For starters, she's a sophisticated little thing, and...''

''She's got her hooks into baby brother.''

Jeri rubbed her palms over her bare knees. ''Yeah.''

Mike laughed. ''That's not the end of the world. Scott needs some education.''

She looked up peevishly. ''At what cost?''

''Easy, Tag. He's not going to do anything stupid. You gotta let him grow up.''

Her shoulders drooped. ''You know what, Mike? I feel like an old woman. I mean I'm barely eleven years older than he is, and I'm acting like a mother hen.''

''A little bossy, are you?''

She threw a pillow at him. ''You know me too well.''

''Okay, so Tiffany's causing you to worry about Scott. What else?''

She bit her lower lip and stared at the ceiling. ''That's it, I guess.''

Mike drained his glass and studied her. ''Hmm, I don't think so.'' He waited. Jeri couldn't bring herself to speak. Any show of sympathy and she was apt to burst into tears. ''Contini?''

She turned and stared at him. ''How'd you know?''

He chuckled. ''Ever since you volunteered with the

fire department, I knew fireworks were coming. Dan's a good-looking lonely guy and you're an attractive lonely gal. It was an explosion waiting to happen." He tousled her hair. "Am I right?"

She grinned ruefully. "An explosion, all right. Until Tiffany doused the fire."

He gave her an *aha!* look. "Trouble in paradise?"

"Oh, Mike, we were getting along so well. I wouldn't tell this to anybody else, but I really thought Dan might be the one. Now I feel stupid."

"How's that?"

"Tiffany has had a lonely life and she resents the divorce and what she perceives as a life deprived of Daddy's attention. I'm trying really hard to sympathize, cut her some slack." She stared at her hands folded in her lap.

"But?"

"But she's a pain in the ass. Before she ever arrived, she'd made up her mind to be as miserable as possible, and she's doing a damn good job of it. Lazy, moody, manipulative. You name it."

"And Dan?"

She snorted. "He may be able to handle a raging forest fire, but he won't stand up to his daughter."

"And you think he should?"

She gaped at him. "She's out of control."

"Sounds to me like she's very much in control."

"I beg your pardon?"

"She's certainly got you right where she wants you."

The truth of his statement resonated in her brain. "But she needs a good shaking up."

"Jeri, she's not one of your basketball players."

"I know. But it's so clear to me what a great kid she

could be if she had some structure, some discipline in her life.''

''And Dan's supposed to provide that suddenly after all these years?''

''She's working him.''

''She's a teenager, for God's sake. Didn't you ever work your folks?''

''I guess. It's just that...that it makes Dan look weak.''

Mike stretched his arms across the top of the sofa and threw his head back. ''Oh, boy. Let me guess. You told him what needs to happen.''

''Well...yes. Somebody had to.''

''You think he could be 'the one,' yet you charged in and questioned his judgment, his manhood? You *do* have a problem, Tag.''

She swallowed hot tears and stared at her lap. ''I thought you were my friend.''

He picked up one of her hands and then let their clasped hands fall between them on the sofa. ''I am.'' He seemed to be considering something. Finally he said, ''You want some advice?''

Still staring in her lap, not sure if she could take any more, she nodded.

''You've always been a champion. A go-get-'em, rough-and-tumble competitor. Frankly there aren't many men who could go head-to-head with you. It's too risky. You scare the hell out of 'em. Dan was an exception, until, of course, you questioned his judgment about his daughter.'' Mike paused. ''Sounds to me like several things are going on here. You love the guy, but you're jealous of his daughter.''

It was true. Mike knew her too well. She remained silent.

"Not of her exactly, but of the hold she has on Dan. And you don't like seeing your man helpless. Something like that."

She mumbled. "I guess."

"You're not only competitive, Tag, you've also always been a fixer. If it's broken, lost or hurting, you're gonna make it right. Your team, your family, your man."

She looked up. "What's wrong with that?"

"Nothing's wrong with the impulse. It shows you care. But you aren't the only one involved. Sometimes you've gotta trust the other guy, give it time. Not be so controlling."

"Controlling?" The word left a sour taste in her mouth. She sputtered. "Maybe, but I feel like...if I don't handle something, it won't get done or won't get done right."

"And what would happen if it didn't?"

"I'd fail."

"Is that so bad?"

She considered his question, feeling the encouraging squeeze of his hand. "For me? Yeah, that's bad."

"How about letting somebody save *you* for a change? Could you do that?"

"I...I really don't know."

"You might want to try. Men appreciate strength in a woman, but they also want to see that she can be vulnerable, too. Needy."

In a small voice she heard herself say, "I do have needs, you know."

"I know." He stood, pulled her to her feet and made her walk with him to the door. In the entryway he turned her toward him and rested his hands on her shoulders. "Tag, don't lose your femininity in the name of feminism. And, remember, the whole weight of the world isn't on your shoulders."

He pecked her on the cheek, opened the door and walked to his car. She stood looking out long after he'd driven off into the night. She felt bruised, diminished, uncertain. But she found it easier to breathe than she had in almost a week.

MONDAY NOON Dan watched as Tiffany picked up the last slice of pepperoni pizza and took a big bite. This lunch was certainly going over better than quiche and fruit salad at the Ozarks Inn. Maybe he was learning. And this morning's trip to the hardware store for paint had been a success, too. He'd been amazed yesterday when she'd showed him the preliminary sketches she'd made on the shed. She had real talent. And if nothing else, he was grateful she'd at last shown an interest in something.

Perhaps his life was simplifying, after all. Ever so slowly he was making progress with Tiffany, and he'd disposed of the Jeri problem—more or less. It was still difficult seeing her at the marina; they circled each other like wary cats. But time would surely take the edge off his discomfort. Breaking off the personal relationship had been in everyone's best interests. Funny, though, how something that was so obviously right could still feel so wrong.

He eyed his daughter as she licked her fingers. Today she had her hair pulled back into a twist, exposing her lovely cheekbones.

"I like your hair that way," he ventured.

She looked up, startled. "It's no big deal."

"Is that how you always handle compliments?"

"What do you mean?"

"It's customary to say thank-you. You have a very pretty face. You shouldn't always hide it."

"Pretty? Not me."

Dan's heart contracted. He reached across the table and tipped her chin. "Yeah, you."

Her eyes glowed and her jaw relaxed. "You're embarrassing me, Dad."

"Honey, that's not my intention. I'm telling you the truth. I have a hunch Scott Monahan shares my opinion."

She looked flustered. "I dunno."

"And I'll bet others have, too. Do you have a boyfriend in Virginia?"

"I thought I did. Tony. But I haven't heard from him lately."

She sounded disappointed. Another rejection. "Maybe that's just as well."

She chewed her bottom lip. "Maybe."

He plunged on. "Do you miss your friends in Virginia?"

She mumbled something he couldn't make out. "What?"

She looked up, her eyes sad and uncertain. "I don't have that many." She paused, then corrected herself. "I *know* a lot of kids and we hang around together, but I don't have, like, you know, any real close friends."

"So who do you talk to when you need someone?"

She began to tear her napkin carefully in long strips. He waited, dying inside. "I dunno."

"Tiff, I hope you'll believe what I'm going to say. I'll always be here for you—only a phone call away." She studied the napkin she was decimating. "Next time you need a shoulder to cry on or somebody to celebrate with, all you have to do is call. I love you, honey."

She continued—one strip, two strips, three strips. Then she looked up and seemed to assess him, as if trying to come to a decision. "Why did you stay away so much of the time?" Her gaze was fixed, impassive, for a moment, then she lowered it.

"That's a valid question." He shoved his plate aside and folded his hands on the table. "Much of it couldn't be helped. But I suppose part of it was by choice." He noticed her chewing the inside of her mouth. "Let's start with what couldn't be helped. The navy is a demanding life, even more so when you're on sea duty. Orders were orders. I was a damage-control officer. Damage-control officers are needed on ships. That's what I was trained to do and what I liked doing. Could I have done something else? I suppose. Would I have been happy? I doubt it. When I finally got tired of the navy, I chose this life. I'm not the kind of guy who can report to a desk job nine to five and find satisfaction. Am I making sense so far?"

Scooping up the paper strips, she wadded them into a ball. "I guess."

"As for my divorce from your mother, I don't think that could be helped, either. It would've happened sooner or later, no matter what. We didn't share the same values, enjoy the same kind of life-style, go into marriage with the same expectations. If we'd stayed together, it would only have been because of you. In the long run, that might have been even harder on you."

"Maybe." She didn't look up, but she stopped rolling the napkin ball around the tabletop. "You and Mom are different, all right." He detected the hint of a smile.

He took a deep breath. "Now for the difficult part—the part I could have done something about. I could have fought harder to exercise my visitation rights. I don't know how to say this without sounding defensive, but, Tiff, your mother didn't make it easy for me.'' His daughter glanced up, as if encouraging him to continue. ''She always had some excuse why the timing wasn't convenient—you were sick, she'd already planned a visit to your grandparents, you'd been invited to a birthday party.''

She seemed to be listening attentively. ''Over time, I began to think it didn't matter to you whether I showed up or not. When I *did* come, it often seemed like we both faked having a good time. You were just a kid, and it was natural for you to act eager to get home to your mother, your friends. After a while I felt like an intruder. You had good cause to resent me. You were a little girl when I moved out, and it must've seemed like I'd abandoned you. Then when I was at sea for long stretches and couldn't get there for dance recitals and school programs, you must've thought I didn't care.'' He picked up her hand and held it gently. ''Nothing could be further from the truth.''

''I guess I've never really looked at your side of things.'' She wore a puzzled little frown. ''You mean you cared about me...all that time?''

''I've never stopped caring about you, honey, never. That's why it's so important to me what happens this summer. I want us to build a good honest relationship.'' He searched her face. ''Do you think that's possible?''

She lowered her lashes, sat very still for a moment and then looked straight at him. ''I don't know.''

He squeezed her icy fingers. ''Why's that?''

''I...it's scary.''

''Scary?'' *Please, Lord, help me through this.*

''What if it doesn't work?''

"You mean, what if we try and I'm a disappointment?"

"No, *me*. What if I can't be the daughter you want?"

Relief surged through him. He chuckled. "Oh, honey, there's no way that can happen. You're already the daughter I want." He released her hand and sat back, smiling. "Unless you want to talk about the matter of underage drinking and late hours..."

"Now?" He could hear the protest in her question.

"No, not now. But isn't that what fathers who love their daughters do? Try to protect them?"

A sunny smile broke over her face. "Yeah...yes. But that doesn't mean I have to like it, does it?"

"Well, don't you...just a little?"

She shrugged, the corner of her mouth quirking. "Maybe...just a little."

Progress—at last. Time to lighten up. "You ready to go back and attack the fish-cleaning shed now that we've bought a whole rainbow of paints?"

She wiped her hands on her shorts and stood. "I need them all, Dad," she said with a hint of defensiveness.

He rose to his feet. "I know you do. And for whatever it's worth, I think you're enormously talented."

"Don't say that." Pain flitted across her features.

Dan raised an eyebrow.

The pain slowly evaporated, leaving a knowing smile. "Okay." She slipped a small hand into his. "Thank you, Dad, for the compliment."

THAT SAME AFTERNOON Jeri entered the casual country-garden dining room of the Ozarks Inn and was ushered to a table overlooking the river. She studied the menu carefully, closed it, then nervously reopened it. She'd finally taken the big step with Celeste. To continue avoiding her, especially after she'd promised Dad she'd make an effort, smacked of cowardice. So here she was, butterflies cavorting in her stomach, wondering what on earth she would say to the woman she'd invited for lunch.

Her nervous state was not improved when, across the river, she spotted Dan and Tiffany coming out of the local pizza joint, hand in hand. She snapped the menu shut. It still hurt that he seemed able to proceed serenely with his life when hers was in total ruin. Mike had not spared her the unpleasant truth. She *was* aggressive, competitive, threatening—in short, nobody Contini or any other man would willingly pick out of the crowd. Though inside she sometimes felt fragile and vulnerable, she apparently projected an image of...what? If she were a man, she supposed they'd say she had balls. *Terrific. Just what a girl needed.*

Was Mike right? Had subconscious competition with Tiffany for Dan's affection played a part in her attitude toward the girl? If so, that was downright immature and made her feel ashamed. She'd always been competitive, always valued winning. Why? In her family she'd been taught losing was acceptable only if you'd given your all. A sudden thought jarred her.

Is the need to prove I'm "one of the boys" how I seek approval from men? Her stomach imploded. Could she be right? Was competing her defense?

"Jeri?" The svelte blonde dressed in charcoal linen slacks and a red-and-white polka-dot blouse stood beside the table. "I'm sorry to have kept you waiting."

Jeri took the hand Celeste extended and looked up into a pair of friendly gray-blue eyes. "Celeste, I'm glad you were free on such short notice."

The woman sat down and picked up the menu. "Have you decided?"

Jeri nodded. "I always end up ordering the same thing here. Chicken crepes and fruit salad."

"Sounds perfect." Celeste set the menu aside. "Let's make it two."

The hovering waiter took the order and disappeared. "I'm glad you suggested one o'clock, Jeri. Most of the businessmen have cleared out, and we'll have a quieter time to get acquainted." She smiled across the table. "Thank you for inviting me."

"You've probably wondered what took me so long."

"Not at all. I imagine the idea of me has taken some adjusting to."

Jeri relaxed her grip on the napkin in her lap. "Truthfully it's been difficult. Don't misunderstand. Not because of you personally, just...because."

"Because you loved your mother and because it seems too soon."

Jeri felt soothed. She nodded.

Celeste smiled thoughtfully. "My son in Fayetteville feels much the same way." Jeri reacted with surprise. She had never considered Celeste's family, their possible feelings. "He thinks my seeing Hank diminishes how I felt about his father."

Jeri's eyes widened. "I can understand that. My mother was a beautiful caring person. I believe my parents had a great marriage. Even though I know Dad's lonely, it still...yes, I guess I feel Dad's dating diminishes Mother, their relationship."

"Thank you for being straightforward, Jeri. Hank and I never set out to hurt anyone, although at times our actions must appear selfish. Do they?"

Her candor was disarming. Jeri heard the tinkle of

glassware at the next table, felt a waft of cold air from the ceiling fan above. "Honestly? Scotty and I have both felt...hurt, I guess. Dad's been preoccupied, not just with you, but with Cedarcrest, too."

"Hank's counted heavily on you, hasn't he?" Jeri saw understanding in Celeste's eyes.

She picked up her goblet and sipped some water. "I suppose he has. But then, that's partly why I came home in the first place."

"Still, it can't be easy. You've been asked to take on a lot. A grieving father who seems to be acting like a foolish old man, and a teenager who resents authority, particularly his older sister's."

"I...I don't know what to say." Celeste's succinct summary of the situation was right on target.

"Jeri—" her right hand fluttered at the collar of her blouse "—I'd like to be your friend, although that may be difficult for you at first...."

"No, I'm not sure it will be. I came here prepared only to tolerate you, Celeste. I'm finding, though, that I *like* you." She bit her lower lip. "But I'd still appreciate knowing what's going on between you and Dad. He doesn't volunteer much."

"To tell you the truth, neither of us knows the answer to that question. I *can* tell you we enjoy each other's company, we have fun together. Seeing each other helps keep the loneliness at bay. But each of us had great love and respect for our spouses. No one will ever replace Jack in my heart, just as no one will replace your mother for Hank. I believe, though, that love is not meant to be locked away in a casket, but exercised and given—over and over again."

Jeri recognized Celeste's sincerity and conviction. "Thank you for your willingness to lay your cards on the table. I'd dreaded the thought of making small talk throughout lunch.'' She smiled.

"Speaking of which, here it comes.'' They moved their silverware aside to permit the waiter to put down the colorful plates. "This looks delicious.''

"It's never failed me yet.'' Jeri picked at a wedge of chilled watermelon.

"One thing more, Jeri.'' Celeste paused. "Hank tells me Scott's not dealing well with his mother's death or our dating. You're probably bearing the brunt of that. How can I help?''

Suddenly the fruit didn't look nearly as appetizing. Jeri lowered her fork. "I honestly don't have a clue what you or I can do. I've certainly tried. But he won't talk about any of it—not Mom, not you.'' Her face fell. At the moment she couldn't think of a way to narrow the gulf between her brother and father, and introducing Celeste into the middle of it was not an option.

Celeste carefully buttered her muffin before meeting Jeri's gaze again. "Sounds to me like it's up to Hank.''

Unexpectedly Jeri felt a sense of enormous relief. *Up to Hank.* She chewed on the idea. Had she been protecting Dad? Excusing him? Letting him off the hook while *she* tried to keep everybody happy? Was that the game? Just pass the ball to good ol' Jeri. Let her go in for the layup, and when she doesn't score, blame the loss on her. She felt her dander rising. Was she her father's keeper? Her brother's keeper?

She nodded and said, "And to Scotty. Celeste, you know what? It's time I stood on the sidelines and let them settle things.''

Jeri couldn't fail to notice the respect and affection in Celeste's eyes when she answered, "I think you're absolutely right." She hesitated. "And, Jeri, I'll be rooting for you."

Jeri's tension eased into a genuine smile. "I appreciate that."

TWO DAYS LATER Jeri sat on the screened porch at dusk trying to concentrate on the physical-education course outline she was studying. Just as she'd pick up the thread, she'd hear the *thumpa-thumpa* of Scotty dribbling a basketball, then the *thwang* of the metal rim vibrating, the sound of the ball ricocheting off the backboard or, most often, the *whoosh* of a clean shot. Then the pattern would begin again—*thumpa-thumpa, thwang. Thumpa-thumpa, whoosh.* She could tell by the vehemence of the dribbling that Scotty was working out frustration. Lord knows, she'd used basketball often enough herself for that purpose.

She probably needed to let off steam, too. It had been nearly a week since Dan had declared his independence. Then Scotty had let her have it. *Don't talk to me about Mother,* he'd said. How long could he go on holding his grief and anger inside? And Dad—who knew where he was coming from? The irony of Celeste's understanding didn't escape her. Chuck and Doug were lucky to live so far away.

She bit her lip. That was an unworthy thought. If her older brothers were here, they'd do what they could. But guiltily she realized it would be comforting to lean on them, to be the little sister again.

Thumpa-thumpa, whoosh! She set the book aside. Maybe a game of H-O-R-S-E would loosen her up—if Scotty didn't snap her head off.

When she reached the driveway and offered him some competition, he shrugged indifferently and bounced the ball to her. She split the cords with a clean corner jump shot. He followed suit. Then she tried an unsuccessful backhanded layup. He scooped up the ball and slowly and deliberately dribbled to three-point range and sank a beauty.

By the time the sun had set, Scotty was ahead three games to two. He turned on the garage light and the contest continued. Not once had he slapped her a high five or expressed admiration for a particularly skillful shot. In fact, the games had been conducted without any of their customary bantering. He eyed the basket with intensity and seemed determined to best her. Ordinarily she'd have risen to the bait. But his aloofness took the fight out of her.

About nine their father turned into the drive, effectively ending the contest. Jeri heard Scotty mutter, "What's the deal? Think you live here or something?"

Hank stepped out of his car, briefcase in hand, and greeted them. "Well, who's winning?"

Scotty turned his back and shot the ball hard against the backboard. "What do you care?" He retrieved the shot and threw the ball up again.

Jeri shrugged. "Scotty is."

Hank set the briefcase on the ground, rolled up his shirtsleeves and held out his hands. "Toss it to me. Let's see what the old man can do."

Scotty pivoted, cradling the basketball against his hip, staring insolently at his father. "I already have a pretty fair idea what 'the old man' can do."

Jeri tensed, like a spectator watching two bullies circling each other, waiting for the first punch to be thrown.

"What's that supposed to mean?" Hank stepped toward Scotty, his hands jammed in his front pockets as if he feared what would happen if he left them dangling at his sides.

Scotty sneered. "Gimme a break. This 'work' you're doing every night? It must be pretty heavy-duty. You're never here anymore. So...I don't need any father-son basketball games so you can prove you're still good old Dad."

Hank turned helplessly to Jeri. "What's he so upset about?"

Scotty bounced the ball viciously. "What am I upset about? Try Mom, for starters. Just because she'd dead doesn't mean *I've* forgotten her, unlike other people I could mention." He glared at his father.

Jeri took a step toward Scotty, tempted to reach out and touch his arm, to do anything to defuse the situation. Then the memory of her conversation with Celeste stopped her. She turned to her father, whose face was suffused with crimson.

"This is between you and Scotty. It's time I quit running interference." She stooped to pick up her father's briefcase. "I'll be inside. As for the two of you—" she looked from one to the other "—deal with it!" Her hand was shaking as she reached for the kitchen door and disappeared into the house.

CHAPTER THIRTEEN

"GO 'WAY." Tiffany pulled up the sheet, rolled over in
the rumpled bed and grumbled sleepily, "I'm tired."

Dan shook her gently. "I need your help this morning."

She pushed his hand away, muttering into her pillow,
"Scotty and Jeri work on Thursdays."

"Jeri just called. They're both going to be late. Some
family problem."

She opened one bleary eye. "I'm on vacation."

Dan's patience snapped. He'd been up since five, it
was after nine, and with vacationers arriving at the marina in unusually heavy numbers, he needed her coop-
eration. "Not today." He ripped the light blanket off
the bed, pulled the pillow out from under her head and
threw her a pair of shorts. "Rise and shine. *Now.*"

She sat up and buried her fingers in the tangle of hair
falling into her face. "It's not my problem Gidget and
Scott flaked out."

Gidget? Dan let that one roll off him; he'd think
about her disrespect later. He unearthed a clean T-shirt
from the middle bureau drawer. "Here. I don't have
time to argue." He checked his watch. "I'll give you
ten minutes. Then I expect to see you in the office,
working."

He wheeled to leave, but not before hearing the spiteful words she spit out. "I hate you. I don't need this

crap. I'm calling Mother. She'll come and get me out of this dump.''

Dan grimaced, tempted to rush back into the room and shake some sense, or at least minimal courtesy, into her. A hundred excuses crowded to the forefront. She'd been up late the night before; Vicki had indulged her; she *was* far from home, far from her friends. He wanted desperately to rationalize her behavior, to avoid taking her attitude personally. But the truth was she was behaving like a spoiled brat.

Damn! Just when he'd thought they were getting along better. He jogged from the house to the dock. Well, he'd been firm, all right. If this morning was an example of what Jeri had meant, darned if he could figure how "firm" and "loving" went hand in hand.

JERI HUNG UP the telephone and faced her brother. "Okay, I've called the marina. Dan's not happy. Maybe Miss Tiffany will have to get off dead center and actually work.''

Scotty looked as if he'd just crawled out of a dirty laundry bag—wrinkled boxers, hair standing in spikes, puffy eyes. He scowled over the piece of cantaloupe Jeri set in front of him. "Shut up about her.''

Jeri folded her forearms on the island counter across from him. "No. I'm not going to shut up. Not about her, not about anything. We've all been doing that for way too long. We're going to get some things out in the open, starting with your conversation last night with Dad.''

"I don't want to talk about it.''

"Too damn bad, Scotty. Because you're not going anywhere until we do.''

He glared at her. "You can't stop me.''

She leaned on one elbow and pointed the other index finger straight at him. "Think again. It's up to you. Either we talk or you'll have to take me on. As you may recall, through the years, I've landed some pretty effective blows."

She pulled up a bar stool and waited while he slumped over the cantaloupe, taking his time eating. The ice maker clunked out some cubes, the refrigerator hummed, the kitchen radio played Kenny G in the background. She waited.

Finally he set down his fork and said, "So?"

She shifted in her seat. "So...did you and Dad settle anything last night?"

"Right, like everything's A-okay?" He curled his lip. "Here's what we 'settled.' He's seeing this Celeste, a 'fine woman,' he said. He'd like me to be more 'understanding.'" Scotty picked up his fork again and jabbed it into the cantaloupe rind. "And I basically told him he was a bastard who thought only of himself. There. Satisfied?"

Jeri's stomach cramped. When she'd left the two of them alone last night, she'd nurtured the crazy hope of a breakthrough. Instead, after twenty minutes, she'd heard the Toyota burn out of the driveway. Her father had passed through the great room, looking downcast, before going directly to his bedroom and shutting the door. He'd been up and gone this morning before she saw him. She had no clue when Scotty had returned, but it must've been very late.

"No, I'm not satisfied." She felt the beginning of a headache. "This family is too important to shrug off. Mother is dead." Her words reverberated in her ears like a shotgun blast. "But Chuck and Doug aren't, you're not, I'm not and Dad isn't. Are you going to hold it against him forever that he's living?''

Scotty still wouldn't look at her, just kept playing with the cantaloupe rind. She continued, ''I know you're angry Mom is gone. I was, too. I can't tell you how many times I shook my fist at God. But you know what? Nothing I did changed a single thing. What we wish is just that—a wish. I, for one, am ready to deal with reality.'' She stood up wearily, reached to remove his plate from the counter and paused. ''Let's move on, Scotty. I can't do it by myself and—'' she saw him slowly raise his head and stare at her with tortured eyes ''—neither can you.''

When he remained silent, she turned to the sink and took her time cutting up the rind and scraping it into the disposal. ''Help yourself to the cereal. I'm leaving for work. Guess I'll see you later. Dan's expecting both of us.''

MERCILESS—THAT WAS the only word to describe the afternoon. Scorching sun, humidity coating every surface of her skin with a moist glaze, and a headache well beyond the reach of two aspirin. But that was far from the worst of it.

Scotty had clumped through the office at ten-thirty, pausing only to put his sandwiches in the refrigerator. Since then, except for retrieving his lunch, he had remained outside.

After a curt ''Good morning,'' Dan had distanced himself, dealing with the minnow supplier, repairing a weakened section of the walkway between boat stalls and now tinkering with a mechanical problem on the twenty-four-foot pontoon boat.

Even when customers had stood four and five deep

waiting to pay for gas, purchase fishing licenses, rent boats, buy chips, had Tiffany helped? No. As soon as Jeri had arrived, the girl had left the office, paint supplies in hand, and stalked out to the fish-cleaning shed.

If only she were *still* there. During the heat of the afternoon, Tiffany had set up camp in the office, where she'd sprawled in one of the vinyl chairs directly beneath the ceiling fan, and, while chewing red licorice sticks, watched soap operas at top volume. Jeri was ready to scream.

She slumped against the counter, blowing down the front of her blouse to dry the moisture gathering between her breasts. For what seemed the hundredth time she checked the wall clock. Three more hours at least to go, depending upon when the rental boats returned.

She really ought to quit this job. More than she'd cared to admit at the time, she'd volunteered because of Dan. Now, instead of pleasure, his presence provoked only pain. Nothing, not even his telling her to butt out of his personal life, had diminished the powerful attraction she still felt. But quit? She'd never quit anything in her life.

"Mom-mie, see the fishies?"

"Do I hafta wear a stupid life jacket?"

Jeri glanced up. Here they came, a veritable Von Trapp family. Children stair-stepped from teenager to toddler, all trying to wedge through the door at the same time, followed by a serene woman and a harried red-faced man. "We want to rent a pontoon boat."

Jeri attempted to look cheerful. "I'm sorry, sir, they're all booked for today."

"What do you mean, they're all booked?" The man pointed to the rental stalls. "There's one right there."

"It's not available."

"Mom-mie, I have to go potty."

"What do you mean it's not available? I promised the kids."

The woman sidled up next to her husband. "Could you tell me where the rest room is?"

Jeri pointed out the door. "Over there, at the campground." She turned back to the man. "I'm sorry, but that boat has mechanical problems."

"Mom-mie, I have to go really ba-ad!"

Tiffany turned up the TV volume and noisily dragged her chair closer to the set.

"Look, lady, I told these kids we were going for a boat ride, I see a boat, and you're telling me no way, José?"

Jeri ground her teeth. "I'd accommodate you if I could, but..."

Out of the corner of her eye, Jeri saw Dan enter from the gas dock.

"Damn. Francine, get these kids back up to the car. We'll try the Lazy River Marina." As the group trooped out, the man threw Dan a scathing look. "You own this place? Helluva way to run a business. See if we ever come back!"

Dan watched them go, then took off his ball cap and threw it down on the table. "Great!" He opened the refrigerated case and reached for a bottle of water, downing half of it in one gulp. "Tiffany, for God's sake, turn that thing down!"

Tiffany hit the volume control on the remote and settled back into her customary position. "Touchy, touchy."

"'Touchy' doesn't come close. The starter's out on the twenty-four footer and it's rented all weekend long. I can't afford not to have it in service." He polished off the water and turned to face Jeri. "I'm driving to Fayetteville to the marine supplier. Probably won't be back until nearly dark. Can you stay?" He nodded almost imperceptibly in Tiffany's direction.

Just what she wanted. More of this day from hell. "I suppose so."

"Okay, then, I'm off." He hesitated and crossed to Tiffany. "Do you want to come along?"

Tiffany smoothed her hands over her faded yellow T-shirt. "To a boat place? And miss Georgine telling Francisco she's pregnant? Get real."

He shrugged. "Just thought I'd ask. I'll be back around seven." He hesitated again, looking at Jeri as if he wanted to say something more, but then picked up his ball cap and left.

Jeri paced to the window and stared out at the lake, afraid of what she'd say if Tiffany made one false move. Should she try more aspirin? Her head felt like the site of a buffalo stampede.

At five Tiffany got up from the chair, helped herself to an ice-cream bar and switched to MTV. Until then, despite a steady stream of customer traffic, she had not moved from her spot nor offered to help.

Mark came in at six, apologizing for having to leave them shorthanded. Tiffany barely acknowledged his departure.

The late-afternoon fishermen began arriving to buy bait; at the same time, pleasure boats returning from the day's outings pulled up to the dock. Scotty could hardly keep up with the demand for gas, and Jeri was at the outer limits of ragged. Still, Tiffany sat.

Finally around six-forty a lull came—the calm before the rental boats, due back at seven, returned. Jeri thought it worth risking, so she approached Tiffany.

"Since we're two men shy here, do you think you could help clean up the rental boats?"

Tiffany glanced up briefly, gathering her hair off her neck, and then stared beyond Jeri at the gyrating vocalist belting out sadomasochistic lyrics. "No. It's too hot out there."

Jeri picked up the TV remote, pressed the power button off and slammed the unit down on the table. "Hot? I'll tell you about hot." The hooves of the buffalo were grinding into her skull. "Would it hurt you to help out around here? Your father's trying to make a go of this place, no thanks to you, and—"

Tiffany stood, a hip cocked to one side. "Look, Gidget, I don't need any lectures from you."

"Yeah? Well, somebody needs to knock some sense into you."

Tiffany's voice rose. "Butt out. You've got no right to talk to me like that. Don't think I can't see through you. You've been panting after my father, but you're history, Gidget. History!"

"Maybe I *am* history." Jeri pointed a finger at the girl's chest. "But you're not—not yet. If you could ever get rid of that huge chip on your shoulder and realize that nobody promised you a rose garden, you *might*, become a decent human being. But right now you're lazy, spoiled, selfish—"

"Selfish? You think I wanted to come spend a month in this godforsaken hillbilly place? Look, Jeri—" she hissed out the name as if it were etched in acid "—I've been a *nice* girl. I've put up with this floating excuse for a business, and I've tried to get along with Dad, but—"

"—but you still don't understand, do you? *The man loves you.* Don't ask me why. And what does he get for thanks? A daughter who, excuse us all to heck, tolerates spending time in Arkansas with him.''

"That's it, I've had it." Tiffany picked up the ice-cream-bar wrapper and sailed grandly toward the door. She made a show of depositing the paper in the trash and then turned to face Jeri, her face the color of her licorice. "You are *not* my parent. Besides, you've been dumped by Dad, so I don't have to listen to you. Believe me, I intend to tell him all about this conversation."

Jeri crossed the room swiftly and stood eye to eye with Tiffany, her hands clamped on the girl's arms. "Forget about me. Tiffany, screw your head on. Your dad loves you. A lot. Don't be stupid. So life's given you a raw deal. That doesn't mean you have to continue fouling up. Bitterness won't get you anywhere."

"It'll get me outta here." Shoving Jeri aside, she ran out the door. "As if anybody really cares!"

The thud of Tiffany's feet hitting the planks of the walkway as she raced toward the house beat like an ominous drum in Jeri's ears. She'd surrendered to the heat, the headache and her own misery, lashing out in a way that she realized would set Tiffany—and Dan—forever at a distance. Tears of frustration, shame and loss welled in her eyes.

"What was that all about?"

Jeri turned around slowly. Scotty stood just inside the door to the gas dock, fists clenched at his sides, his eyes a stormy gray.

Jeri collapsed into a chair, swallowing hard, blinking away the threatening tears. "How long have you been listening?"

"Long enough to learn I'm not the only one you're bossing around." He jerked his head in the direction of the house. "Long enough to hear you rag on her until she couldn't take it anymore.'' He strode toward her and leaned his palms on the desk, his face just inches from hers. ''Tiffany's right. You *aren't* a parent. Get a life, Jeri. And fast, before you screw up everybody else's.''

The whine of a powerful motor penetrated the stillness, but they continued staring at each other. Finally Scotty straightened. ''I've gotta go back to work. But you better figure out what you're gonna do about Tiffany. Because, unlike you, I *do* care!''

He turned and pushed out the door. Jeri dug in the pocket of her shorts for a tissue. Then came the tears.

TIFFANY STOMPED into her bedroom, turned her boom box to full volume and threw herself down on the bed. Bull followed her, nails clicking on the wood floor, and jumped up beside her. She curled one arm around the dog's neck. ''I *hate* her, Bull. She's been on my case all summer. I'm not one of her damn students.'' She pounded the pillow in frustration. ''And Dad? Is he blind? What did he ever see in her?''

She sat up suddenly, shoving the dog aside. ''You're too hot.'' The room was an oven. She went to the dresser, hunting through the mess on top for a rubber band. She had to get the weight of her hair off her neck. Once it was secured in a ponytail, she walked into the kitchen, heading straight for the freezer compartment. She pulled out a cherry popsicle, tore off the paper and curled up on the divan. *Huge chip on my shoulder? You got that right.* She studied this dismal excuse for a living room—secondhand furniture, worn braided rug, mismatched fabrics. *Rose garden?* Right. Like living with her mother was a barrel of laughs? Moving from apartment to apartment? Thinking maybe *this* time

Mom would actually settle down with someone? A normal family? God, what would *that* be like?

She sucked on the popsicle, visualizing Gidget with that know-it-all look on her face and remembering her accusations—*lazy, spoiled, selfish.* She scowled. She'd come to Arkansas, hadn't she? And Dad wasn't really so bad—especially if he'd just quit looking at her with that worried look, like...like he was checking to see if he'd made her happy yet. She'd even tried to help—she was painting that old fish shed, wasn't she?

She licked her tongue along the popsicle stick and tossed it toward the wastebasket. It missed, and Bull ran over and sniffed it, then sprawled in the middle of the rug looking at her with sympathetic eyes. She hugged her knees to her chest. *The man loves you,* Jeri had said. But how was he going to react when he heard about this afternoon's argument? After all, Dad had yelled at her, too, just before he'd left. She couldn't do anything right—not for her mother, not for Dad and certainly not for stupid Gidget!

She stood up decisively and walked to the phone, punching her mother's latest motel number. The mechanical voice on the other end politely informed her that "Mr. and Mrs. Purd Fields" had checked out and left no forwarding address.

Terrific. She couldn't even locate her own mother to come rescue her from this hellhole. She began pacing the floor, muttering, "I've gotta get outta here. I can't stand it anymore. I don't wanna see Dad tonight. I don't wanna see anybody!" What was she supposed to do? Stick around and let them all take another swing at her?

Hell, no! If she couldn't get away for good, at least she could get away for tonight. Maybe *somebody* would actually care when they couldn't find her.

She went into her father's room and grabbed the extra set of keys to his personal ski boat. She could be out of here before anyone even noticed.

She watched from the porch until she saw Jeri go out on the dock to help Scott clean one of the rental boats. Then stealthily she made her way past the office and down a long row of stalls to her father's boat. Quietly she untied the mooring lines and stepped carefully into the driver's seat. Using the dock, she silently pushed the boat out into the channel. She glanced up at the sky. Not quite sundown. She'd have plenty of time to get to the cliffs on the south shore of the lake. She could be by herself there. Away from everybody.

She started the engine, putt-putted out into the lake and then gave the boat full throttle. With the engine roaring in her ears, she failed to hear the rumbling of distant thunder.

"WHO THE HELL is that?" Scotty jerked up in annoyance as a ski boat streaked past the gas dock toward open water, churning up a huge wake, despite the clearly posted warnings.

"That's *Dan's* boat!" he exclaimed.

At the same moment, Jeri wailed, "Oh, God, it's Tiffany!"

Scotty didn't spare her. "Dammit, now look what you've done!"

Jeri vaulted over the railing of the pontoon boat and took off at a dead run for the nearest Wave Runner.

Scotty ran after her. "What're you doing?"

"Going after her."

Scotty grabbed the handlebars. "I'll go. You've done enough damage."

Jeri wrested the craft away from him and straddled

the machine. "You're right, I've screwed everything up. So I'm the one who has to go after her. Besides, other rental boats are due back, and you need to be here to handle them. We've gotta think of Dan, too."

A menacing streak of lightning speared the tallest hill across the lake as Jeri shoved the Wave Runner away from the dock. "Any idea where she might go?"

Scotty stood, jaws working, impotently running both hands over his head. "I dunno. She could be anywhere. She doesn't know the lake that well." He looked frantically out into the main channel. "Try the cliffs."

Jeri gripped the handlebars as the Wave Runner accelerated rapidly. The wind was picking up, and threatening inky clouds were massing on the horizon. In the distance she spied four boats, all racing in different directions ahead of the approaching storm. She squinted. With the light in her eyes, she couldn't make out which boat to follow. The cliffs. She'd have to begin there and hope to God Scotty had been right.

She saw an awesome display of sheet lightning behind the hills. This was no time to be on the lake. Belatedly she realized she'd torn off without a life jacket.

She closed her eyes as a fount of spray doused her. What might the girl do? Grimly Jeri pressed the accelerator harder, aware that her self-righteous high-handed attack had caused Tiffany to flee. Dan would be furious! Dan. She hurt clear down deep in her gut at the thought of him.

As she jumped like a showboating daredevil across the waves rolling diagonally at her, another thought, so painful it tore an audible cry from her, penetrated her brain. She cared about Tiffany! Not because she reminded her of some of her students, not because she was Dan's daughter, but because...she reminded her of herself! Competitive, aggressive and...lost. God, was this what it was like to be a parent? To care so desperately for the safety and happiness of your children? To feel such pain when they shoved you aside, asserted independence, failed to meet your expectations?

The sky had darkened to an ominous moss green, and Jeri knew it was only a matter of minutes before the fury of the storm broke over the lake. Oh, God, what if Tiffany wasn't at the cliffs? A savage whitecap hit the Wave Runner broadside, and only by sheer physical strength was Jeri able to right the craft and continue toward the limestone cliffs.

There! She thought she spotted a boat bobbing wildly near the shoreline where the steep well-worn path started up to the Rakestraw cabin at the base of the cliffs.

She veered toward the boat, praying Tiffany was safe. ''Tiff-a-nee!'' she screamed into the wind as she drew near the ski boat. When she came within ten feet, she saw the boat was empty and drifting, the bowline dragging limply through the water. Dread seized her. Had Tiffany fallen out? Had she worn a life jacket? Surely she wouldn't do anything stupid?

Maybe Tiffany had secured the boat and the wind and wave action had broken it loose. Jeri glanced at the shore. Through the thick woods at the base of the trail, she spotted a flash of yellow. Tiffany? Thunder, crashing and echoing, rolled around the hillsides. It had to be her! The boat could wait. Tiffany was more important.

Jeri raced in, ground the Wave Runner on the gravel bar and quickly pulled it up on the shore. Surely the girl was headed for the cabin. Jeri started up the path, praying she'd find Tiffany, knowing she had to set things right somehow, and knowing, with complete certainty, that Tiffany needed her. And that she needed Tiffany.

Tree branches raked her face and her thigh muscles felt like mush, but still she pushed on. Reaching a rock ledge above the forested shoreline, she paused to catch her breath. Overhead the turbulent clouds boiled and the trees below her whipped in frenzied reaction to the wind.

She began running along the rocks toward the Rakestraw cabin, which sat on a prow of land jutting out just below the massive limestone formations. Another flash of yellow. Tiffany! Oblivious to the loose rocks beneath her feet, Jeri hurried on. Within fifty yards of the cabin, she saw Tiffany nudge the front door open and disappear inside. She cried the girl's name again, but another clap of thunder, right on top of her, muffled the sound.

Just then, as if the sky had been ripped open, a bolt of lightning cracked down over the top of the cabin, so close Jeri instinctively hunkered down and covered her head. When she looked up, sheer terror snaked through every sinew of her body. A giant pine tree just above the cabin had been split in two, its dry needles and branches transformed into a fiery torch. The smell of charred wood and damp earth assaulted her nostrils as, in horror, she watched the blazing tree fall onto the cabin. Forks of flame immediately engulfed the aged cedar-shake shingles.

Jeri raced over the remaining distance, hoping against hope she would see Tiffany run from the burning structure. Where was she? Dear God, it couldn't end like this!

She pulled open the heavy door and, staying low, searched the smoke-filled cabin, oblivious to the heat and flames. Aware only that Tiffany had to be in here.

CHAPTER FOURTEEN

As he approached the marina, Dan noted with relief that all the rental units were in their slips. He backed into his parking space, rolled up the windows of the Jeep and dashed to the office. The lake was deserted, the oncoming storm having sent boats scurrying to safety. He set the new starter on the office counter and looked around. The lights were on, but no one was there. Jeri's car was still in the lot. Tiffany? Scott? He felt suddenly uneasy.

Stepping onto the gas deck, he saw Scott, facing the lake, his body taut. Dan walked toward him. "Where is everybody?"

Scott turned, worry imprinted on his face. "I wish I knew! We've gotta do something. Tiffany and Jeri are out on the lake."

"Out on the lake? What do you mean?"

"They had a fight. Tiffany took off like a bat outta hell in your boat."

"Jeri?"

"She went after her on a Wave Runner."

"Where?"

Scott shook his head wearily. "I dunno. Tiffany had a good head start. I told Jeri to begin looking at the cliffs. We've been to a couple of parties at the old Rakestraw place. Tiffany'd know how to get there."

Wind and swells rocked the dock beneath their feet. "Why didn't you go, too?" Dan asked.

"Jeri said somebody had to stay here to check in the rentals. She told me she was responsible for what happened and took off before I could do anything."

Fear, raw and corrosive, immobilized Dan before years of training kicked in and he shifted into his emergency mode. "Get the powerboat ready. I'll grab the radio, flashlights, some blankets." He took off toward the office, shouting back over his shoulder, "Hurry!"

Inside he turned on the two-way radio and reached the dispatcher, who assured him they'd had no calls about any problems but agreed to alert the lake patrol. *Small comfort!* He rummaged quickly through the supplies, snatching up a first-aid kit, bottled water and some life jackets. A helluva storm was bearing down. He could only hope they'd find Tiffany and Jeri first or that somehow the storm would blow over. He couldn't stop to think the worst. They had to be all right.

What had gone on between the two of them? There was no time to indulge in the frustration and anger that swept over him, in the questions that pounded in his brain. He had to be calm. In control. Find them.

He locked the office doors and handed the gear to Scott, who was already in the boat with the engine started. Dan climbed aboard, then took the controls and opened the throttle.

Ten minutes to cover the five miles to the cliffs. Ten minutes when anything could happen! Punctuating this thought was a jagged streak of lightning, illuminating the slate-colored surface of the lake, followed by a violent thunderclap. Water splashed over the bow as Dan, hunched over the console, drove on. If Tiffany had gone to the cliffs, to the cabin, she'd be safe, out of the storm.

Jeri, too? He hoped to God. The two people he cared most about in the world. He closed his eyes briefly. His daughter and—the truth struck him at the same moment the boat catapulted over a whitecap—the woman he loved.

He blinked rapidly, clearing his vision. Only a few minutes more and they'd round the point where the cliffs would be visible.

What had Scott said? A fight? He should have seen it coming. He leaned toward Scott and shouted, "What did they fight about?"

"Jeri was on Tiffany's case, you know, about not helping out and—"

"What'd Tiffany say?"

Dan could barely hear Scott's response. "Something about getting outta here. That nobody cared."

Dan clenched his hands on the steering wheel, his insides going bone-cold. *He* cared. Hadn't she realized that?

Beside him in the seat, he heard the beeper of the emergency radio. He held it up to his ear, listening intently as the awful words came through the static. "Alert all units. Lightning strike near the Rakestraw place off county road 345. Smoke's been spotted. Paradise Point department is responding, but may need backup."

Just then they rounded the point; and midway up the far hill, just at the base of the cliffs, he saw it—a gray-white spiral of smoke coiling into the sky just above the Rakestraw place. Lord, the cabin was miles down dirt roads from the Paradise Point fire station. How long would it take them to respond?

Dan pushed the engine to its limit. Surely if Tiffany and Jeri had been in the cabin, they'd escaped, run down the path to the lake or found shelter in one of the rock overhangs.

Then he saw something that caused both hope and fear to crest within him—his ski boat, buffeted aimlessly by the waves, bobbing like a cork between him and the shore. He headed toward it, searching the water for Tiffany...and for a Wave Runner.

SATISFIED THAT TIFFANY wasn't in the front room, Jeri held her breath and ran into the kitchen. Through the smoky haze she made out a form. Panic bubbled into her mouth. Dear God, Tiffany?

She fell to her hands and knees and scrambled across the floor, reaching the inert body. Her fingers, searching the head, encountered long hair, a bump on the right temple and, thank heaven, a pulse. The girl, lying half on and half off a couple of old thin mattresses, was unconscious. Looking behind her toward the front door, Jeri saw the living room burst into flames. A back door? Where? She groped frantically toward where she remembered it had been and, instead, encountered a glowing mass of sticky pine bark. Scuttling back across the floor, she squelched the rising tide of nausea. She had to do something. Tiffany was not Cora Hunnicutt's dog, and Dan was not going to appear like Superman to rescue them. *Think, dammit, think!* She had to get Tiffany out of here, get to safety. As if mocking her reason, she heard the crash of timber falling in the living room.

Mattresses—why? Parties? Kids? Then the answer came. *Beer! The springhouse.* She shifted Tiffany's body onto the mattresses, groped for the handles of the bottom one and dragged them down the closed-in walkway between the kitchen and the springhouse. In the cavelike opening, cool drafts of air revived her as she reached under Tiffany's armpits and stretched her out on the rock floor beside the small spring-fed pool.

Behind her she could see flames moving inexorably toward them. If she didn't act quickly, the smoke would be sucked into the springhouse, venting through the very air holes in the rock they needed to breathe. Somehow she had to block the entry before they were overcome by smoke.

Tiffany groaned beside her. *Coming to, thank God.* Jeri swallowed hard, her head ringing with the sound of crackling, hissing, raging fire. *Do something!* Water. The pool. Something to block the entry. *Dear Lord, the mattresses. Do I have time?*

Summoning all her firefighter training, she reached into the walkway for the two mattresses and hauled them into the springhouse. She grabbed hold of the top one and threw it into the pool to soak it. Then she heaved it up against the entryway, stuffing it into any apertures, praying it would stand upright long enough for her to soak the other one. Exhausted, she felt momentarily disoriented, incapable of rational thought or action.

Beside her, Tiffany groaned again, giving her one last surge of will. If she could prevent the smoke from seeping into the small cavern, the air and water in the springhouse would buy them some time.

Gasping for air, she tossed the second mattress into the small pool, then dragged it across the floor and pushed it upright against the first. At last she sank, gasping, onto the floor, leaning her back against the cool jagged rock wall.

"Who's there?" Tiffany's voice echoed hollowly in the small chamber.

"Jeri."

"I...I can't see you. Where are we?"

"In the springhouse behind the cabin."

"My head hurts. Cabin?"

"The Rakestraw place. Do you remember coming here?"

"The boat.... I was running away, but...what happened?"

"Do you remember the thunder and lightning?"

Tiffany didn't immediately respond. Then she said, "Lightning? I'd just come into the cabin when...right on top of me. But that's the last thing I remember."

"You must've tripped over something, maybe the mattresses, and hit your head. Whatever happened, you were knocked out." She paused. "We'll just have to wait. Surely someone will be coming soon to rescue us."

"I'm scared." A muffled sob accompanied Tiffany's admission.

"Me, too." Jeri felt a spasm of dizziness erupt inside her skull. She lowered her head between her knees, clenching clammy hands together. Her breaths came in short pants. Claustrophobia, black and grasping, engulfed her. *Spiders. Mice. Locked in.* She gagged. *I'll be all right, I'll be all right. Someone will be coming, someone will be coming. Mom...help!*

Then above the roof of the cave and through the thickness of the mattresses, she heard an unearthly sound like boulders crashing down a mountain, like...a rock slide.

"Mom!" The sharp scream reverberated in the cold springhouse. Just before she fainted, Jeri realized the scream had come from her own mouth.

DAN HAD NEVER FELT so helpless and so terrified in his entire life. But clear thinking was essential for taking the right action, and he had somehow to control his panic. He couldn't assume Tiffany was in the cabin— or in the water. He clicked on the handheld radio and alerted the lake patrol of the location of the drifting boat, then confirmed the Rakestraw-cabin fire with the emergency dispatcher. As an afterthought, he said grimly, "Better notify Hank Monahan, too."

Scott was spread-eagled over the bow, searching the water. Suddenly he reared up, gave Dan a rev-it sign and pointed to the shoreline. The Wave Runner, beached near the base of the path up the hill!

Dan took several deep breaths. Jeri had gone after Tiffany. The Wave Runner's location was consistent with the idea Tiffany had been heading for the cliffs. Surely they were together. Nervously he glanced up at the burning cabin. Dear God, they had to be all right!

With lightning flashing intermittently followed by great crashes of thunder, he cut the engine and let the boat glide up onto the gravel bar. Scott leaped out and secured the bowline to a sturdy sycamore. Dan grabbed the supplies, then clambered out after Scott, who was already racing up the path.

When they reached the rocky ledge, they stopped dead. The cabin was an inferno. The roof had caved in and the flaming walls were sending smoke and burning cinders high into the air. Because the cabin sat on a rock promontory, the fire fortunately wasn't endangering any nearby vegetation. In the distance Dan picked up, with relief, the wail of the first fire engine.

But if Tiffany and Jeri had been in the cabin, it was too late.

No! He refused to think that. They'd have run out, sought shelter somewhere, maybe beyond the house in the other direction. Glancing toward the lake, he saw the patrol vessel circling the area between the drifting ski boat and the shore.

"Where *are* they, Dan? Where *are* they?" Dan recognized the tone—Scott was on the brink of hysteria.

"C'mon." Dan signaled the boy to follow him as he began crashing through the forest below the rocks. "Let's search on the other side. They've got to be there."

"You think?"

"Yeah." A sharp pine branch snapped back, scratching his cheek. He hurried on. If they weren't there, huddled somewhere under the rocks, he'd have to make a horrifying suggestion to the firemen. A splat of water hit his forehead, then another and another. Rain. Too late to save the cabin, too late to save...

You can't think like that. They'll be all right. They have to be. He knew the danger of losing heart, giving up hope. Jeri—resilient, defiant, resourceful. Surely she would have taken care of his little girl! He choked on the sobs threatening to unman him.

JERI'S EYES fluttered open. She saw only darkness, suffocating, impenetrable. She felt woozy, totally disoriented. When she tried to sit up, she couldn't distinguish up from down, left from right, so she curled herself into a ball, clutching her knees to her chest. Cold. She was so very cold. She could sense a scream, deep in her abdomen, gathering momentum, force. She clamped her teeth and waited—

"Jeri?" *The voice. Tentative, worried. Whose?* "Are you okay?"

She tried to answer, but her jaws seemed paralyzed. Then she felt hands—soft, gentle, like a mother's stroking the tender skin of an infant—on her arms, her shoulders, her face. "Jeri?" The voice sounded close. "It's Tiffany." Fingers gently traced her cheek. "Say something."

Tiffany? Who? What's she doing...in this blackness? The caress was calming. She was connected to somebody. She wasn't alone. Instead of a primal cry, a vast expulsion of air, pushed by a giant interior bellows, left her body. She could breathe! She felt her jaws relax. She tried to speak. "Tiffany?" The voice came from far away and didn't sound like hers. She tried again. "Tiffany? Where are you?"

"Right here." The words were whispered near her left ear. *Right here. Someone's right here.*

"I'm afraid. It's so dark. What happened?"

The hands kneaded her shoulders, then moved down her forearms, warming her icy skin.

"You saved me. The fire. Remember? We're in the springhouse."

Springhouse? Fire? Suddenly she reached out and clutched Tiffany's arm. "Tiffany?"

"I'm right here."

The argument, the cabin, the smoke—it all came back. And...the springhouse. Vomit rose in her throat. *Trapped. Oh, God, I'm trapped!* She struggled to sit up, swallowing the bile. Her breath came in ragged pants. *Tiffany! Dan's daughter. My fault. I have to take care of her.* "Are you okay?"

"I bumped my head. But I'm alive. Jeri, you saved my life." She sensed Tiffany sitting back on her heels.

Saved...but for how long? Jeri's head gradually cleared. They didn't dare try to leave. The fire might be raging, smoke might be sucked into the springhouse. No, all they could do was wait. "Are you scared?"

A small voice answered. "Yes. You?"

She didn't dare admit pure terror. She had to be strong. Somehow. "Yes."

"You called out for your mother right before...before, I guess you fainted."

"I did?"

"Yeah." Tiffany hesitated, then began speaking louder, faster. "I always thought you were so, you know, in charge. That nothing fazed you. And there you were, like a scared little girl, wanting your mom. She's dead, isn't she?"

Jeri froze. *Dead.* Her mother wouldn't be coming to unfasten the padlock, fling open the utility-shed door and carry her to safety, hugging her close, murmuring soothing words in her ear.

"I guess you don't wanna talk about it, huh?"

Jeri heard the hurt in Tiffany's voice. Suddenly she knew she not only wanted to talk about her mother, she needed to. "Yes, I do. I think talking will help us keep calm while we wait. The time'll pass faster."

"But...we don't have to talk about your mother. We could talk about something else."

"It's all right. My mother..." Jeri paused, myriad images floated before her in the darkness. "Mom was...special."

"What do you mean?"

"She loved life. Embraced it. She was fun. She'd do wacky things, like dressing up herself on Halloween to go trick-or-treating with us. One year she was Batman and I was Robin. She also played in the snow, went water-skiing, made funny faces at us when we sulked. Laughter. I remember lots of laughter."

With surprising suddenness, tears streaked down

Jeri's face, running salty over her lips. They kept coming and coming.

When at last her tears began to ebb, she wondered at
the outpouring of emotion. Had she been so busy tending to everyone else, trying to please her father, that
she'd failed to grieve properly herself?

"Your mom sounds nice," Tiffany murmured wistfully. "There's not much laughter in my mother's
house."

"But surely she loves you," Jeri said.

"Sometimes I wonder. I feel like I'm always in the
way. Mom works all day. When she comes home, she's
either so tired she can hardly fix supper, or she can't
wait to go out dancing with some bozo. Sometimes I
think her life would be much easier if I wasn't—"

Jeri interrupted. "Don't even say it. So you don't live
a Good Housekeeping Seal of Approval life? Nobody
does really."

"*You* did!"

Jeri considered her response carefully. "It probably
seems that way to you, but there were rough times for
me, too."

"Name one." A hint of the old cynicism sounded in
Tiffany's demand.

"Growing up with three brothers and a father who
expected me to do everything better than any girl. I've
always suspected he was secretly disappointed I wasn't
another son. I did my damnedest to please him. I was
competitive, busting my butt to bring home medals,
awards, anything to prove I could hang in there with
the boys. It's probably one reason I have trouble with
men."

"Trouble?"

"I'm too aggressive, too pushy, too opinionated. You

name it." Jeri thought she heard a muffled laugh. "You, of all people, can't argue that. You got a big dose of it today yourself."

The giggle faded into silence. "Did your parents ever rag on *you* like that?"

"Oh, yes. I didn't escape scoldings in my so-called charmed childhood. You probably aren't interested in the numbers of times I was grounded in high school."

"Grounded? Really?"

"Broken curfews, taking the car without permission... Let's see, skipping school—"

"You?"

"Yeah, me."

"Didn't their nagging make you mad?"

"At the time. But now I'm really glad."

"Glad?"

"They cared enough to say no. To let me know I was a better person than that."

"You think 'no' means somebody cares?" The earnestness in Tiffany's voice suggested this was a concept she'd never considered.

"I'm sure it does." Jeri felt Tiffany's fingers tentatively touch the back of her hand.

"Then...maybe Dad, you know, loves me." There was wonder in her voice.

Jeri turned her hand palm up, laced her fingers through Tiffany's and squeezed gently. "Beyond any doubt. You have no idea how much he looked forward to your visit, to having it go well."

"I've been kinda...bitchy, haven't I?"

Jeri felt on the spot. "Well, kinda."

"So...if somebody gets on your case, then that could mean they care?"

"People who don't care don't get involved."

"Then—"Jeri sensed the smile even though she couldn't see it "—maybe you care, too?"

Jeri felt all her resentment, jealousy and anger melt away. "When you look it at that way, yes, I guess I do." Her voice softened. "More than I was willing to admit."

"Why?"

"Because...I care so much about your father and you're part of him. But he's... That's history."

"No! Wait a minute. Listen to me, Jeri." Tiffany's voice was excited. "People who love you say no, right?"

"Yes, but—"

"Don't you see? Dad's said no to you. That big jerk. He's trying to discipline you, too. You know why? Because he's crazy in love with you and won't admit it."

"Tiffany, no. It's not like that."

"Sure it is. I've been the big glitch. Dad thinks he can't please me and have you, too. But *you* know, and *I* know...he needs us both. I'll work on him. He'll see."

"Tiffany, it's too late for—"

"Uh-uh. It's never too late when the Tiffer gets an idea!" Suddenly she gave a sharp intake of breath. "Wait! Quiet."

Jeri listened intently. "What?" she whispered.

"Digging. Doesn't that sound like a shovel hitting rock?"

The faintest clink syncopated with the drips of the springwater into the pool. Then another clink. And another! Jeri hugged Tiffany. "I think we'll soon be out of the dark."

EMERGENCY LIGHTS cast an eerie glow over the damp smoking timbers. Dan stood, one arm firmly around

Scott, trying to keep the youngster from falling to pieces. Weary firefighters trudged up and down the narrow trail leading to the top of the ridge, the closest the vehicles could come to the scene. All any of them had been able to do was stand helplessly in the pelting rain until the fire burned itself out.

Exhausted, miserable and more frightened than he'd ever been, Dan watched Hank Monahan, his face ashen in the ghostly light, struggle toward him and Scott.

"Jeri?" he wheezed, reaching for Scott. Dan stepped away, watching as the boy, eyes filled with tears, shook his head and then let himself be gathered into his father's arms. "Oh God, oh God. I can't lose another one of you," Hank murmured.

And neither can I, Dan thought. Tiffany, the daughter he was just beginning to know. And Jeri—amber eyes, burnished gold hair, jutting chin, smart mouth and all. He felt an ache so deep, so biting it caused him to close his eyes and clench his fists. *Control.* He was losing it. Any minute now he'd let out the piercing scream building within him.

"Dan?" He opened his eyes and looked into the compassionate face of the Paradise Point fire chief, Elliot Mann. "Good news. No bodies in the debris."

Dan sagged against the other man, overcome with relief. Then he straightened, worry replacing the all-too-temporary reprieve. "Then...where, Elliot? The lake?"

"No. Nothing there. The patrol's still searching, and so are we." He clapped a hand on Dan's shoulder and returned to his men.

Dan repeated the new information to Hank and Scott. The boy grabbed his father's arm. "So maybe Jeri's...?"

"Yeah, son. She's strong." He gave Scott's shoulder

a loving squeeze. "There's nothing that girl can't do. If there's a way, any way at all, for her and Tiffany to come through this, she'll find it."

Yeah, Dan thought, *Jeri's got what it takes. Staying power, resourcefulness, loyalty, she's got it all.* Why hadn't he seen it before? Vicki hadn't had in her little finger the courage and devotion of Jeri. And though he loved his mother—passive, compliant, doting—she didn't have the fire, the passion he now admitted he'd always craved. What he'd needed all along—a strong woman—he'd denied. Not only denied, but turned his back on when she stood right in front of him, pleading.

Abruptly he turned to Scott and Hank. "They're here somewhere. There has to be a place we haven't thought of."

Scott lifted his anguished face, his eyes slowly focusing, and stared at the void where the cabin had stood. Suddenly he started running. "Beer!" he shouted. "Hurry!"

"Beer?" The incongruity of the word temporarily paralyzed Dan. Then, like Hank, he sprinted after Scott.

"Over here." Scott stopped in front of the firemen. "Quick! The springhouse! They're in the springhouse. They've gotta be. Under those timbers and rocks!"

Dan looked at the face of the cliff where, behind the burned trunk of the pine, rocks and dirt had tumbled down, loosened apparently when the tree fell, then set in motion by the collapse of the hillside. He scrabbled around, frantically trying to find a shovel. He'd claw with his fingers if he had to!

He felt a restraining hand on his arm. "No, Dan. It's our call. We'll handle it. Besides—" for the first time Elliot Mann's eyes showed the glint of a smile "—you're not dressed for it."

Sheepishly Dan looked down at his soggy deck shoes and cutoffs. Elliot was right. But it was torture to stand on the sidelines while the Paradise Point boys sawed away the tree, branch by branch, and began removing the slide, stone by stone.

Scott edged as close as he could, bouncing on the balls of his feet, as if body language could move the project along faster. Hank looked heavenward, oblivious to the rain, now gradually abating. Dan's eyes never left the firefighters, who, slowly, carefully, were making an opening.

Finally a rangy soot-begrimed fireman threw both hands over his head, fists pumping, his thunderous voice booming in the tense quiet. "They're here! They're okay!"

Dan found himself surrounded by Scott and Hank, the three huddled in a triumphant hug. "Thank God!" Dan heard Hank say quietly. "And thank Scott!"

TIFFANY DIDN'T KNOW about okay. Her head still ached something fierce and Jeri must be exhausted. But it sure beat being dead.

"We're widening the hole. Can you crawl out or do we need to come get you?" the fireman called.

Tiffany turned and made out Jeri's face. "Whaddaya think?"

Jeri managed a grin. "We got in under our own steam—"

"No, yours!"

"—and we'll get out the same way." She raised her hand in a limp high five.

Tiffany met it. God, Gidget had guts. How come she hadn't seen it before? What had caused the two of them to get off on the wrong foot? Well, jeez, yeah. That first day it *had* been kind of a shock to walk in on two nearly naked people—one your own father and the other a strange lady. Any daughter might feel weird about that. And Jeri seemed to know all about the marina, how things worked, where they were. *And then she tried to tell me what to do. Nobody tells me what to do. Or maybe it's just I never listen. Maybe I should start.*

While the two of them wrestled the mattresses loose, she heard the steady clink of shovels. In her wildest dreams she'd never imagined feeling this close to Jeri. Heck, did it take something as drastic as being trapped, near death, in a springhouse for the truth to hit her over the head? Duh.

And Dad. He'd tried, really tried, to please her, almost to the point that at times, he was pathetic. Like taking her to that cave and that fancy-schmantsy place for lunch. Like teaching her to water-ski and letting her drive the boat. But would she let any of that affect her? God, what a butt-head she'd been!

She moved up to the hole and hollered, "Can we try to come out yet?" Her patience had run thin. All she wanted in the whole world was to be in her father's arms.

"Yes, ma'am. You ready?" The deep reassuring voice outside was an answer to her prayer. A brawny hand reached down to assist her.

"You go first, Tiffany." Jeri's voice was faint but calm.

Tiffany looked back. "Thank you, Jeri. I think you're the best!" Then with the aid of the steadying hand, she eased herself through the opening.

She staggered against the fireman, blinking in the sudden light, feeling isolated raindrops strike her face. Then she saw her father running toward her. In moments she felt herself embraced in a huge bear hug. Tears streamed down her cheeks. "Daddy, I...I love you so much," she managed to stammer.

"Oh, honey. I love you, too. I was so scared."

She drew back and looked at him, instinctively taking in all at once the concern, the strength, the love in his eyes. "It was Jeri. She saved my life." He looked up at the sky, and she felt him shudder just before tears trickled down his face. "We're okay, Daddy. *Really*."

JERI STOOD, supported by her father and brother, her legs still trembling. Only now did she admit how close she and Tiffany had come to the unthinkable. The relief was palpable, like having five-hundred pound barbells removed from your shoulders.

Her father wrapped her close and said quietly, "I've never been so proud of you, Jeri. I had confidence all along. You've always been the strongest, most competitive of the Monahans. I knew if anybody could do it, you could."

There they were—the words she'd waited for all her life. Affirmation from her father. She was the best of the boys! She sniffled and turned to hug him. His belief in her meant everything.

She felt a tentative hand on her back. She turned to see Scotty's tortured face. "I'm sorry, Jeri, for all the things I said." He stared at the ground. "And I took you for granted." He looked up, his face solemn. "I'll never do that again. Not with you. Not with anyone I—" he strangled on the word "—love."

She put her arms around his neck and drew his head down close. "I love you, too." Then she stepped back and linked arms with her father and brother. "Let's go home."

CHAPTER FIFTEEN

WHEN JERI AWOKE the next morning, it was to intense sunlight streaming in through the window. Rubbing her eyes, she pushed herself to a sitting position. On the desk across the room stood a colorful bouquet—yellow snapdragons, pink carnations, rosebuds and baby's breath.

She swung her feet to the floor and crossed to the desk, then read the signature on the small pasteboard card propped against the vase. She felt fleeting disappointment—it was Celeste's, not Dan's. She'd written: "I'm sorry it took such drama to get Scott and your father talking, but it worked! They love you very much. Breakfast's waiting in the kitchen."

Jeri ran a brush through her tangled curls and glanced at the clock. Ten-fifteen. She dimly remembered Scotty and Dad bringing her home, and someone—Celeste?—tucking her into bed. Her muscles ached in unfamiliar places, as if she'd cycled the entire Tour de France all in one night. Before going to the shower, she took a moment to lean over the bouquet and inhale the delicate fragrance of the roses.

When she emerged from her room after her shower, she was surprised to find Scotty and her father sitting at the kitchen counter talking and laughing as if a pixie from a Disney film had sprinkled fairy dust over the grouchy pair and—poof!—transformed them.

"Dad? Why aren't you at work?" She stared at her brother. "And Scotty—what about you?"

Her dad and brother got up and took turns hugging her. "Work?" her father said. "Why would I be at work? This morning nothing's more important than taking care of you."

Taking care of me? The words had an unfamiliar ring. Taking care of others she knew about, but *being* taken care of? By her father?

Scotty patted her back. "You scared me to death!"

Jeri leaned against him. "That makes two of us. I was scared out of my mind." Images of the fire, of Tiffany lying prone, of the suffocating claustrophobia, threatened her composure. "Tiffany—is she...?"

Her father took her by one arm, propelled her into a chair at the table and sat down beside her. "I talked with Dan about an hour ago. Just a bump on the head, that's all."

Behind her, Scotty bustled about the kitchen and then awkwardly put a plate in front of her. Cheese strata, melon wedges and a blueberry muffin. She looked up. "Who...? Surely not you!"

"In your dreams! Nah, Celeste brought us breakfast." Scotty ducked his head. "She's really an okay lady." As if cutting off any surprised reaction from her, he hurried on. "Did you see the flowers?"

"They're beautiful. But how—?"

Her father interrupted. "I called her last night when I got the word. She waited here at the house to help. This morning she showed up with the flowers and food."

Jeri dug in. Breakfast was hitting the spot. "Where is she?"

"She didn't stay," Scotty volunteered.

"That's because I asked her not to," Hank said simply.

"Oh?" Jeri eyed her father warily.

"Scott, have a seat." Hank gestured to an empty chair. "I have some apologizing to do, and I'm not going anyplace until I get some things off my chest." The seriousness of his expression caused Jeri to put down her muffin and nervously wipe her mouth with her napkin. "You kids have suffered more than your share." His hands lay on the table, clenching and unclenching, as he looked from one to the other of his children. "It was bad enough your mother died, but then I abandoned you emotionally. I've been no help to anybody."

He paused. Scotty studied his fingers. Jeri didn't know how to respond. The truth of his words provided a powerful exclamation point to the silence.

"Let me start with you, son." Scotty licked his lips nervously. "Pat's death knocked me for a loop and numbed me for a long time. I just hope it's not too late to say something I should've said back then. Scott, you were not responsible for what happened. There was absolutely nothing you or anyone else could have done to save her."

Scotty blinked his eyes, his lashes moist. "I miss her."

Jeri sensed a shifting. Something critical was taking place. She sat silently, watching, listening.

Hank reached across the table and gripped his son's hands, gently pumping their joined fingers against the glass surface. "Oh, God, I do, too. I always will. But I still have you and Jeri and Chuck and Doug."

"What about Celeste?" Scotty looked impassively at his father.

"Yes, *and* Celeste."

Scotty's gaze fell to their clasped hands, then he expelled a long sigh and raised his face. "It's okay, Dad. It's not Celeste. She's a nice person. I just wasn't ready for..."

"For seeing your old man already turning to another woman?"

"Yeah, I guess. But..." Jeri held her breath. An obvious struggle was going on within Scotty. "But I've been thinking about it quite a bit. I needed somebody, too. That's why Tiffany and I are close. I needed her. She understands."

Jeri swallowed hard. *I need, too. I need Dan.* Suddenly it occurred to her. Maybe need wasn't the healthiest basis for a relationship...

Scotty continued. "So, Dad, I'm willing to give Celeste a chance. See how it goes, if that's what you want."

Hank pumped their hands once more before releasing his grasp. "Thank you, Scott. That's all I ask."

Then he faced Jeri, leaning his elbows on the table, genuine concern in his eyes. "Honey, I appreciate all you've done since you've been home but I put way too much on your shoulders. You made it so easy for me just to go about my business, taking your help for granted, not giving the two of you much thought. It wasn't fair."

"Fair has nothing to do with it, Dad. I wanted to help. But—" she could admit it at last "—I didn't know how. I was convinced I could fix everything. And when I couldn't..." She shrugged and grinned weakly. "Failure is something I don't do well."

Her father's voice was firm. "You haven't failed. And your heroism—that's the only word for it—last night showed what a brave wonderful woman you are. You will never know what went through my mind. I could have lost you, too. I'm like that stupid mule that has to be hit on the head with a two-by-four before you can get his attention." He picked up her hand and rubbed her fingers with his thumb. "Jeri, Scott, you've *got* my attention. From now on."

Jeri sagged with relief. She didn't have to save the world all by herself.

"Dad," Scotty said, "thanks, you know, for telling us..." His voice trailed off awkwardly.

"Son, we'll talk some more. But now you and I need to get to work." He looked at Jeri. "Will you be okay?"

She mustered a smile. "I'll be fine. Nothing a day's rest won't cure."

As they started to leave the table, the phone rang. "I'll get it!" Scotty vaulted into the kitchen. He turned around, grinning. "It's for you, Jeri. Dan." He handed her the receiver.

A chill slithered from the base of her neck all the way down her spine. She held the phone in her icy fingers. Her dad walked over to her, squeezed her shoulder and whispered in her ear, "I'll see you tonight." He winked. "For dinner."

Still holding the phone, she walked slowly out onto the screened porch, struck by the brilliant kaleidoscopic colors of the lake, trees, sky, clouds. Inhaling deeply, she put the phone against her ear. "Hello, Dan."

His voice was low, husky. "Jeri, are you all right?"

She exhaled. "Tired, that's all."

"I can't thank you enough for what you did. When I think what could have happened to Tiffany...well, you saved her life."

This conversation, formal and ritualized, felt surreal. She fulfilled her role. "I'm just the one who happened to be there." Did she dare confess that her angry words had precipitated the whole affair?

"I'm glad you were. I'll never be able to thank you enough."

"Dan, please, this isn't about thank-you's. Is Tiffany okay?"

"Just a nasty bruise. Other than that, she's fine. Slept late and ate like a horse this morning. Jeri, I—"

"I'll see you tomorrow at work," she interrupted.

"Sure you'll feel like coming in?"

Some of her old fight surfaced. "It takes more than a fire and a cave-in to keep me out of action."

"That's my girl!"

My girl? "So—"

"Wait. There's one more thing I want to say. It wasn't just Tiffany I was worried about." He paused. "It was you."

"Dan, I..." She felt guilty enough about what had happened to Tiffany; she didn't want him feeling obligated to her. Besides, she needed time to process what had happened, to make sense of her own emotions.

"Maybe we can find some quiet time tomorrow to talk."

"We'll see. Dan, I need to go." The lie provided her best defense against the wistfulness in his voice, against his mistaking his feelings of gratitude for something deeper. For something she wasn't ready to deal with yet.

She could barely hear him. "Tomorrow, then. Bye."

Setting the phone down, she sank into the hammock swing, eyes closed, slowly rotating the swing and then letting go, unwinding. And doing some serious thinking.

DAN ADJUSTED the blinds and locked the doors of the marina office. It had been difficult to concentrate on work today. His mind kept recalling last night's frantic scene, the sour taste of pure panic in his mouth. He could handle dangerous situations at sea, rely on training and procedures, take action. But last night's helplessness, the endless waiting and dark speculation...there weren't words for it.

Once Tiffany had awakened and eaten, she'd hung around the marina, staying close to Scott and him. He'd been aware of her eyes following his movements. And, he admitted, he'd not wanted her out of his sight.

Weary though he was, he needed to spend some quiet time with Tiffany. See how she was doing, what she was thinking. Scott had mentioned an argument with Jeri, but what had really caused her to run off in the boat? Was it so horrible here? Was he somehow responsible?

He started toward the house through the twilight when he heard a soft splash-splash. He turned, and there, at the far end of the dock, sat Tiffany, idly kicking her bare feet in the water, Bull nestled close beside her. She had one arm around the dog and seemed lost in thought. Dan paused to study her. She had pulled her hair back in a French braid. The effect was striking, emphasizing her high cheekbones and sun-kissed complexion. She seemed, at the same time, both childlike and womanly. Then it struck him. She looked serene, beautiful! The startling effect threw him off balance, and he stood for several seconds just observing her before walking toward her.

She glanced up at him just as he removed his deck shoes and sat down beside her, dangling his feet in the water, too. "How you doin', bambino?"

She smiled at him. "You haven't called me that in years."

He considered. "I guess not. When you were eight, you told me you hated me to call you that. That you weren't a baby."

"Sounds like something I'd say." She smiled shyly. "But, Dad, I like it now."

He settled an arm around her. "What changed?"

She pulled her feet out of the water and wrapped her arms around her knees. "Lots. I've been thinking today. About things—you, Mom, this place, Jeri." She leaned her forehead on her knees. He could barely hear her next words. "I've been a real butt-head, Dad."

He gently massaged her shoulder. "Maybe we all have."

"I'm gonna try to get my act together."

He waited. Finally she raised her head and stared out across the cove to the far hilly shoreline, its forested green turning to shadowy black as the sun sank. A last faint streak of silver made a V across the calm surface of the lake.

"It's beautiful, Dad. Look." She gestured at the scene before them. "I've made fun of Arkansas all summer, but—" she seemed to be searching for words "—now that it's almost time to leave, well, I'll miss it."

Dan felt a lump in his throat. "I'm glad. This kind of peace, quiet—it's partly why I'm here, you know."

She snuggled closer. "I know."

"And you can come back as often as you want to."

She looked at him, her eyes liquid with affection. "I know, Daddy. And I will, but..."

"But?"

"I'm worried about Mom." Her eyes lost their glow.

"How's that?"

"I think…she's very unhappy. She doesn't seem able to just *be*, you know what I mean?" He knew, but thought it unwise to interrupt. "I think, kinda like me, she's been looking for love, but in all the wrong places."

"We've all been unhappy. Like the rest of us, your mother will have to find her own way."

She seemed to chew on that idea. "What can we do?"

"Change."

"What? How?"

He pondered his response. "Start talking to each other. Honestly. About feelings, like we're doing now." He paused. "For instance, did you know I've been scared ever since you came?"

"Scared?" Her look suggested the idea seemed preposterous. "Whaddaya mean?"

"I had a huge stake in your visit. In trying, somehow, to make up for all those times through the years I was out of the picture. In proving I love you."

Tiffany nodded. "Oh, Dad, I realize that now. I also realize that saying no to someone means you care about them."

He looked at her in amazement.

"That's what Jeri told me," she said.

Dan felt chagrined. That was what she'd told him, too. But he hadn't trusted her. Hadn't trusted himself. "Why did you run off in the boat like that? Scott said you and Jeri had a fight."

Tiffany let her feet fall back into the water. "I pushed her to the limit, I guess, and she fired away. She called me selfish and lazy and spoiled. I told her where she could put her opinions. I was really pissed off. All I wanted was to get away—from everything and everybody.''

''So why the turnaround now?''

Tiffany studied her toes. ''Because she's just like me. Doesn't take any guff from anybody, even the smart-mouthed daughter of her boyfriend. And because...she's the bravest lady I know. And you know what else?'' She looked at him expectantly.

''No, what?''

''Her life hasn't been all that great sometimes, either. But she isn't a whiny-ass like me.''

Dan hugged her close. ''Oh, you're not such a bad kid.''

She stared seriously into his eyes. ''I'm going to try to be better. Don't expect miracles, but I'll do the best I can.'' She jumped to her feet. ''Let's go fix some popcorn. I'm starving.''

Dan stood up slowly, delighted and bewildered by his wise child.

''Oh, Dad, one thing more. *You'll* be the butt-head if you let Jeri get away.''

WHEN JERI REPORTED for work Saturday, she felt shaky. Weak. And seeing Dan, when she first arrived, did nothing to improve her condition. He stood at the end of the dock, scanning the lake, his back to her. He wore khaki shorts and a navy T-shirt; every familiar muscle and sinew of his body was a reminder of simpler times—when emotions and responses had been uninhibited. Now, snarled in guilt, doubt and confusion, she felt helpless. What was going on inside her?

She collapsed wearily into the desk chair. She'd have to tell him about her argument with Tiffany. How would he react?

He remained on the dock, attending to the first few fishing parties, until Scotty and Mark showed up. She gripped the counter tightly when she saw him walking toward the office. Her jaw felt rigid. She couldn't have smiled if her life depended on it.

"Morning, Dan." She kept her eyes lowered, studying the boat-rental reservation book.

He rounded the counter and wrapped an arm around her. The warmth of his hand through the thin jersey of her tank top, the faint whiff of his aftershave, the cobalt of his eyes when he tilted her chin so she could no longer avoid his gaze set up a muffled buzzing in her head.

"God, am I glad to see you!" His voice, husky and intimate, penetrated her daze. "I had to be sure you were okay." His concerned look drove straight into the core of her guilt. "You *are*, aren't you?"

She backed away from his touch—dangerous in its comfort. "Fine." She struggled for composure. "I'm fine."

"Sure you feel like working today? I can call Raymond."

The screen door opened suddenly and slammed shut. "Don't call Raymond." Tiffany, her hair caught up in a ponytail, stood grinning at them. "I'll help." Then Tiffany leaned over the counter and gave Jeri a wink. "Besides, we have stuff to discuss, and, Dad, it doesn't involve you."

"Well, you may have to stand in line. Because I have some stuff to discuss with Jeri, too."

Jeri felt her stomach muscles tighten. She didn't feel like herself. Maybe she *had* come back to work too soon. But it wasn't the work; it was the realization that she had to face the music. She tried a light laugh that didn't quite come off. "Tiffany, if you don't mind, I think I'd better start with your father."

Tiffany looked from one to the other. "Tell you what. Have the morning rentals all gone out?" Dan nodded. "Then I can handle the rest for a while. How hard can it be?" She moved behind the counter, poured two cups of coffee and handed one to each of them. "Take this with you. Shoo!" She flapped her hands at them.

Dan shrugged and grinned at Jeri. "Surely she can't screw things up too much. C'mon. We'll go over to the house, sit on the deck and talk."

Jeri wanted to forestall the discussion, fight off the inevitable. But sometimes the game began whether you'd practiced enough or not. And this was one time no amount of experience was going to help. "Okay," she murmured.

Dan opened the door for her, then paused to look back at Tiffany. "Holler if you need us."

Jeri clutched the coffee cup in both hands and trudged beside him, the image of a scaffold looming in her head. He spoke casually. "I don't know what happened in that springhouse, but something did. Tiffany has changed, mellowed. I owe you a big thank-you."

She couldn't stand it. It wasn't credit she deserved. They had reached the steps to the deck. Jeri settled on the top one, setting her coffee down beside her, locking her hands around her knees. "Please, Dan, you don't owe me anything except a tongue-lashing." She waited, heart pounding.

"Tongue-lashing? For saving my daughter's life?"

"No. For putting her in danger in the first place."

He settled two steps below her, leaning against the railing, his legs crossed at the ankles. He looked at her. "How's that?"

She squeezed her eyes shut and then stared into his. "We had a fight."

"I know."

"I caused the whole thing. I really ripped into her. I don't know if it was the heat, the soap operas or what. But something snapped." She struggled for breath. "I accused her of being thoughtless and lazy and uncaring…"

He set his cup down. "Sounds like a pretty accurate call to me."

His words stopped her. "Huh?"

"You tried to tell me, help me to see that she was manipulating all of us."

"But I had no right. She's your daughter, and you didn't need me telling you what to do. I've never been a parent."

He smiled. "Yeah, and I resented your telling me the truth. I didn't want to hear it."

"It wasn't my place."

"Who else was going to jerk my chain?"

"Dan, I'm sorry. All of that is between you and Tiffany. But I'm telling you, I chased her away—into the storm, into the cabin…"

He reached up, unclasped her hands and held them gently. "If you hadn't ticked her off, something else would've driven her to rebel."

"But it wouldn't have nearly killed her."

He moved up one step, increasing the pressure on her hands. "We don't know that. All I know is that you risked your life to save hers." He brushed his lips across the back of her hand, his mustache tingling against her skin. "Jeri, I think you saved more than her life. Something happened in that springhouse, and my daughter came out of it with a whole different attitude."

He tugged on her hands, drawing her down beside him. "*You* made that happen."

"Dan, don't. I—"

Before she could utter her denial, he dropped her hands, pulled her against him and kissed her like a man who meant business. It felt so good and at the same time so wrong. She didn't want his gratitude. She hadn't earned it. She couldn't afford the luxury of being held, of wanting him fiercely, when it wasn't going to work. Summoning her strength, she pushed gently against his chest until his lips parted from hers and his eyes came into focus, wide with puzzlement. "Sweetheart, what is it?"

The endearment stiffened her resolve. She stood abruptly. "I have to get back to work. Look, you're relieved, grateful. I understand." She swallowed convulsively. "But let's not confuse the issues. I overstepped my bounds and nearly caused a tragedy. That's something I'll simply have to live with. But from now on, I think our relationship should be strictly business."

He grabbed her arm. "Business? You can't be serious! This isn't just about Tiffany. It's about you and me. About needing each other. More than I ever admitted to myself until Thursday night."

She shuddered. "I wish it were different. But gratitude, guilt, need—that's not love." She gently removed his hands from her shoulders, caressing them as she did so. "Needs. Mine have been pretty overwhelming. Right now, I don't know how much of what I'm feeling is grief about Mom, confusion about Dad. And how much of my reaction to you was physical. Was I using you to fill up the empty spaces in me?" She ignored the anguish on his face and hurtled on to the conclusion.

"None of those is much of a basis for a relationship. I'm sorry, Dan."

She turned away, started down the steps, then paused. "Maybe I should give up the job for the rest of the summer. School's starting soon and I need to get prepared."

Dan continued to stare at her. "Jeri, I..." He seemed to struggle to find a neutral tone. "Okay. Do what you have to do. But if you have to quit, could you wait till Tiffany leaves next week? She needs you right now, even more than she needs me. Please?"

"For a week, then." She rubbed her hands nervously on her thighs and then thrust them into the pockets of her shorts. "I'm sorry, Dan," she said again, then turned and ran down the path to the marina.

PEACE AND QUIET? He'd asked for it. Now he was going to get it. He sank onto the steps, picked up his coffee. He could hear Bull scratching at the door to come out. But he didn't want company, not even the dog. Tiffany. Jeri. Tiffany *and* Jeri. Linked in his mind. Embedded in his heart.

Vicki would be picking Tiffany up a week from Sunday. Jeri would quit the marina. He wouldn't see her—except for fire-department business. He'd have his peace, all right. After Labor Day, the pace at the marina would slack off, he'd be into winterizing boats, making repairs, undertaking renovations. By himself. Unencumbered. Alone.

He didn't understand Jeri. Tiffany had been the real obstacle between them, hadn't she? But now that condition had changed. So what was Jeri's deal? One look at her this morning—shadows under her eyes, worry lines wrinkling her forehead, a lower lip that quivered

ever so slightly when she thought no one was looking—
had sliced him right down the middle. He loved her!

Submissive, doting, passive—like his mother? Not
hardly. Jeri was a fighter. Had that been part of the
problem? Had he wanted to put her in her place, tame
her? Mold her into the kind of woman he'd always ide-
alized? Well, she sure as hell hadn't held still for that.

She'd mentioned physical need. But though she'd
come on strong, he hadn't objected. Had that assertiveness bugged him?

But without that same drive and sheer gutsiness,
where would Tiffany be? Had he felt—he hated to say
the word—somehow *threatened* by Jeri? By that fierce
independent spirit?

Yeah, maybe. But what had happened just now, when
Jeri had run off leaving him sitting here, had felt like
disaster—like a ship capsizing, its stern slowly sinking
into a watery grave, bow pointed at the sky.

He struggled to his feet. Was he going down with the
ship? Not if he could help it. Peace and quiet were
illusions; he'd have neither without Tiffany...and Jeri.

CHAPTER SIXTEEN

MIKE BURST into the marina office Saturday evening at a dead run. "Jeez, Jeri, why didn't you call me right away? I had to learn the news from Doug. He just called. You could've been killed!" His face was flushed and he paced back and forth in front of the counter. "Are you okay?"

Okay? The aftermath of the fire was nothing compared to the misery of working side by side with Dan. Worse, now when it was too late, Tiffany followed her around chatting animatedly about boys, pop music, school, her friends, even soliciting Jeri's advice about how to get along better with her mother. Guilt about the fire was bad enough, but the hope she saw burning in Tiffany's eyes broke her heart. Dan's gratitude, Tiffany's expectations and her own neediness were taking their toll.

"Yes, thanks, Mike. I'm fine."

"How come you look like hell, then?"

A faint smile flickered across her face. "You never did mince words. Is it that bad?"

"Miss Arkansas's in no danger of being dethroned." He gestured toward the clock. "When does Contini liberate you from this place?"

"Seven-thirty."

"Great." He retrieved a root beer from the refrigerated case and plunked three quarters down on the counter. "Only fifteen more minutes, Tag, and then you and I are going fishing. Like old times. It'll do you good." Before she could protest, he cut her off. "No arguments. Set us out a carton of worms, a six-pack of sodas and some chips while I get my cooler. Catfish are biting."

Later, sitting in the bow of the boat bobbing along the rocky shoreline, she began to relax, the peacefulness of the twilight and the lulling motion of the water easing her tension. The croaking of the tree frogs, the cooler evening air fanning her skin and the gentle drag on her line evoked memories of a childhood that, right now, seemed light-years ago. Dear Mike. He had a way of knowing just when she needed rescuing. He'd often stood up for her when her brothers were being...well, brothers.

She reeled in and found that while she'd been daydreaming, a wily fish had nibbled at her worm, bit by bit, until there was nothing left. She opened the carton, dug in the damp dirt and extracted another juicy night crawler, threading it onto her hook. She cast toward a submerged log and let the weight take the line down.

Mother. An ache, like a boulder wedged in a crevice, cramped her stomach, and tears stung her eyes. She'd been so busy trying to straighten Scotty out, running interference for her father, elevating herself to the role of savior that only since the springhouse had she gotten in touch with her own overwhelming need to mourn.

Mike tied the boat to a tree spiking above the lake's surface. "Any nibbles?"

She attempted a smile. "Just one. You?"

"Nah." He fastened a spinner-bait to his swivel and cast toward the shore, then leaned back in his seat. "Ah, this is the life. Glad you came?"

"Yes. I really am. Thanks."

"Don't mention it." Across the cove, a buck thrashed to the edge of the water, dipping his head for a drink. "Tag, were you scared?"

"Scared?"

"In the springhouse. It must've been horrible for you to be trapped like that."

"You mean my claustrophobia?"

"Yeah."

"Mike, I...I totally lost it in there." Her throat constricted. "If it hadn't been for Tiffany..."

"From what I hear, you didn't 'lose it' before then, though. You saved her life."

"I'll never believe that."

"Why not?"

"Because she'd wouldn't have run away that night if it hadn't been for me."

Mike reeled in and recast farther down the shore. He waited quietly, slowly retrieving his line.

"I told her off."

"So you're taking the weight of the world on your shoulders again? Blaming yourself? As if the girl didn't have a load of problems before you ever met her?"

"I guess that's what I *am* doing." Jeri felt another tug on the end of her line and reeled in ever so slightly.

"Still in control, eh?" He studied the setting on his drag, not looking at her. "What about Contini?"

She felt another tug on her line. A definite strike. She reared back, trying to set the hook. "Damn! He got away."

"Contini or the fish?" This time Mike was staring straight at her, challenging her.

"Oh, God, Mike, don't do this to me."

"Do what?"

"Make me talk about him."

"Give you a physical feat to perform and you'll go for it every time, but you're scared as hell of emotions."

"Terrified."

"Especially when it comes to men?"

She lowered her head, letting the rod slip through her fingers and rest across her legs. Dammit! Was he going to make her cry?

"Tag, what are you so afraid of? Can't you let down those barriers long enough to feel, really *feel?*"

The night sounds echoed loudly in her ears. *Barriers?* She didn't like this conversation. Yet there was no place to go, unless she swam. And she *was* afraid. "What barriers?"

"Your competitiveness. Your need to take care of everybody else. Your inability to let others get close enough to take care of you." He hesitated. "Intimacy. I think you're afraid of intimacy. And I don't mean sex. There's a big difference between sex and intimacy."

The boat rolled gently in a swell, and she felt suddenly naked, exposed. All this time had it been fear rather than strength that had motivated her?

"Jeri, what about Dan?"

She buried her face in her palms and sat motionless, her heart thudding. "I...I don't know."

"Reel in. We'll try another spot." Before Mike untied the line and backed away from the tree, he smiled at her. "He's a good man, Tag. Don't let *him* get off the hook."

THURSDAY AFTERNOON Tiffany sat cross-legged on the dock, paintbrush in hand, shading in some deeper blue to give the lake depth. This old fish shack might smell putrid, but the mural was looking halfway decent. She should be able to finish before Mom and Purd arrived

Sunday. They'd probably had themselves a whoopdee-doo of a time. They'd sent her postcards from all over the place—Las Vegas, Hollywood, Tijuana. When Mom had called last night, her voice had been all throaty and kind of muffled. She'd actually said she'd missed her, like maybe she was happier or something.

Tiffany dabbed at the mural, then leaned back to take in the result. Okay. When she'd started, it had been a way to get out of the office, away from—she winced—Gidget. But now, she wanted it to show all the colors, from the deep blue-green of the pines to the silver-aquamarine of the lake's surface sparkling in the morning sunlight. For some reason, it was really important to get this done just right. Heck, she was going to miss the place—smelly catfish, unshaven fishermen, whiny kids and all.

She wiped the brush with a turpentine-soaked rag. She was going to miss more than that. Scott. He was possibly her best friend in the whole world. She felt a little thump down deep. He'd promised to write. She hoped so. He made Tony look like a jerk. Even the other kids here weren't so bad. Bubba and LaFaye were having a farewell party for her Saturday night. Sometimes she thought maybe they even liked her.

And, of course, Dad. It was hard to believe she'd made him scared. But she understood it now. And she also understood that he loved her.

She'd developed a definite mushy spot in her heart for him, too. You could do a lot worse for a father. Except for one thing—the breakup with Jeri. He must be stupid or something. Jeri, too. It didn't take a rocket scientist to see they were in love. But oh, no, they both moped around, avoiding looking at each other. Jeri was

okay with her, but the minute Dad was around, she just
sort of clammed up and got real busy all of a sudden.

And in the evenings Dad would sit on the deck, staring at the stars, nursing a beer. Finally Tiffany had had
it and asked him what their story was. "We've broken
up," he said. "We aren't right for each other."

Crap! Tiffany thought. She dipped the brush in gold
paint, needing to get the color of the sycamore foliage
just right. Adults! How dense could they be? She dotted
the undersides of the leaves. Well, they'd reckoned
without the Tiffer. She wasn't leaving here until she'd
gotten them back together—somehow. She grinned,
feeling devilish. They wouldn't know what hit 'em!

JERI DREADED IT. The bimonthly Thursday fire-
department meeting was tonight. Smitty and several
others had called during the week, trying to make her
out as some kind of heroine for rescuing Tiffany. She
felt like a fraud. She'd thought about skipping the meeting, but that would only generate questions. She stared
into the mirror, tucking the sleeveless red blouse into
her white shorts and thinking how downright weepy she
felt. It wasn't like her. Where was her fight? *Face it.
You don't want to see Dan. Not in a situation where
everyone will be watching the two of you.* It was hard
enough working at the marina—and she still had two
more days of that before Tiffany left.

The old Jeri would have taken the situation as a challenge, would have waded right into the meeting,
wrested control and won. *Won?* Was that what her life
was all about—winning? What? Hollow victories? The
reflection in the mirror showed wide tentative hazel
eyes. Afraid of intimacy? Mike had confronted her, not
once but twice. "Trust the other guy," he'd said. "Let

him save you for a change." But she was too confused, too proud, too stubborn, too...vulnerable.

She picked up her billfold and keys and walked reluctantly through the house. Celeste and her father sat on the couch holding hands and watching a movie on TV. Scotty sprawled on the rug, his arms clutching a throw pillow. Jeri exhaled. This area of her concern, at least, had diminished.

All three looked up and smiled, as if they shared a bond. "Have a good meeting, honey," her father said.

"I'll try." She walked out the door and climbed in behind the wheel of the Explorer. She sat for several seconds, her nerves wired, before she turned on the ignition and backed down the driveway.

DAN, CORNERED BY Carl Rojas in a boring conversation about types of riding mowers, sipped his coffee and, over Carl's shoulder, eyed the door. No Jeri. Not yet. Disappointment curled in his stomach. Painful as it was to be around her, he missed her like hell when he wasn't. He didn't know how much longer he could stand by keeping his feelings in check. But nothing in her demeanor since Saturday had suggested a way to break through to her. It was as if an invisible hand, palm defiantly held up, signaled "Stay away."

He glanced at the clock. Time to begin. He excused himself and walked to the front of the room, taking his position at the podium. The men gradually straggled toward the chairs. Tonight Carl Rojas was reviewing flammability of household chemicals and preventive measures. Just as Dan called the meeting to order, he noticed Jeri slip in and quickly take a vacant chair next to Earl Gunderman in the last row. She took out a pen and pad and began taking notes as if preparing for a final exam. Never once did she look up at him.

At Smitty Dingle's request, the business meeting and program had been deliberately abbreviated. Dan didn't know how Jeri would react to what was going to happen. But he knew it wouldn't go over if he had any part in it, so he had deferred to Smitty and the others.

As Carl outlined the dangers of household cleaning agents, Dan leaned against the wall, trying to appear interested. All he could see of Jeri was the top of her head, honey gold curls still damp from her shower, and the curve of her cheek. Damn! He wanted to stride back there, gather her up and carry her, caveman-fashion, back to his house and make love to her till she was senseless.

God, is there anything more boring than types of chemicals?

With Smitty making frantic slashing gestures across his Adam's apple, Carl finally took the hint and drew his monologue to a close just before eight-fifteen. Meanwhile Smitty nodded to Ted Allison, who slipped from his chair and ducked outdoors. Yielding the floor to Smitty, Dan took a seat on the front row.

Just then the door burst open. Carrying a huge cake, Tiffany entered, followed by Scott, Hank, Celeste and Ted. Earl Gunderman pulled Jeri to her feet, circled her waist and began singing, "For She's a Jolly Good Fellow."

Dan watched as realization dawned on Jeri's face and the crimson of her skin bled into the color of her blouse. What the firemen lacked in musical ability they made up for with enthusiasm and volume.

The voices faded into thunderous applause as Earl led Jeri to the front of the room and ceremoniously turned her over to Smitty. Dan could see her fingers curling into fists, her teeth biting her lower lip as she fought for control.

Tiffany set the cake on the table next to the coffee-maker, and Celeste hastily arranged napkins, plastic forks and a stack of paper plates. Hank and Scott leaned against the rear wall, grinning proudly.

Jeri, shaking her head vehemently, tugged on Smitty's arm as if pleading with him to activate a trapdoor for her to fall through. Dan could sense her discomfort as strongly as if it were his. He heard her whisper, "Please, Smitty, I can't—"

"Hush up, everybody." Smitty waved his arms over his head and the room quieted. Those who'd been standing eased back into their chairs. "Now, lots of us have known this little gal a long time. She's always been a firecracker. And I'll tell ya, our chief wasn't the happiest man on the lake when I brought her here to be a firefighter. But—" he looked straight at Dan "—I'll bet now he's damn glad I did." Applause broke out again. Dan tried in vain to catch Jeri's eye, but she kept her head averted, her throat moving in jerky swallows.

Smitty turned back to Jeri, holding her by both shoulders. "Now, Jeri, I know how important it is for you to feel like...well, like you're one of the boys. And that rescue you made last week, hell, if you ever felt you didn't qualify before that, you damn well do now."

Tiffany let out a "Yeah! Way to go!" and pumped her fist in the air.

Dan was sitting close enough he could see the tears gathering on Jeri's lashes. She needed to escape, needed a hug, needed taking care of, but he had to sit by helplessly.

"Me and the boys, well, we don't have medals or

nothin' like that. But we did get together to buy you a present. Sort of a token of how we feel about you.'' Carl Rojas disappeared into the men's room and came out lugging a big wrapped package, which he brought to the front. "Open it!" Smitty urged.

Dan watched her, saw the debate going on within her. He sighed with relief when grace won out and she slowly began unwrapping the package. When she lifted the lid, Smitty couldn't contain himself. "See? Size-eight boots!" He insisted that she step into them and then pulled out a fireman's coat—one that fit her—and helped her into it. "Now you're official! The hero—" he looked around at the crowd "—er, heroine of the Eagle Point Volunteer Fire Department!"

The crowd erupted and Tiffany sprinted from the back of the room to envelop her in a big hug. Dan swallowed hard as he stood with the others and applauded, wanting desperately to hug her, too.

Smitty waved his arms again and the men fell silent. Jeri took a small step forward. "I—" her voice quavered "—I don't quite know what to say. That rescue shouldn't have been necessary. If it hadn't been for me—"

Tiffany grasped Jeri by the shoulder and interrupted. "If it hadn't been for her, I wouldn't be here." Facing Jeri, she gave her a little shake. "Shut up, Gidget. You're spoiling the party."

Jeri stared hard into Tiffany's eyes, then turned to the crowd. "I'm...honored—" she seemed to struggle for the next words and then gazed with irony straight at Dan "—to be one of the boys!" The men stood, stomping and hooting.

"How's about cutting into that cake, Jeri?" Earl shouted.

As SHE DROVE toward the marina Saturday morning, Jeri felt rested, more like herself than she had since before the fire. It was one of those breathtaking days when land formations appeared sharper, colors more vivid. A gentle summer rain the night before had banished the oppressive August heat and humidity, the sky was a cloudless blue, and trails of wispy fog rose from the creek arms.

She rolled down the window and breathed deeply of pure mountain air, containing the slightest hint of autumn. School started in ten days. She was looking forward to the new job, meeting the girls who were going out for basketball, being caught up in the enthusiasm of those first days of the semester.

The busy-ness would be therapeutic. Although she would never have believed it two weeks ago, she would miss Tiffany, wise-ass attitude and all. She had endured plenty in her life, but Jeri would lay odds that the girl's strong sense of self and her courage would carry her far.

And she would miss Dan. The fishbowl atmosphere of the fire-department meetings didn't really count. But how many times could she use the excuse of sailing to go to the marina? Why was she even thinking about it? It seemed as if the summer had been divided, emotionally, into two distinct phases: the first when she'd avoided the realities of her own life, her own feelings by seeking comfort—escape?—in Dan's arms; and the second, when realities blindsided her. Realities like her smug assurance she knew what was best for everybody. Like the emotional void her mother's death had created. Like her realization that pain and need were not a healthy basis for a relationship. In fact, they made of love a demand rather than a gift.

She eased into her parking place, rolled up the window and locked the car. As she walked toward the office, Tiffany's mural caught her eye. Something about it—the whimsy of its concept—revealed a whole new side of Tiffany. A side that made her infinitely more likable.

When Jeri stepped into the office, she was surprised to see Raymond Bell, along with Mark, Scotty, Tiffany and Mike—Mike?—lounging around the table, looking at her expectantly. "Mornin', Miz Jeri," Raymond said. Scotty studied his shoes, trying to suppress a grin, and Mike had his arm casually draped over the back of Tiffany's chair. Tiffany, knees pulled up to her chest, looked like the cat that ate the canary.

Jeri's mouth gaped. "What...what're you all doing?"

"Tendin' the store today," Raymond offered.

"What do you mean? Where's Dan?"

Mike's face took on a look of mock despair. "Funny thing about that. Your brother here—" he hooked a thumb at Scotty "—discovered a problem with the motor on your sailboat. Asked Dan to take a look."

She glanced down and noticed Mike was rolling some objects around in his hand. She seized his fist, eyeing him suspiciously. "What've you got?"

"This?" Mike looked up innocently and opened his fingers, revealing spark plugs. Then he looked at Raymond. "Whaddaya think? Has Dan had time to diagnose the problem?"

"I reckon."

"Here." Mike handed Scotty the plugs. "Guess you'll need these."

Jeri stared from one to the other, dumbfounded. Something was going on and she wasn't in on it.

Mark stood. "Here comes a boat. I'll be out at the pump." Then he gave Jeri a small salute. "Good luck!"

"Good luck?" She put her hands on her hips. "All right, what's up?"

Tiffany eased her feet to the floor, stretched and crossed the room to Jeri. "Ever read *Julius Caesar?*"

"Shakespeare! What in—"

"Well, did you?"

"Yes, but—"

Tiffany put her hand around Jeri's waist and slowly walked her to the door. "Well, we have us a little conspiracy here." She winked at Scotty. *"Et tu, Brute?"* He nodded emphatically, stood and retrieved a picnic basket from behind the counter and trailed them out the door.

Jeri planted her feet and confronted the teenagers. "Okay, you two. Out with it. What do you think you're doing?"

"Doo-ing?" Tiffany drawled the word as she studied the sky. Then she hooked an arm through Jeri's and began propelling her toward the slip where the Monahan sailboat was berthed. "We've seized power, taken over the marina for the day with Mike's and Raymond's help.

"But, why—"

"Shut up, Jeri, and move." Scotty nudged her backside with the picnic basket.

"Because—" Tiffany paused for emphasis "—we're tired of you and Dad acting like pouty little kids. You're supposed to be the adults around here. We figure a nice day-long sail together might help."

Jeri felt her face flushing. She floundered for a comeback. "Don't you think, uh, we're capable of handling our own business?"

"That's a definite no!" Scotty said as he gave her another push along the walkway.

Dan reared up and watched them approach. He looked disgusted. "Okay, wise guys. Which one of you took the plugs?" His eyes darted back and forth from Tiffany to Scotty.

Scotty placed the basket in the boat while Tiffany, exerting pressure on Jeri's arms, forced her into the cockpit. Dan turned, scowling, to Jeri. "What the hell—?"

She shrugged. "Ask them."

He turned back to his daughter. "So?"

Tiffany was casually untying the bowline while Scotty loosened the one at the stern. "Great day for sailing, don'tcha think?" She shoved the bow away from the dock.

Scotty held out his hand and tossed the plugs toward Dan. "Here, in case you need them."

Tiffany stood up waving gaily. "Bon voyage." She grinned roguishly. "And don't come back until you two butt-heads get something settled."

For good measure, Scotty leaned over the water and gave the stern a push.

DAN TOSSED the spark plugs up and down in his hand as the sailboat drifted away from the dock. "I don't suppose we have much choice, do we?" He did not look pleased.

More for something to do than out of acquiescence, Jeri, her back to Dan, started removing the sail cover. "I guess it won't kill us to humor Tiffany and Scotty." Talk about awkward! It was one thing for her and Dan to get together to talk, but this plan, devised by two scheming teenagers was Machiavellian. She took her time folding the cover before she stowed it and turned around. Dan was fiddling with the motor, inserting the plugs. "Are we going to sail her out or use the motor?"

"It's your boat," he said as he screwed the last plug into position.

So it's going to be like that, is it? "Let's be sure the motor works. Anyway, we won't have enough wind until we get into the main body of the lake."

He started the motor and yielded his position at the tiller to her. He sat, portside, his ball-cap visor pulled low over his scowling face, as she piloted the boat past the marina out into the cove. To add insult to injury, the entire marina "staff" was standing on the gas dock waving farewell, like proud parents sending their children off to camp for the first time.

"This wasn't my idea, you know," she said primly.

"I believe you. After all, you made yourself pretty clear the other day." His voice was neutral, but he avoided her eyes. "I'll hoist the damn sails." He lurched to his feet and began unfurling the canvas.

Jeri turned the vessel into the wind, cut the motor and went to help. They worked efficiently for several minutes, neither of them speaking. This was beyond awkward. What on earth were they going to do all day? Stare at one another? As Dan hoisted the mainsail, he muttered, "It was never about gratitude."

A puff of wind sent her to the tiller while he trimmed the sheets. The unspoken question resonated with the soft luff of the jib. She eyed the telltale and set course across the broadest expanse of the lake. He settled back, the sheets held loosely in his tanned hands.

"So *don't* ask." His voice was hard.

Damned if I will. Mike and his fear theory. Intimacy? How could she ever have thought she loved Dan? *Look at him. Sitting there like a grizzly bear with a thorn stuck in his paw.* She felt something of the old combative Jeri surfacing—and something of the new Jeri who was trying like mad not to run from her feelings. "Okay, what *was* it about?"

He cocked his hat back on his head and looked directly at her. "You. It was about you."

Was it the wind at her back or the way he was looking at her that made her shiver? The shoreline was closing in fast, but the impending collision was in her heart. He wasn't going to make this easy. "Prepare to come about."

As Jeri shoved the tiller and gave the command, he ducked under the boom and came up on the starboard side. She felt, somehow, as if his eyes had never left her face. She squinted into the sun, adjusting their course. She felt his foot nudge hers, then again. She turned to him.

"You can run, tack, beat or reach, Jeri," he said, "but I'm still gonna be right here."

He'd hit the bull's-eye. She *was* evading, dodging, escaping. Not her style. Suddenly, decisively, she let go of the tiller. Sensing her intention, Dan loosened the sheets until the prow headed into the wind and the boat rocked aimlessly in the middle of the lake.

"Why?" she asked.

He rubbed a finger over his mustache. "Why? Because I'm thirty-six years old and I'm unwilling to spend the rest of my life wondering what in hell went wrong with us. You can give me all the bullshit you want about gratitude and pain and...Lord knows what else. I don't buy it. We had a good thing going. And you can't use Tiffany as an excuse anymore. She thinks you hung the moon." He leaned forward, his arms dangling between his legs. "So…as long as the kids have put us out to sea, I, for one, intend to use this time to chart a course, with or without you."

Jeri had no place to look, nothing to do, except sit there, fear pounding in every cell of her body. Not the stifling claustrophobic kind, but something infinitely more permanent, more damaging. She knew beyond the shadow of a doubt that Dan was dead serious. He wanted answers. Yet fear held her in its clutches. To face it would be to strip away her lifelong stock-in-trade—cockiness, assertiveness, command. To risk failure and…rejection. *Fine, butt-head. Just give up. Atta girl!* That's exactly what Tiffany would say. So would Mike—and the old fighting Jeri.

She rubbed her hands nervously up and down her thighs. "Okay. Let's get it over with."

"Damn, Jeri, it's not a dose of castor oil we're talking about." He took hold of her hands, the warmth and pressure stilling her nerves, sending a tremor of relief through her. "It's us."

She fought for honesty. "I don't know if there *is* an 'us.'"

"Okay, let's start there. Why not an us?"

The funny feeling in her stomach had to be the rocking motion of the boat. "I came on to you way too strong. Practically threw myself at you." *There. It was out.*

"Did you notice me complaining?" The corners of his mustache twitched with humor.

"But it was my motives, don't you see? I—"

"You mean there was something else besides my irresistible body?" The smile had lifted to the creases around his eyes.

She couldn't squirm away. He was still holding her

hands tightly. "Well..." Damn, she could feel herself blushing. "Seriously, Dan—"

He interrupted. "Sweetheart, I'm just teasing. I *want* you to be serious, for both our sakes. I'm listening."

She gazed for a long moment at the distant haven of the shoreline. Then she turned to him. "When I came home back in June, I thought I was over my grieving, that I could help Scotty and Dad. I thought I knew what I wanted."

"Like being on the fire department? Proving yourself?"

"That's the way I've always been. Now, though, after handling Dad and Scotty all wrong, treating Tiffany—as if I had any right—like one of my mouthy students, and then..." She faltered.

"Go on. You're doing fine."

She collapsed against the stern. "Using you to get my needs met emotionally and, uh, physically..."

He dropped her left hand and moved beside her circling her with his arm, kissing her gently on the temple. "That's what it's all about, sweetheart."

The stroking of his mustache across her skin, the feel of his lips nibbling on her earlobe, made it hard to concentrate. A gull flying overhead let out a shrill cry, but the roaring in her ears had a different origin altogether. She struggled to sit upright. "What *what's* all about?"

"Trust. Love. You trusted me to care for you, to honor you. What's happened to change that?"

She paused, scrabbling for reasons, excuses. Instead, lightninglike images rolled in her mind: Dan rescuing her from Cora's house; Dan running interference the first time she saw Dad and Celeste together; Dan, his head thrown back in ecstasy, when they made love. What was she afraid of? Relinquishing control? Admitting the truth? *No game face for this. Just from-the-gut honesty.*

Her voice surprised her. It was strong, clear. "Nothing," she said, then slipped her grasp from his, turned toward him and framed his face with her hands. "Dan Contini, I love you." *Out loud. By God, out loud.*

He stroked her arms and nestled her against his chest, chuckling. "I've been wondering what's taken you so long to figure it out."

She peeked up at him in mock consternation. She didn't like being bested. "Do men always have to be right?"

He smiled indulgently. "Maybe not always. Just most of the time. And I know one other thing I'm right about."

"What's that?" Her heart kept rhythm with the waves knocking against the hull.

"I love you, too. And you're not going to get away again, lady."

She sighed and cuddled closer, feeling his fingers beneath her T-shirt exploring the bare skin of her back, his lips crushing hers. She was drowning right here in a boat in the middle of a lake.

Then he pulled back and cocked an eyebrow at her. "Wanna give the kids their money's worth?"

"What do you mean?"

He pointed dead ahead. "See that cove over there? Nobody's in it. We could run in there behind that big overhanging willow and—"

"Chief Contini, are you thinking what I'm thinking?"

"What're you thinking?"

Go for the basket! Jeri ran her hands up under his

shirt, rubbing his chest seductively. "I'm considering starting a little fire."

"I was thinking more like a major conflagration." He trailed his fingers across her shoulders and down over her arms before he straightened and put the tiller in her hand. "Here, Captain."

Jeri started to take charge, then released the tiller and stood up. "Not me." She gave him a nudge with her hip. "I trust you. You be the skipper." She took her position, gathered the sheet and smiled with satisfaction. Intimacy. It had a lot going for it!

As the sun rested on the rim of the mountain to the west, Tiffany put the finishing touches on the mural and signed her name with a flourish. Scott walked up behind her, glancing nervously at his watch. He frowned. "Jeez, I didn't think they'd be gone so long. I've already finished cleaning up the rentals."

Tiffany folded her feet under her and stood up, wiping her hands on her paint-splattered shirt. "Long is good, Scott." She smiled smugly.

"I dunno. Maybe something happened to them."

"Maybe." She arched her brows knowingly, the smile broadening. "Probably took 'em a while to eat that lunch we fixed, drink the champagne Mike brought, talk things over, and, uh, you know."

He gestured helplessly. "But your party. We gotta leave for Bubba's pretty soon. You gotta change."

She placed a placating hand on his shoulder. "I know. Why don't you run along? Pick me up in an hour. I'll be ready."

"But what if they're not back?"

"They will be. Trust me." He shrugged and took off

toward his car. She stood back and took one last look at the mural. Perfect, if she did say so herself.

With Bull trailing along after her, she hurried to the house, jumped in the shower, shampooed her hair and dried it quickly, pulling it up off her neck with a ribbon. She dropped a scoop-neck white blouse over her head and tucked it into green-and-white striped shorts. She started out of the room, then turned back and hastily sprayed cologne below her ears and on each wrist. She hated to think about this being her last night here. She'd miss Dad and Jeri. And Scott.

Her heart turned over. She'd fallen for him, big time. It couldn't have been only a month ago she'd thought he was the biggest rube she'd ever clapped eyes on. She felt a catch in her throat. When she'd given up fighting Arkansas, it'd begun to feel like home. And now it was already time to leave. Climbing back into the motor home with Mom and Purd would feel weird.

Bull jumped off her bed and cocked his head. "What is it, boy?" Then she heard it, too, the hum of a boat motor. She raced to the window. The bare-masted sloop, sails secured, motored slowly toward the marina. Two figures, nearly inseparable, were visible in the stern.

"We did it, Bull!" She chuckled to herself all the way to the dock. She could hardly wait to spring the last surprise!

She stood at the end of the Monahan stall while her father maneuvered the craft into the slip. Jeri threw her a line. While she secured it, Tiffany noted with satisfaction their relaxed manner and the loving way her father assisted Jeri—perfectly capable of doing almost anything for herself—onto the dock. Tiffany stood her ground, forcing them to speak first. Damned if she'd ask.

She didn't have to wait long. Jeri walked straight toward her and enveloped her in a big hug. "You're some special kid, you know that?" she whispered in Tiffany's ear; and before she could answer, Dad hugged the two of them. "I'm a lucky guy to have such a beautiful armload of women!"

After a moment Tiffany pulled away. With a little skipping motion, she stepped ahead of her father and backpedaled toward the fish-cleaning shack, chattering all the way. "You know how I wanted to finish my paint project before I leave tomorrow? While you were gone today, I had some time and, well—" she stood aside and gestured with a sweep of her arm "—here it is."

Her father wrapped an arm around Jeri's waist, and the two stood studying the scene. Her dad's voice, when he spoke, was husky. "Pretty sure of yourself, weren't you, bambino?" But he held out his other arm and she curled up against him, snuggling close.

"Do you like it?"

"It's great," her father said.

"And accurate," Jeri added.

Tiffany noticed the tears in her eyes and smiled. "I did good, huh?"

The painting showed a rocky shoreline beneath a tall pine tree, with a brown A-frame house in the background. In the foreground stood three figures, arms entwined. A tall man with a mustache in a U.S. Navy T-shirt, a gangly teenager with long ash-blond hair and a smiling woman with short curly honey-colored hair. Beside them sat a boxer, looking for all the world as if he was grinning. Above the figures, in bright blue paint, were the words "The Contini Family."

EPILOGUE

November 16

Dear Dad and Jeri,

I'm sitting here in study hall bored out of my tree. Yeah, yeah, I've finished my homework, but Old Man Dietrich is giving me the eye, so I have to look like I'm busy. What a drag! But I haven't talked with you guys in a while, so I decided it wouldn't kill me to write a letter.

Here's a miracle for you. Purd and Mom seem to be getting along great. 'Course you know I wasn't thrilled when they wheeled into River Falls and Mom broke the news. Not like I'd have had any say about it, anyway. Married. In one of those dumb wedding chapels in Las Vegas. But I've decided Purd's not so bad. I mean, he's not cool like you, Dad, but he treats Mom like she's Dolly Parton or something, and he doesn't butt into my life. Except to buy me stuff. So what's not to like about that, right?

School is okay. I actually made four B's and a C this quarter. Sorry, Jeri. The C was in gym class. I just can't get into sweating up a storm and then trying to look halfway decent the rest of the day. Good news, though—my art-class project was picked to be in this big show they're having in Richmond, an all-state youth exhibit or something.

Sorry I can't come out for Thanksgiving. I doubt Mom will do the big turkey dinner, though. Purd will probably take us to the Officers' Club for some gross buffet with a lot of old people. Oh, well. It won't be long before I'll be coming to Arkansas for Christmas and—ta-da!—your wedding! Jeri, I'll try not to embarrass you as maid of honor by falling on my butt or something.

I can't wait to see Scott again, too. He'll be a handsome best man. I miss you guys. Don't forget I'm planning to spend all of next summer with you. What if I started a mural on the office, Dad? I've got some great ideas. Maybe one where Jeri's holding a baby?

Oops, I have to run. The bell just rang. Ugh, chemistry.

Love,
Tiffer

EVER HAD ONE OF THOSE DAYS?

TO DO:

☑ late for a super-important meeting, you discover the cat has eaten your panty hose

☑ while you work through lunch, the rest of the gang goes out and finds a one-hour, once-in-a-lifetime 90% off sale at the most exclusive store in town (Oh, and they also get to meet Brad Pitt who's filming a movie across the street.)

☑ you discover that your intimate phone call with your boyfriend was on company-wide intercom

☑ finally at the end of a long and exasperating day, you escape from it all with an entertaining, humorous and always romantic Love & Laughter book!

ENJOY
LOVE & LAUGHTER
EVERY DAY!

For a preview, turn the page....

Here's a sneak peek at
Colleen Collins's RIGHT CHEST, WRONG NAME
Available August 1997...

"DARLING, YOU SOUND like a broken cappuccino machine," murmured Charlotte, her voice oozing disapproval.

Russell juggled the receiver while attempting to sit up in bed, but couldn't. If he *sounded* like a wreck over the phone, he could only imagine what he looked like.

"What mischief did you and your friends get into at your bachelor's party last night?" she continued.

She always had a way of saying "your friends" as though they were a pack of degenerate water buffalo. Professors deserved to be several notches higher up on the food chain, he thought. Which he would have said if his tongue wasn't swollen to twice its size.

"You didn't do anything...bad...did you, Russell?"

"Bad." His laugh came out like a bark.

"Bad as in *naughty*."

He heard her piqued tone but knew she'd never admit to such a base emotion as jealousy. Charlotte Maday, the woman he was to wed in a week, came from a family who bled blue. Exhibiting raw emotion was akin to burping in public.

After agreeing to be at her parents' pool party by

noon, he untangled himself from the bedsheets and stumbled to the bathroom.

"Pool party," he reminded himself. He'd put on his best front and accommodate Char's request. Make the family rounds, exchange a few pleasantries, play the role she liked best: the erudite, cultured English literature professor. After fulfilling his duties, he'd slink into some lawn chair, preferably one in the shade, and nurse his hangover.

He tossed back a few aspirin and splashed cold water on his face. Grappling for a towel, he squinted into the mirror.

Then he jerked upright and stared at his reflection, blinking back drops of water. "Good Lord. They stuck me in a wind tunnel."

His hair, usually neatly parted and combed, sprang from his head as though he'd been struck by lightning. "Can too many Wild Turkeys do that?" he asked himself as he stared with horror at his reflection.

Something caught his eye in the mirror. Russell's gaze dropped.

"What in the—"

Over his pectoral muscle was a small patch of white. A bandage. Gingerly, he pulled it off.

Underneath, on his skin, was not a wound but a small, neat drawing.

"A red heart?" His voice cracked on the word *heart*. Something—a word?—was scrawled across it.

"Good Lord," he croaked. "I got a tattoo. A heart tattoo with the name Liz on it."

Not Charlotte. Liz!

Let's Celebrate!

LOVE & LAUGHTER™

invites you to the party of the season!

Grab your popcorn and be prepared to laugh as we celebrate with **LOVE & LAUGHTER**.

Harlequin's newest series is going Hollywood!

Let us make you laugh with three months of terrific books, authors and romance, plus a chance to win a FREE 15-copy video collection of the best romantic comedies ever made.

For more details look in the back pages of any Love & Laughter title, from July to September, at your favorite retail outlet.

Don't forget the popcorn!

Available wherever Harlequin books are sold.

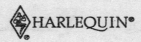

Look us up on-line at: http://www.romance.net

LLCELEB

HARLEQUIN AND SILHOUETTE
ARE PLEASED TO PRESENT

Love, marriage—and the pursuit of family!

Check your retail shelves for these upcoming titles:

July 1997
Last Chance Cafe by Curtiss Ann Matlock
The most determined bachelor in Oklahoma is in trouble! A
lovely widow with three daughters has moved next door—and
the girls want a dad! But he wants to know if their mom needs
a husband....

August 1997
Thorne's Wife by Joan Hohl
Pennsylvania. It was only to be a marriage of convenience—
until they fell in love! Now, three years later, tragedy
threatens to separate them forever and Valerie wants only to
be in the strength of her husband's arms. For she has some
very special news for the expectant father...

September 1997
Desperate Measures by Paula Detmer Riggs
New Mexico judge Amanda Wainwright's daughter has been
kidnapped, and the price of her freedom is a verdict in
favor of a notorious crime boss. So enters ex-FBI agent
Devlin Buchanan—ruthless, unstoppable—and soon there is
no risk he will not take for her.

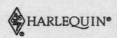 

If you love medical drama and romance on the wards,
then our new medical series by bestselling author
Bobby Hutchinson will bring you to fever pitch....

August 1997—THE BABY DOCTOR (#753)

by Bobby Hutchinson

Dr. Morgan Jacobsen is a skilled obstetrician.
Unfortunately, outside of work she's a klutz. Her
new partner at The Women's Center, Dr. Luke Gilbert,
brings out the worst in her, but Morgan brings out
the best in *him*—and his daughter—until their
children become friends. Then there's more
trouble than even Morgan can handle....

Look for *The Baby Doctor* in August wherever
Harlequin books are sold.

THE FRAUDULENT FIANCÉE
(#751)
by Muriel Jensen

Amnesia. A marriage of convenience.
A secret baby.

Find out what it's all about in August 1997.

Available wherever Harlequin books are sold.

FORTUNE COOKIE

Breathtaking romance is predicted in your future with Harlequin's newest collection: Fortune Cookie.

Three of your favorite Harlequin authors, Janice Kaiser, Margaret St. George and M.J. Rodgers will regale you with the romantic adventures of three heroines who are promised fame, fortune, danger and intrigue when they crack open their fortune cookies on a fateful night at a Chinese restaurant.

Join in the adventure with your own personalized fortune, inserted in every book!

Don't miss this exciting new collection!

Available in September
wherever Harlequin books are sold.

HARLEQUIN®

HE SAID

♥

SHE SAID

Explore the mystery of male/female communication in
this extraordinary new book from two of your favorite
Harlequin authors.

Jasmine Cresswell and Margaret St. George bring you the
exciting story of two romantic adversaries—each from
their own point of view!

DEV'S STORY. CATHY'S STORY.
As he sees it. As she sees it.
Both sides of the story!

The heat is definitely on, and these two can't stay out of
the kitchen!

Don't miss HE SAID, SHE SAID.
Available in July wherever Harlequin books are sold.

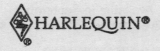

HARLEQUIN®